Barrows noted the display on one of the screens at T'Pril's workstation. "Despite what at first looks like an erratic course, there's a more or less straight line cutting across the system's outer edge." She entered a string of commands into her console. "If I had to guess, I'd think the thing was heading toward Neptune."

T'Pril replied, "A logical deduction, despite the lack of evidence."

"For now, I'll take it," said Masilamani.

Continuing to study the computer-generated track of the still-unidentified anomaly, Barrows said, "What if we redirect stations A55 through A61 and attempt to surround it?"

"Triangulation." T'Pril punctuated her simple answer with an arching of her right eyebrow. "It is an unorthodox suggestion. We must also consider the risks of leaving unattended the sectors overseen by those remote stations."

"If we can lock it down," said Barrows, "long-range sensors should be able to track it until we can get a ship or two out there to investigate. Let's do it."

"There is another point to consider, Commander," said T'Pril. "The object may interpret our redeploying of the monitoring satellites as an aggressive action."

STAR TREK®

THE ORIGINAL SERIES

ELUSIVE SALVATION

Dayton Ward

Based upon *Star Trek*
created by Gene Roddenberry

POCKET BOOKS

New York London Toronto Sydney New Delhi New Roswell

Pocket Books
An Imprint of Simon & Schuster, Inc.
1230 Avenue of the Americas
New York, NY 10020

This book is a work of fiction. Any references to historical events, real people, or real places are used fictitiously. Other names, characters, places, and events are products of the author's imagination, and any resemblance to actual events or places or persons, living or dead, is entirely coincidental.

First Pocket Books paperback edition May 2016

POCKET and colophon are registered trademarks of Simon & Schuster, Inc.

For information about special discounts for bulk purchases, please contact Simon & Schuster Special Sales at 1-866-506-1949 or business@simonandschuster.com.

The Simon & Schuster Speakers Bureau can bring authors to your live event. For more information or to book an event, contact the Simon & Schuster Speakers Bureau at 1-866-248-3049 or visit our website at www.simonspeakers.com.

Manufactured in the United States of America

10 9 8 7 6 5 4 3

ISBN 978-1-5011-1129-7
ISBN 978-1-5011-1130-3 (ebook)

As always,
for Michi, Addison, and Erin

Historian's Note

The "present day" portions of this story take place in 2283, approximately two years prior to Khan Noonien Singh's escape from the planet Ceti Alpha V and the *Starship Enterprise*'s battle with the *Reliant* in the Mutara Sector (*Star Trek II: The Wrath of Khan*).

BEGINNINGS

One

Sol System
Earth Year 1845 (CE)

Warnings were increasing in number as well as volume, their shrill tones growing more insistent with each passing moment. Drevina swept the three long fingers of her left hand across the controls overseeing the alert system, muting the din that was fast becoming bothersome in the restricted space of the control pod. Her action did nothing to alleviate the mounting problems, as a host of status indicators still glowed bright orange, communicating the severity of the ever-worsening situation.

"Drevina," said Glorick, her systems operational specialist and friend, "we continue to lose power in primary propulsion. If we cannot correct the problem, we will be unable to achieve superluminal velocity."

Without moving her gaze from her controls, Drevina replied, "Then make your corrections." It was a useless directive, she knew, but stating it helped to alleviate her mounting irritation, if only for a moment.

"It is not a control systems failure," Glorick countered, and Drevina heard him drawing a deep breath. "The problem is with the drive itself. We cannot make an attempt at repair without landing. There is simply too much damage."

Drevina was aware of this, of course, just as she knew that the propulsion was not the only issue they faced. The life-support system was also beginning to issue advisories, which meant that if they did not find a suitable location for landing in short order, nothing else would matter. She suspected that the last skirmish with their determined pursuers had inflicted more damage to the ship than she and her companions would be able to repair.

"This system contains nine planets," reported Glorick. "According to my scans, only one contains an atmosphere comparable to our own. It is the planet third closest to the local star."

"Is that world inhabited?"

Glorick nodded. "It appears so, though I will not be certain until we get closer."

"Assuming that is possible," said another voice. Glancing over her shoulder, Drevina saw that Canderon, who despite any formal training served as the ship's mechanical technician, had entered the control pod. "The propulsion system is beginning to overheat. We need to put down somewhere, soon." Despite his passive expression, the strain of his voice betrayed his nervousness to Drevina. The flashing of the alarm indicators across various consoles reflected across his face.

She spared the briefest of moments to eye him with annoyance. "We are endeavoring to do precisely that."

"At least allow me to reduce power," said Canderon, his bright eyes widening in alarm. "That will remove some of the strain from the damaged systems."

Releasing a resigned sigh, Drevina replied, "Very well. Glorick, do your scans reveal any signs of pursuit?"

It required several more moments before Glorick said, "Negative."

"What about the third planet? Are you detecting any signs of technology or weapons that might pose a threat?"

Again, Glorick replied, "Negative. I am detecting no indications of any vessels anywhere in this system, and the planet itself appears to lack any sort of orbiting satellites or other space-based technology. Perhaps the world is home to a preindustrial civilization."

"If that is true," Drevina said, "then it will be our first taste of good fortune since setting out on this voyage. Alter our course toward the planet. Continue your scans as we approach, and locate a suitable landing area well away from any population centers."

As Glorick set about the tasks she had given him, Drevina heard the reduction in the ship's main power generation systems and felt a mild reverberation channeled through the console beneath her hands. She could tell just from the sound made by the craft's engines that they were ailing and in desperate need of repair or, at the very least, a cessation of the abuse they had endured to this point. They had been traveling at high velocity for far more cycles than recommended by the ship's technical specifications as well as Canderon's stern warnings. There had been no choice; eluding their pursuers was of paramount importance. Having accomplished that goal—for the time being, at least, and at great cost to the health of her ship—her focus along with that of her companions now shifted toward the simpler yet still dangerous mission of hiding until help arrived, assuming it ever did.

Until then, we cower in a hole and wait.

Drevina hated running, hated leaving behind her family, friends, and everyone she had ever known while they continued to stand and fight against tyranny and slavery. Despite what her friend and mentor, Anardrin, had told her in the moments before ushering her and her shipmates aboard this vessel and defending its escape with his own life, Drevina did not feel like any sort of potential savior. It was a sentiment shared by Glorick and the others fleeing with her, as well as the others of her people who had taken flight in similar fashion. How many of her fellow Iramahl had been lost to the resistance against their oppressors, the Ptaen, to protect her and others like her? There was no way to ever be certain. All she knew was that the Ptaen would not stop until every last Iramahl was back under their control, or dead. This was especially true for those like Drevina and her companions, which was why they had traveled so far into the depths of unexplored space in a desperate bid to escape the Ptaen Consortium's influence.

Drevina also knew that she would die before returning

to that loathsome existence, and that Glorick and the others felt the same way. So, they had run, not just for their own lives but perhaps the very future of all Iramahl, and in the hope that the sacrifices of good people like Anardrin and countless others would not be in vain. They had followed a tortuous path through the void, passing system after system that contained no worlds capable of sustaining them. Even when a planet was detected that might offer even temporary sanctuary, if it harbored an indigenous society, then Drevina was reluctant to go there for fear of exposing some innocent civilization to Ptaen oppression. How many worlds had they put at risk just by virtue of their headlong flight?

Such caution was no longer an option.

Another alert tone sounded in the cramped control pod, and Drevina directed her gaze to the indicator now flashing on her console just as she felt the entire vessel shudder around her.

"Drive system is going offline," reported Glorick. "Internal temperature in the drive core is approaching dangerous levels. I have no choice but to reduce power further."

Looking through the control pod's forward viewing port, Drevina saw the planet they now approached. Brilliant blue oceans and thriving green-and-brown landmasses were highlighted by swipes of bright white cloud formations. In many ways, the world reminded her of their own Yirteshna, or at least the visual recreations she had seen in historical documents and other contraband materials she had managed to obtain at rare, irregular intervals. It was fortunate that this planet seemed so beautiful and inviting, given that it soon would be her new home. This assumed she and her friends survived the next few moments.

"Reduce power to the minimum needed to control our descent," she said. Another review of the navigational system showed that the ship's orientation for entering the planet's atmosphere needed further adjustment. As she entered those instructions to the console, it became apparent that the ailing vessel was going to fight any efforts at control all the way to the ground.

Glorick confirmed her suspicions when he reported, "I think we may need to abandon ship."

"He is correct," added Canderon, who had moved to the control pod's remaining seat and begun using that workstation to monitor the craft's onboard systems. "We will not be able to maintain control once we enter the atmosphere."

"Very well," Drevina replied, dividing her attention between her companions and her controls. "Alert the others, and prepare a distress message with our location for transmission. I will begin the separation procedure." Though she and everyone else aboard the ship were experienced pilots and space travelers, their indoctrination into this particular vessel's operation had been hurried and incomplete. The onboard computer had assisted in negotiating those knowledge gaps, but there were still aspects of the ship's configuration and capabilities that Drevina did not yet understand. Key among those deficiencies was an understanding of the emergency separation protocols for the control pod.

Consider this your final test.

"Lvonek and Mranzal are in the berthing compartment," said Canderon, "and they've sealed the hatch. We are ready."

Nodding at the report, Drevina replied, "I have programmed the ship's onboard computer to attempt a water landing once we separate. Scans show the planet has several undersea regions that are deep enough that the wreck will likely never be found." She could not be sure the onboard computer would survive on its own once the control pod left the rest of the ship behind, but there was little she could do about that now. Either the main hull section would carry out its final instructions, or it would not. For the moment, she had far more urgent concerns. "Glorick, is the distress message ready?"

"Yes. It has been encrypted and prepared for broadcast on the coded frequency."

Would the message be heard by friends, or enemies? Given the distances the transmission would have to travel, it was inevitable that unwanted ears would hear it. Drevina knew there could be no avoiding such things.

"Send it," she said, reaching up to wipe away perspiration from the side of her smooth head before instructing the computer to proceed with the separation sequence. The control pod, along with adjacent compartments for habitation and storage, was designed to operate as an independent craft in the event of an emergency. It lacked the necessary propulsion systems for interstellar travel, but it did contain provisions and other equipment to sustain the crew while they awaited rescue.

Or recapture.

The wayward thought was pushed aside as yet another alarm flashed for attention on her console. Studying the indicator, Drevina released a vulgar term for a sexual act she had heard her father employ on frequent occasions during her childhood, in defiance of her mother's constant protestations.

"What is it?" asked Glorick.

Drevina replied, "The pod's own navigational system appears damaged. We will have only limited maneuverability once we separate from the ship."

"It is still more than we will have if we stay," said Canderon. "We have no choice."

Any response Drevina might have offered was lost as the ship once more trembled around them, and she felt the straps of her chair binding against her clothing and her shoulders as she and the others were tossed about inside the tiny control pod. "Increase power to maneuvering thrusters," she said. "That will help us during our descent." The blue-green world now filled the viewing port, and the ship was beginning to protest the collision of heat and energies as it fell from space through the planet's atmosphere.

"Wait until we are clear before separating," warned Canderon, and Drevina heard the anxiety in his voice.

"If we do it sooner, the stresses of atmospheric entry may force the rest of the ship into a tumble as we pull away." Drevina looked over her shoulder to meet his gaze, and he added, "I would suggest avoiding that."

The shaking increased for the next several moments, to the point that Drevina was sure the ship would tear itself apart, and she gripped the edge of her console in a desperate bid to keep from being thrown from her seat. As the intensity grew to the point that she expected to hear the alarm signaling a hull rupture, the tremors began to subside. This was greeted by a host of new warnings and alerts erupting from different consoles around the control pod.

"I am losing maneuvering control," warned Glorick, his voice tight. "We need to separate, now!"

"Did you transmit the message?" Drevina asked, her hand hovering over the control that would jettison the control pod free of the ship.

Glorick nodded. "Yes!"

"Commencing separation." Drevina dropped her hand onto the control, feeling it depress under her fingers, and an instant later she felt the ship lurch somewhere beneath her. There was a momentary sensation of forward motion being interrupted, and she noted how the sky ahead of her fell out of view as the pod arced away from the rest of the ship. She felt them pitching forward, and there was a fleeting glimpse of the jettisoned vessel plummeting toward white ground far below.

"Scanners detecting no appreciable higher-order life

signs," reported Canderon. "The region we are approaching is glacial, and there are no signs of significant technology or habitation."

Drevina asked, "What about the main drive section?"

"It is maintaining its final course. If that continues, it will fall into an area of the ocean that is one of the deepest on the planet. I cannot believe anyone looking for us will be able to find it."

"Good." That, at least, was one less thing for Drevina to worry about.

"Maneuvering thrusters are only partially functional," said Glorick. "I am having trouble stabilizing our descent."

Seeing that issue on her own console, Drevina asked, "Have you selected a landing site?"

Glorick grimaced. "I do not believe we will be able to maintain full control long enough to get us to the first location I chose." He paused, his hands moving over his controls before he shook his head. "It is requiring most of our available power to prevent us from crashing."

"Just put us down," advised Drevina as she glanced once more through the viewing port. The frigid region where the control pod soon would crash was not her first choice, but a controlled landing anywhere was better than risking an attempt to reach a more hospitable climate with their compromised systems. The area they looked to be approaching at least had some merits, being far away from any sizable concentration of indigenous intelligent life-forms. If the climate was as uninviting as Canderon suggested, it would afford them a decent place to hide.

The pod lurched with sufficient force to pull Drevina from her seat, and while her restraints kept her from being heaved out of the chair, they did so with no small amount of abuse. She gritted her teeth and bit back pain as the straps cut into her skin, and her back ached from the abrupt impact. The resulting alarm siren was silenced in a moment by Canderon.

"I am losing control," called out Glorick.

Outside the viewing port, the ground seemed to be rushing upward with greater speed, even though her controls told Drevina that the pod's rate of descent was slowing. She tried not to dwell on the fact that the readings were describing a scenario whereby they would still crash into the ice below, only at a slower speed.

"Firing braking thrusters," she said, stabbing at the appropriate control. The effect was immediate as ports on the pod's hull bottom flared to life, pushing upward against the small survival pod and arresting its plummet from orbit.

Then the thrusters shut down.

"No!"

Her shout was accompanied by renewed wailing as more alarms sounded in the cockpit, followed by a noticeable shift as the pod began to bank to one side. Without thinking, Drevina pushed herself back in her seat even as the onboard artificial gravity and inertial damping systems struggled to compensate for the abrupt change in the ship's attitude.

"Braking thrusters are offline!" Canderon turned in his seat. "I cannot restore them. We have no way to slow our descent!"

That was not entirely correct, Drevina knew. Tested piloting techniques for reducing the pod's speed were still available to her, but only if the remaining maneuvering thrusters remained functional, unlike so many other shipboard components.

"I am leveling our trajectory," she said. Reviewing her console's status displays that showed information about the pod's current speed and altitude, she began calculating how much time she had to execute whatever maneuver she hoped to bring them down in something that resembled a controlled landing. "Tell the others to brace themselves for impact."

Engaging the ship's remaining thrusters, Drevina felt the pod responding to her commands. For the first time, she sensed a connection with the craft as it plunged through the atmosphere. Now subject to gravity as well as the air it was displacing, the pod communicated to her its reactions to these external forces, allowing her to make necessary flight adjustments based on instinct and training rather than relying only on instrumentation. This was flying, something she had done since she was a child, first under her mother's guidance and later once she joined the resistance and—

One of the pod's remaining maneuvering thrusters selected that moment to fail, and the effect on the descending craft was immediate as it pitched to one side. Outside the port Drevina caught sight of blue sky where

she should be seeing the white of unending frozen t͡
rain. Both Glorick and Canderon shouted in alarm but
she ignored them, her hands playing across her console
in a frantic attempt to bring the pod back under control.

"Everyone brace yourselves," she said, her attention
riveted on her controls as she did her best not to stare
at the ground that was growing ever closer. "We are
landing."

This truly was a beautiful planet, Drevina decided.

She hoped she would live long enough to call it
home.

AFTEREFFECTS

Two

Tonia Barrows had no idea what was in her mug. She knew only that it could not be coffee.

"Commander?"

The voice of her yeoman, Dominic Schlatter, was tinged with concern, and Barrows looked up to see the younger man's worried expression.

"Somebody call medical," she said, placing the coffee mug on her desk and sliding it out of her reach. "I think I've just been poisoned."

Stepping toward her desk, Schlatter retrieved the mug. "I heard that maintenance was working on the food slots earlier today." He eyed the mug and its contents. "Maybe they need to go back and check it again."

The bitter taste of the bad coffee still on her tongue, Barrows made an exaggerated face. "Or just notify the weapons division that we're onto something new here."

"I'll check one of the other processors, Commander," Schlatter said, turning toward the door.

Barrows waved away the suggestion as she rose from

her seat. "I'll do it. I need to get out of this box for a bit, anyway." Her day had begun earlier than normal, as she had hoped to tackle the growing backlog of status reports, logs, and other correspondence sent to her by the station's various section heads. She also had her own reports to complete before her first meeting with Jupiter Station's new commanding officer, Captain Kevin Wyatt. Charged with overseeing not just the early warning network but also one of Starfleet's preeminent medical and scientific research facilities, Wyatt had a reputation for being unforgiving toward inefficiency of any sort had preceded him. With that in mind, Barrows had been putting in extra hours to make sure the Early Warning Monitoring Center and all of her people were squared away ahead of the incoming CO's first inspection.

Accomplishing that goal was going to be much more difficult if she could not find some decent coffee. Maybe she would use this opportunity to drop in on Leonard. Looking at her desk chronometer, she figured that he likely would be in his office by now. Leonard McCoy was an early riser, but she had known better than to wake him at what he would have called an "unholy hour" when she opted to start her own workday early. Though he could be grumpy with little or no provocation, having his sleep interrupted for anything less than a full-blown crisis was just asking for trouble. Smiling at the image her thoughts conjured as she stepped around her desk, Barrows straightened her uniform jacket on her way across her office.

The doors parted at her approach, and she stepped into the EWMC operations center. Though somewhat larger than a starship's bridge, the circular room was configured in much the same manner. Ten workstations formed a ring around the Op Center's perimeter, broken only by the doors to her office and the turbolift on the room's opposite side. Those stations surrounded a smaller hub of four consoles situated in a recessed deck area. Gray railings separated the hub from the upper deck area, broken by four sets of steps leading down into the center well. The bulkheads extended above the perimeter workstations, and set into them were eight large display screens. Between those screens and the smaller displays at each of the individual consoles, the Op Center was a constant hive of information.

"Greetings, Commander," offered one of her junior analysts, Lieutenant T'Pril. A tall, even statuesque Vulcan, she stood at one of the hub stations in the middle of the room, and it took Barrows an extra moment to remember that the lieutenant was the day's watch officer. Indeed, it was her first time taking on the role since her arrival aboard the station earlier in the month.

"Good morning, T'Pril," Barrows replied, nodding in greeting. "How was your first night in the hot seat?"

The Vulcan's eyes narrowed. "My first duty shift as watch officer proved largely uneventful. Thank you for the opportunity. I look forward to my next scheduled posting."

Despite her recent arrival, she had wasted no time

acclimating to her duties, and Barrows had been eager to get her into the watch rotation. Overseeing the Op Center and all of its inherent activity was a duty Barrows preferred to rotate among her officers. It gave those in her charge an opportunity to refine their own skills at managing multiple demands on their time as well as the team of subordinates under their temporary command. The latter task often proved the most challenging, as each member of the EWMC team was responsible for myriad responsibilities that required them to operate individually and independently for lengthy periods. Coordinating their efforts, and ensuring that nothing was lost in the soup of information they all worked to interpret and understand, was one of the more taxing and insightful tests of leadership and command presence Barrows had ever seen, short of attacks by enemy vessels. To that end, their performance in these situations was a significant component of the regular personnel reviews and fitness reports she was required to submit for each of the men and women under her command.

Barrows said, "Uneventful? That's an interesting way to put it." She glanced around the room, taking in the various display monitors. "What they didn't tell you when you got your orders, Lieutenant, is that the days start to blur together after a while."

"There was one incident, Commander," said T'Pril. "Station maintenance did dispatch a message earlier this morning that they were diagnosing an issue with the food processor systems. We were advised to use the food slots with caution, as the system might produce unexpected results."

"Yeah, I met one of those already." Barrows offered an embellished shake of her head. "I don't recommend it." She glanced around the room. "But, if that's the worst problem we had, I won't complain."

T'Pril said, "The only other item of note is that the third wave of software upgrades for the outer boundary stations completed at zero-two-thirty-seven hours. Verification and diagnostics are still in progress, with an expected completion time of zero-nine-hundred. All stations have remained operational throughout the process."

Nodding in approval, Barrows said, "Outstanding. Three down, four to go. Glad to hear it didn't cause any problems in here. I'd hate for our people to be bored."

As was the case at any hour of the day, members of the EWMC team occupied all fourteen stations, each of them tasked with reviewing and analyzing the constant streams of incoming information. Data collected by Jupiter Station's array of long-range sensors as well as the network of automated satellites forming an artificial boundary at the solar system's outer edge was routed here, where Barrows and her teams—with considerable help from the station's computers—reviewed and analyzed the continuous influx of information. The computers handled the bulk processing, sifting, and summarizing of data received from the various inputs, and sophisticated software protocols were more than capable of identifying threats or other issues of potential concern. Despite the impressive abilities of such autonomous processes, just about anyone who worked in this field, or even with sensor arrays and their accompanying decision support systems, agreed that such tools could not replace the eyes, reasoning, and intuition of a well-trained analyst. Tonia Barrows was one of those believers, and so was everyone under her command.

"Once the upgrades are done, let's run a full diagnostic on our own systems, just to make sure there aren't any sneaky problems with the interface between us, the main computer, and the boundary network." Barrows paused, considering the task she was about to have her people undertake. Looking at the people currently operating the different workstations, she knew that most of them had reported several hours early for the start of their shifts in order to support the upgrade processes under way at the time. They could use a break, she decided. "The diagnostic should probably eat up the bulk of the day, so let's get beta shift in here early this afternoon and be ready to hand off to them by thirteen hundred hours."

T'Pril nodded. "Understood."

"Good. Now, if you'll excuse me, Lieutenant, somewhere on this station is a food slot with a cup of coffee, and I want it."

Barrows had moved to within a few steps of the Op Center's turbolift when she heard an alert tone from one of the consoles behind her.

"What's that?" she asked, turning toward the sound even as similar indicators began sounding around the room. She noted how everyone had refocused their attention on their respective workstations, hunching over sensor viewers or computer interfaces. For a moment, Barrows imagined she could sense the tension level rising in the very air around her.

Easy does it, Commander. Let's not jump the gun here.

Stepping down into the hub, Barrows moved toward T'Pril, who was already back at her station and had elected to remain standing before her console. The Vulcan's long fingers moved across the rows of controls arrayed before her, and her gaze was focused on the station's array of eight display monitors. On each screen was a litany of data streaming almost too fast for Barrows to follow.

"Observation Station A47 has detected an anomaly," T'Pril reported. "It appears to be an intermittent energy distortion. Long-range sensors first detected it when it came within twenty million kilometers of the system's outer boundary."

Barrows frowned. "First detected? Where is it now?"

"It was last detected at a range of approximately four million, six hundred thousand kilometers, and appears to be traveling at warp speed, but the method of propulsion is unknown. The readings to this point have been erratic, which is why the computer did not alert us before now." T'Pril tapped a short sequence of controls. "At first, it was attempting to ascertain whether it had acquired a faulty reading. Only after the subsequent contacts did the protocols ascertain that it was not an irregularity in our systems."

"Are you saying we can't track it?" asked Barrows, already dreading the answer she knew was coming.

T'Pril shook her head. "Not with any consistency, Commander. Whatever it is, it appears capable of eluding our sensors, at least enough to mask its movements. As such, we are unable to pinpoint its course or probable destination."

"Sound yellow alert." Moving past the Vulcan, Barrows tapped a control to activate the intercom system. "Early warning center to Captain Wyatt."

A moment later, the gruff, stern voice of Kevin Wyatt came through the workstation's communications panel. "*Wyatt here. Commander Barrows, is that you?*"

"Affirmative, sir. We've got what looks to be a situation brewing up here." After using as few words as possible to describe what the long-range sensors seemed to be tracking and the difficulties being experienced, Barrows added, "We're issuing a stationwide alert, but I think you'll want to apprise Starfleet Command, sir."

The Jupiter Station's commanding officer said, "*Agreed. Continue your scanning efforts and keep me updated. I'm on my way up to you.*"

"Acknowledged. Barrows out." Severing the connection, she was aware that the rest of her team was dividing their attention between their respective stations and her. Looking to T'Pril, she asked, "Anything new?"

"Negative, Commander. The energy reading remains sporadic and elusive."

"Let's get Masilamani on this," said Barrows, gesturing toward one of the perimeter stations near the Op

Center's turbolift. "I want him sifting through whatever mess of data the computer pulled this from."

"I have already assigned him that task and routed the necessary data clusters for his review, Commander."

Upon hearing his name, Lieutenant Senthil Masilamani turned from his station, rising from his seat before moving to the railing encircling the hub well. A young man of Indian descent, the sensor officer's features were such that even when his expression was composed, he seemed to still be smiling. "I've only just started my analysis, Commander. Whatever that thing is, it's not like anything I've ever seen."

"I think we can safely assume it's not a naturally occurring phenomenon," said Barrows. "Not if it's traveling at warp. I'm also not too happy that our warning systems didn't detect this thing earlier than they did, and the fact that we can't seem to keep a decent track of it makes me wonder if it's alone out there." If what they were seeing was a ship, had the sensors and early warning stations failed to detect the presence of additional vessels? Assuming that was true, where were those other craft now? Despite such troubling thoughts, Barrows's gut was telling her that the anomaly was a single occurrence, because she could not bring herself to believe that the most advanced sensor array and detection apparatus at Starfleet's disposal had failed to such an astounding degree.

Gut, don't fail me now.

Barrows noted the display on one of the screens at T'Pril's workstation. "Despite what at first looks like an erratic course, there's a more or less straight line cutting across the system's outer edge." She entered a string of commands into her console. "If I had to guess, I'd think the thing was heading toward Neptune."

T'Pril replied, "A logical deduction, despite the lack of evidence."

"For now, I'll take it," said Masilamani.

Continuing to study the computer-generated track of the still-unidentified anomaly, Barrows said, "What if we redirect stations A55 through A61 and attempt to surround it?"

"Triangulation." T'Pril punctuated her simple answer with an arching of her right eyebrow. "It is an unorthodox suggestion. We must also consider the risks of leaving unattended the sectors overseen by those remote stations."

Masilamani replied, "We can expand the coverage with other stations to close the gap, Commander. We're only talking about a short time, just enough to get a fix on . . . whatever that is."

"If we can lock it down," said Barrows, "long-range sensors should be able to track it until we can get a ship or two out there to investigate. Let's do it."

"There is another point to consider, Commander," said T'Pril. "The object may interpret our redeploying of the monitoring satellites as an aggressive action."

Barrows nodded. "That's true, but on the other hand, we can replace those. If this thing is a threat, I'd rather it demonstrate that on automated drones than a starship or something else out here with a crew."

A tone sounded on T'Pril's console, and she touched another control. "Security reports the station is on yellow alert. Defensive shields are online, and weapons are on standby."

"So much for your uneventful duty shift, Lieutenant," said Barrows. "Carry on with our redeployment plan, and while we're doing that, start prepping a data packet for transmission to Starfleet Command. We definitely need to call this one in."

Three

The Northwest Passage
May 30, 1851

If there was any chance of ever being warm again, Thomas Dunning was certain it would require his death and descent into Hell. This, he decided, was looking ever more like an inviting proposition.

Quit your crying, buddy-boy. You've made it this far, and the end is looking to be right there in sight. Don't be giving up now.

Such thoughts, and others like them, filled Dunning's mind as he trudged across the unending field of white. Ice and snow as far as the eye could see, at least in this direction. In the distance ahead of him and to either side were jagged formations where ice had collided on the floe, creating the equivalent of small hills, atop which piled still more ice. The effect was that Dunning felt as though he was wandering through a diminutive mountain range. Though the sun had been shining during the previous three days, the weather had seen fit to make today, the day he was assigned to the hunting detail, a depressing slate gray that seemed to him the color of death.

"You doing all right, Tommy?"

Looking up from where he realized he had been focused on nothing besides putting one foot in front of the other as he made his way across the frozen terrain, Dunning saw his companion, William Holmes, staring back at him. Like Dunning, Holmes was dressed in layers of tattered, heavy clothing that only partially served to keep the brutal cold at bay. Resting on his right shoulder was a Colt carbine rifle that was a match for the one Dunning carried and, like its owner, had seen better days.

"Yeah, I'm fine. Just cold. And hungry. And tired of looking at all of your ugly faces." He smiled at that last part. "I've spent more nights sleeping with you slobs than with my wife."

Holmes released a hoarse laugh. When Holmes grinned, Dunning could see the gaps from the teeth his friend had lost, and it made him run his tongue around the inside of his own mouth. He had lost five teeth to scurvy, the same disease that had ravaged nearly every member of the crews of the *Advance* and her sister ship, the *Rescue*, during the ten months the two United States Navy vessels had been trapped in the ice floe. With fresh fruits and vegetables long depleted from the ships' stores following their departure from New York more than a year earlier, the crews had been subsisting on the cured and salted meat that made up the bulk of their provisions, along with dwindling supplies of dried grains. Their meals were supplemented and the scurvy beaten back on rare occasions with sauerkraut and lime juice, though both of those were also in limited supply and thus were used sparingly. Instead, the *Advance*'s doctor, Elisha Kane, had prescribed fresh meat to combat the disease's effects. To that end, regular hunting parties were dispatched from both vessels in search of birds, foxes, seals, the occasional polar bear, and anything else that presented itself as a target of opportunity.

"Let's keep moving," said Holmes, who for the current hunt had taken the lead on their departure from the ship, setting a pace Dunning knew would get them in short order to the area that had proven fruitful for hunting. "If we hurry, we can find something worth eating and get it back to the ship before dark."

Dunning nodded as he shifted his rifle to a more comfortable position on his shoulder. "Lead on, mate." He knew he would feel better once he had a decent meal. While the raw meat procured from whatever they might shoot today would serve to bolster what had long since become a maddeningly boring diet, it would succeed in its primary purpose: keeping the men alive.

Still, Thomas Dunning longed for the day he could sink his remaining teeth into a fresh apple, pulled from a tree in the orchard on his family farm. Imagining the crisp, sweet taste and the juice running down his chin brought forth another smile. Such thoughts and momentary diversions filled both his waking hours and his dreams. Would he see home again? What about his shipmates or his brothers on the *Rescue*? Would either of their vessels sail again into New York Harbor?

The skipper's seen us this far. He'll get us home, all right.

What had begun the previous spring as a search and possible rescue mission for the *Advance* and *Rescue* had turned into an odyssey of survival for the crews of both vessels. Dispatched from New York at the behest of Henry Grinnell, a shipping merchant with enough money to buy and loan them to the navy to do his bidding, both ships traveled north with the mission of determining the ultimate fate of a British expedition into the Arctic. For whatever reason, Grinnell had become fascinated with the story of Captain John Franklin, who in 1845 had led two ships on a voyage to chart those areas of the Northwest Passage that had not been navigated. A previous expedition by the British had failed to turn up any traces of the lost expedition, after which Grinnell had approached the U.S. Navy about a search party of its own.

At least, that was how it had been explained to Dunning and the rest of the men crewing the *Advance* and the *Rescue*. Scuttlebutt aboard both ships was that one or both vessels had become trapped in Arctic ice and crews were forced to abandon them in an attempt to survive the harsh winter weather on land. That idea seemed to become more likely when evidence of encampments were found in the area of Devon Island, where no previous British expeditions were known to have ventured. This seemed to galvanize the *Advance*'s captain, Lieutenant Edwin De Haven, as well as the *Rescue*'s commanding officer, Samuel Griffin, to continue the search. It was obvious that both shipmasters believed that they had to be within striking distance of finding Franklin and the more than one hundred twenty men who had accompanied him into this vast, unexplored region. It was this sense of looming success that also had motivated the crews of both ships. Dunning had been surprised to learn that in addition to the two American naval vessels, ten other British ships on separate expeditions also were charting the region in search of Franklin's party. This, of course, had led Dunning to wonder just how important this fellow might have been, or whether he may have possessed untold riches that justified such efforts to find him.

Dunning's interest in such matters, along with that of the rest of the men, withered and died once the *Advance* and *Rescue* both became trapped in the same sort of ice floe believed to have captured Franklin's ships. From that point forward, there had been only one mission: stay alive long enough to break out of their prison and return home. Days had stretched into weeks and then to months, as both crews worked to keep their vessels from being torn apart by the always-shifting ice. The floe in which they were entombed had drifted first north and then back to the south, and after months of this, salvation seemed as though it might be at hand. Open water was visible beyond the ice pack, and the efforts of the crew to cut with long saws through the ice around the ships was bearing fruit. Lieutenant De Haven was predicting that both vessels might be free of the floe within the week. This news had raised the men's spirits, though only to a modest degree. The un-relenting monotony of their predicament had worn on them all, to the point that even a deviation such as this, the possible final hunt of their ordeal, was not sufficient to elevate Dunning's mood. Holmes had expressed a similar sentiment as the two men departed the ship, and the gray, gloomy skies felt like fate slapping them just one more time before releasing them and their shipmates to set sail for home.

In actuality, he was thankful for the fickle elements on this day. Navigating the ice packs in bright sun-light brought its own risks, not the least of which was how the harsh rays of the sun illuminated the inces-sant blanket of white, all but blinding anyone luckless enough to be assigned to a working party or other de-tail off the ship. On those days, Dunning preferred not to go ashore but instead see to any of the ever lengthy list of tasks to be carried out aboard the ship. There was always something to do, in particular anything that contributed to combating the effects of the relentless winter weather.

"Almost there," Holmes called over his shoulder.

Dunning was about to reply when something ahead of them caught his eye. Squinting to make out what he at first thought might be an exposed outcropping of rock fifty or sixty yards ahead of them, he realized that the dark object contrasting with the surrounding snow and ice was *moving*.

"Will!" he said, pointing, but by now Holmes also had seen it and was lifting the carbine from his shoulder even as the dark object changed direction and ran away from them.

"Is that a bear?" Holmes shouted, dropping to one knee and sighting down the length of his rifle's barrel. "No, wait. That ain't no bear. What the hell . . . ?"

It was running upright like a man, but something about its silhouette just seemed wrong, somehow. For a moment, Dunning thought they might have come across an ape. What would the rest of the men back on the *Advance* think of that? However, even as he pondered that notion he realized how crazy it had to be. Apes and monkeys and things like that were found in warmer regions like Africa, thousands of miles from here, right? This was something else, either a man in odd clothing or something he had never seen or even heard about before this minute.

"Wait," Dunning said. "That looks like—"

Holmes fired his rifle and the Colt roared like thunder, the report echoing across the ice. The man or animal or whatever it was kept running, and Holmes cocked the carbine with a speed born of skill and practice before firing again. This time Dunning saw the runner stumble and fall to the ice.

"You hit him!" he shouted, running past Holmes with his own rifle held to his chest. "Come on!"

Could it be a member of Captain Franklin's expedition? That unwelcome thought made itself known as Dunning heard the runner utter what could only be a shout of warning, but in a language he did not understand. Dunning lumbered over the ice, feeling his boots slipping despite his scored soles and the burlap tied around his feet and legs. Ahead of them, the figure disappeared around a mound of broken ice that jutted upward where parts of the floe had come together.

"Wait!" he shouted, wondering why he bothered. Whoever the person was, he had just been shot at and possibly struck without provocation. It made perfect sense that he would keep running. By this point, Dunning had closed the distance to less than twenty yards, and he was certain he could hear the sounds of feet running ahead of him. He glanced to the ground he was traversing and saw no sign of blood. Had Holmes not hit the man?

Moving around the ice cropping, Dunning raised his rifle to his shoulder, looking for a target. There was nothing ahead of him but ice.

What in the name of all that's holy . . . ?

He heard the sound of labored breathing from behind him, and Holmes lurched into view. His face was flushed, and his breaths were coming in deep, rapid gasps. Lifting his rifle, Holmes pulled the weapon to his shoulder and stepped around Dunning, who had swept the area ahead of them and seen no sign of their quarry. Likewise, there seemed to be nothing of consequence that could be used for concealment. The ground ahead of them was all but flat.

"Where the hell did he go?"

Drevina listened to Glorick's strained attempts at respiration as her friend struggled to recover from his exertion. Her hand was on his arm, signaling him to remain quiet as the two of them along with Canderon watched the two humans who were standing a body length in front of her. Both males were turning in circles, their projectile weapons at the ready.

"Damn it. I know I hit him," said the human whose weapon had grazed Glorick's arm.

His companion replied, "He fell, all right, but I didn't see no blood."

Drevina glanced to her friend and saw that Glorick was holding his other hand over the superficial wound. Whatever blood it was producing seemed to be absorbed by the layers of his protective clothing, but she looked to the ground just to be sure. She did not think her ability to influence the thoughts of these primitive beings extended to masking the presence of spilled blood or anything else they might drop, and she did not want to test the limits of her gifts just now. The muzzle of the human's weapon was close enough that she could reach out and touch it, or even take it from him.

"You think he's got a camp near here?" asked the second human. "Maybe he's one of Franklin's men."

"That's what I was thinking," said his colleague, "but why would he run? We're supposed to be out here trying to find him, right?"

"Because you shot him? That ain't real friendly, mate."

Even with the translator units Drevina and her friends wore around their necks, understanding the nuances of human language had proven difficult. Their furtive study of the previous groups of humans they had encountered in this region had helped the translators build a linguistic database from which to work, but the process was far from perfect. As was the case among her people, the denizens of this world appeared to employ numerous languages, and within each there existed any number of regional variations.

That seemed to be the case here, as well. Drevina and the others had been observing this group of humans at regular intervals for hundreds of days, based on their calculations of the planet's rotation. The two sailing ships in which they had arrived in the region had been icebound even prior to the Iramahl's discovery of them. She and her companions had watched the vessels' crews work not only to survive but also to free their ships from the ice, or at least keep them from being destroyed as they moved with the ice floes. As their food supplies dwindled, and they began suffering from disease due to lack of proper nutrition, the humans had ventured out onto the ice and to the adjacent land, hunting lower life-forms for sustenance. They had persevered, and from Drevina's observations at least, they had done so with remarkable spirit.

"Come on," said the first human. "We should get back to the ship. The skipper will want to know about this. We can get more men for a bigger search. Whoever he is, if he's running around out here with no gear, his camp can't be far."

His companion grunted something Drevina could not understand, despite her proximity. Neither human harbored any suspicion that their prey stood before them. Drevina could sense the man's thoughts, and she detected no hint that their presence had been detected. The gift with which she had been born and which she had mastered throughout her life was serving her here in the manner she had used it against Ptaen soldiers during her time with the resistance. It was a rare ability, one possessed only by a fraction of her people, and numerous theories had attempted to explain the phenomenon. Drevina had stopped paying attention to the debates long before joining the resistance movement, satisfied that she carried within her at least one more weapon to use against the Ptaen oppressors, and that was before her science knowledge became an even greater asset.

She had discovered her ability worked during earlier observations of another group of humans whose ships had become similarly trapped. Unlike this party, however, the first group had abandoned their vessels and moved to land in their bid for survival. Drevina and her friends had found the encampment they had established and used for a time before forging onward over land, and she also had discovered where three of their number had apparently been interred. The text carved into wooden markers at the burial site was indecipherable, but the intent seemed obvious enough, based on what she had been able to glean regarding human death rituals.

"Yeah," said the second human, lowering his weapon. "You're right. Let's get back." Drevina watched him shake his head. "Damnedest thing I ever saw."

The three Iramahl waited in silence as the two men turned and began retracing their steps. Only when they were out of sight, and Drevina could no longer feel the proximity of their thoughts, did she allow herself to relax.

"Are you injured?" asked Canderon, moving to Glorick and gesturing to the operational specialist's arm.

Glorick shook his head. "It is a minor wound, easily treated, but we should not waste time. This may be an opportunity, Drevina."

"I think you are correct, old friend." After the seemingly unending string of days they had spent coping with this inhospitable terrain since crashing their ship, she had wondered if they might spend the rest of their lives here. There were advantages to such a choice, of course. The climate here made it uninviting to all but the hardiest of this world's higher-order life-forms, but shelter and food were a constant challenge. Drevina and her friends had debated attempting to travel to a warmer region, and even one that was home to more people, but the prospects of doing so on foot were remote, at best.

Only when they had encountered the first expeditions attempting to navigate this region's hazardous, ice-stricken waterways did a plan begin to take shape. They might be able to secret themselves aboard one of the vessels making such a transit, but even that idea was fraught with obstacles. One group of ships had already fallen prey to the ice floes, but this newer contingent had fared far better. Now, after drifting toward

comparatively warmer waters for numerous days, it
seemed that the two trapped vessels were on the cusp
of reclaiming their freedom, and with that might come
the chance Drevina and her companions were seeking.

"If those two are correct," she said, gesturing in the
direction of the departed humans, "they will bring others to search for us. That may be our best opportunity
to board one of their vessels."

Canderon frowned as he worked to treat Glorick's
wound with a suturing instrument from their emergency medical equipment. "Should we not wait a while
longer? It is impossible to predict when the ships will
be free of the ice."

It was a risk, of course, but their observations of
the ships and their crews as the ice in which they
were trapped approached open water had convinced
Drevina that escape was imminent. A handful of days
at most, based on her scanner readings, during which
the humans would be finalizing their preparations as
well as doing whatever they could to accelerate the
process of breaking free. She had watched them toiling
with cutting tools to weaken the ice around the two
ships and seen them celebrate their progress even as
their emotions rose at the sight of the water that was so
very close. Escape was within reach, they knew.

"Now is the time," said Drevina. "We can always abandon the plan if discovery becomes a possibility, but we
were going to have to face the risk. At least now we can
have a decent chance of finding a better place to hide,
while the bulk of the crews are away from their ships."

"Very well," said Canderon. His treatment of Glorick's injury completed, he returned the suturing tool to a pocket of his clothing. "If we are to do this, we should wait for darkness."

Glorick replied, "We will have to abandon some of our belongings. There will be limited capacity to store such things on the ships."

"Agreed," said Drevina. Almost all of their possessions had been utilized to affect their survival since arriving on this world, but they could make do with essentials such as weapons, scanners, medical supplies, and a few other items. Even this desolate environment had served them well, allowing them to forage for food and other things necessary to sustain and protect them. They would have similar success, she knew, once they relocated to a more welcoming climate.

Where these unsuspecting humans and fate chose to take them, Drevina did not know.

Four

San Francisco, Earth
Earth Year 2283

"How is it possible to be this busy and this bored, all at the same time?"

Leaning back in his chair, Admiral James Kirk studied his day's schedule. He waded through the time stamps, messages, notes, and suggestions from the numerous people who sought to provide him with all manner of unsolicited yet hopefully helpful advice. What was left? Inspections, paperwork, staff meetings, paperwork, personnel reviews, and still more paperwork.

Somehow, without his noticing, let alone attempting to put up a fight, this is what had come to define his existence. How had that happened? How had he allowed it to happen?

"It's my understanding that admirals are required by regulations to be bored, sir," said his aide, Lieutenant Commander Shanna Gilkeson, from where she stood on the other side of his desk while holding the data padd that Kirk had come to view as an extension of her left arm. Rare was the occasion that she went anywhere without the ubiquitous device. "If you don't mind my saying so, I think you're handling it far better than most of your peers."

Kirk smiled. The easy familiarity between him and Gilkeson had taken time to build. Upon her assignment to his office as his aide and despite her best efforts, she had been unable to suppress what she later admitted to feelings of "hero worship," as she had described it. Though he tried to take such confessions in stride, Kirk had never grown accustomed to the celebrity that had been foisted upon him. Never was he more uncomfortable with such attention than when encountering young, eager officers on their first assignment, or when he found himself addressing a class of enthusiastic, idealistic cadets at Starfleet Academy. That sort of thing had been much more common in the months following the *U.S.S. Enterprise*'s return to Earth after the completion of its five-year mission of exploration. Starfleet had wasted no time or effort promoting the significance of this accomplishment, as though no other starship crew or commander in the history of space travel had ever carried out their orders. There was much about which to be proud as far as what he and his crew had accomplished. However, Kirk remained troubled by the romanticizing of the *Enterprise*'s missions, which tended to overlook the less pleasant aspects of what happened during those five years. Whenever he felt himself sliding in that direction, he reminded himself of the ninety-four men and women who had perished under his command.

"Are we still on schedule for this afternoon?" he asked, eyeing the computer screen perched on one corner of his desk. Was it his imagination, or were the words and numbers streaming across the screen a bit blurry?

Gilkeson replied, "Yes, sir. Commandant Rouviere said this year's class has been talking about your lecture for weeks. He instructed me to warn you to be ready for an onslaught of questions."

Unable to deal with a small flush of pride, Kirk turned his chair so that he now faced the large, curved windows that served as his office's rear wall. Twenty stories above the ground, he was afforded a spectacular view of San Francisco Bay as well as the Starfleet Academy campus just a short walk from the headquarters complex. Even from this distance, he was able to see people moving about the walking paths that wound around and through the lush, well-maintained lawns and other green spaces. Tiny figures, most wearing maroon uniforms identifying them as cadets, traversed the trails or partook of various outdoor activities.

It was a spectacular day to be outside, Kirk concluded.

"Do you think the commandant would let me hold my lecture in the park?"

"Only if he doesn't care about seeing any of his cadets for the rest of the day." Looking up from her data padd, Gilkeson added, "Your reputation does precede you, Admiral. That's sort of the point."

Kirk sighed. "Thanks for reminding me." Though

his apparent notoriety for bending or flouting rules was by no means unearned, he preferred to think that the choices he had made on those occasions were in service to the greater good. Now that he was in a position of leadership as well as teaching and mentoring thanks to his frequent visits to the Academy, the last thing he wanted to do was instill in the latest crop of cadets a desire to emulate his behavior to such an exacting degree. On the other hand, neither did he wish to dampen their enthusiasm as they prepared to travel to the stars as representatives of their homeworlds and the Federation. He wanted them to learn from their instructors to remember the spirit as well as the letter of the laws and regulations they were expected to uphold, but he also hoped that they would not ignore their gut, their instinct to do what was right regardless of the rules standing in their way.

Sometimes, it's better to seek forgiveness instead of permission.

"Admiral Morrow just sent a message," said Gilkeson, her attention once more focused on her data padd. "He's requesting a meeting with you following your lecture." She smirked. "So much for playing hooky the rest of the afternoon."

"It's like he's a mind reader." Kirk turned his chair from the window. "What's he want to talk about?"

"Fleet redeployment along the Neutral Zone. He mentions your report about the recent spike in activity from the Romulans."

Nodding, Kirk replied, "Let him know I'll be there."

The report in question had been the result of several late nights spent poring over data gleaned from numerous sources. Log entries from starships assigned to patrol the zone, long-range scanner telemetry from observation outposts positioned along the border, and even unofficial accounts from civilian shipmasters operating in adjacent sectors had contributed to his analysis. Once the patterns began to emerge, Kirk still did not know if the Romulans were up to something or were simply modifying their own patrol patterns in an attempt to gauge Starfleet responses, but both of those scenarios factored into his thinking. With all of this swirling in his head, he had consulted his closest friend and trusted counsel, Captain Spock, and the two of them polished the final report Kirk submitted to the Commander of Starfleet, Admiral Harrison Morrow. Their recommendations included new patrol patterns for ships on the Federation side of the zone, as well as a series of exercises starship commanders could employ in order to observe the responses of their Romulan counterparts.

And the game plays on.

Kirk had for the most part been unable to affect how his status as a playing piece on the ever-evolving board changed over time. Now far removed from his former life as a starship captain, his role as chief of Starfleet Operations included sending other starship commanders to push outward the boundaries of both territory and knowledge, dispatching them as explorers and defenders of Federation security. Meanwhile, Kirk's lengthy career and hard-won experience, and even the notoriety that had come his way over the years, had seen to it he now was "too important" or "too valuable" to risk being lost in space.

We need you here, as put by his friend and mentor, Admiral Heihachiro Nogura, when trying to mollify Kirk while telling him about his new assignment at Starfleet Command following a brief flirtation with retirement earlier in the year. *I need you. I need your ability to grasp the bigger picture the way very few of these other rear echelon managers and analysts possess. None of them has been out there, or if they have, then it's been years or decades since they sat in a center seat. I need somebody with fresh eyes and fresh ideas. That's you, Jim. I need you, and so does the next generation of starship captains. I want them to learn from officers like you.*

It was Nogura. There were very few people Kirk could outright refuse when called to serve. Admiral Heihachiro Nogura was one such person. Besides, though he had opted to retire from Starfleet several months ago, it had not taken him long to grow restless. Even the companionship of Antonia Salvatori, the woman he had met while visiting his uncle's farm in Idaho, had failed to shield him from the desire—no, the *need*—to serve, to be useful. He tried to escape it, retreating to a secluded mountain cabin he had built in the Sierra Nevada region of California, but the call could not be denied. The retirement and his life with Antonia ended at the same moment. While Kirk held no regrets about returning to Starfleet, losing her had been painful; part of him suspected it eventually would have happened one way or another. He had long ago come to understand that being unable to sustain a long-term romantic relationship was one of his many failings.

You should stick to what you're good at.

Of course, Kirk had been unable to do just that for a while, now. How many years had passed since he had occupied the captain's chair on the bridge of a starship? Sure, there was the occasional one-off mission, but how long had it been since a ship and its crew were his to command?

Too long.

Something beeped, and Kirk looked from his desk to see Commander Gilkeson once more consulting her data padd. "It's time, sir. Commandant Rouviere says he'll meet you at the Academy's VIP transporter station."

"I thought I'd walk," Kirk said.

"Then you probably should have left ten minutes ago."

Ignoring the remark, Kirk rose from his chair and brushed the front of his uniform tunic to smooth away the wrinkles. "How do I look?"

Gilkeson offered a nod of approval. "Ready to kick cadet butt and take names, sir." She glanced again at her data padd. "If you're serious about walking, I can alert him that there might be a slight delay."

"Perhaps you can call downstairs and have my wheelchair standing by."

"Maintenance reports they're still reconfiguring its dilithium matrix, sir, so it's only good for impulse speeds."

The lightning-quick comeback prompted a chuckle, and Kirk rendered a mock salute. "Well played, Commander."

He was halfway across his office and heading for the door when the chime of his desk communicator panel beeped. Though tempted to ignore it, a skeptical look from his assistant stopped him from leaving. "Answer it. Maybe the Romulans are invading, and they'll cancel the lecture."

"No one's that lucky, sir." Moving to Kirk's desk, Gilkeson tapped the control to activate its embedded comm interface. "Admiral Kirk's office. Lieutenant Commander Gilkeson speaking."

The soft, gruff yet stern voice of Admiral Heihachiro Nogura erupted from the speakers installed in unobtrusive locations around the office. "*Starfleet Academy's still standing, Commander, so I'm assuming he's not left yet.*"

"I'm here, Admiral," Kirk said, waving Gilkeson away from the desk and nodding at her expression of relief. "What can I do for you?"

"*You can haul yourself up to my office, Jim. We've got ourselves an actual emergency, right here in our own backyard.*"

Kirk directed Commander Gilkeson to make apologies on his behalf to Commandant Rouviere and the waiting class. The cadets likely would hate him for not rescuing them from an opportunity for their other professors to assign them additional work and study. He then made his way to the top floor of Starfleet's main headquarters building. He entered the foyer of Nogura's office, and the commander working at the desk reserved for the admiral's assistant rose from his chair, snapping to a position of attention. Kirk struggled to remember the man's name, but failed.

Bennett. Beyer. Bonanno. Something like that.

"Good morning, sir," said the young officer. "Admiral Nogura wants me to send you right in."

Gesturing for him to return to his seat, Kirk replied, "As you were, Commander. Thank you."

He paused to straighten his maroon uniform jacket and verify that the buckle for his wide black belt was in place before proceeding to the doors, which parted at his approach to the suite's inner sanctum and allowed him to enter the room without breaking stride. Modest yet tasteful furnishings adorned the office, beginning with the oval-shaped obsidian desk positioned at the room's far end along with a matching round conference table and chairs situated along the wall to Kirk's left. A large rectangular viewscreen of the size one might find aboard the bridge of a starship was mounted on the wall opposite the conference table, with a pair of plush recliners positioned before it. Freestanding shelves in the office's corners held books and an assortment of mementos and other personal items, all of them speaking to their owner's long, distinguished career.

As with Kirk's own office, the view of the bay afforded from this location and its concave, full-length windows was magnificent, with the higher elevation offering him a look at Alcatraz Island out beyond the Golden Gate Bridge. Standing before the windows, hands clasped behind his back as he contemplated his vantage point was Heihachiro Nogura.

A human male of Asian descent and indeterminate age—despite Kirk's best efforts to access that information—Nogura had been a Starfleet flag officer since well before their first meeting years earlier, back when Kirk was a captain and commanding the *Enterprise*. Further, he had always occupied some key position within the Starfleet Command hierarchy. Twenty years ago, when the Federation and the Klingon Empire appeared locked in a perpetual war footing, Nogura was one of the prime voices directing Starfleet responses and policy at a time when it seemed conflict would erupt at the slightest provocation. Kirk had always found him to be a measured, thoughtful man who communicated much by what he did not say about any given topic, and Kirk believed the reason the Federation was able to prevent all-out war with the Klingons was because of his steady, firm leadership and convictions.

"Good morning, Admiral," Kirk said, standing just inside the doorway of Nogura's office. "You wanted to see me?"

Turning from the window, Nogura seemed to swim within the confines of his Starfleet uniform. He had always been slight of build, but Kirk could not help noting how time at long last was beginning to catch up with the man. His thin hair, once jet black with streaks of gray when Kirk had first come to work for him at Starfleet Headquarters, had within the last few years gone completely white. The lines in his face now were longer and deeper, but they did nothing to conceal the fire that still burned in the admiral's cobalt-blue eyes. Likewise, age had done little to slow him down, as evidenced by the commanding stride with which he crossed his office. He did not slow as he regarded Kirk.

"Do you believe in ghosts, Jim?"

Uncertain as to how to reply, Kirk frowned but said nothing. Nogura, content to let the question go unanswered, walked toward the large viewscreen.

"We appear to have a ghost, right here in our own solar system." Moving to the keypad set into the wall next to the screen, he pressed a control and the display activated, offering a depiction of the Federation seal. "Computer, open the file marked *Anomaly Alpha*." In response to his command, the image shifted so that it now depicted a computer-generated representation of the Sol system. Without further instructions from the admiral, the schematic zoomed in to highlight Neptune and its family of moons.

"Less than two hours ago, our early monitoring people out at Jupiter Station detected an unidentified energy distortion beyond the outer boundary, traveling at warp. Since then, it's shifted its course to enter the system."

Kirk frowned. "An artificial energy signature?"

"That's the logical conclusion. The Jupiter Station teams are still sorting through the data trying to find additional clues."

"Commander Barrows," said Kirk. "Good to know she's overseeing this." Tonia Barrows had served her first tour of duty as a yeoman aboard the *Enterprise* during his tenure as that ship's captain. Their paths had crossed on more frequent occasions in recent years, owing to Barrows having continued her career path in starship operations, advancing to different positions within Starfleet's operations division. She had taken over as commander of the Early Warning Monitoring Center on Jupiter Station two years earlier, working in close proximity to one of his oldest friends, Leonard McCoy. Barrows and McCoy had enjoyed an on-again, off-again romantic relationship over the years, which apparently had returned to on-again thanks to their posting.

Nogura tapped the keypad and the schematic zoomed in again, highlighting one of Neptune's tiny moons. "Whatever this thing is, it's playing hide-and-seek with our sensor buoys and long-range detection grids, but the Jupiter Station team managed to track it for a bit before losing it. After dropping out of warp, it took up position on the far side of Halimede, but when I sent a couple of ships that way to investigate, it disappeared. Sensors have picked up the occasional return, but whatever it is, it's able to avoid our scans for the most part."

Recalling his earlier joke with Commander Gilkeson, Kirk said, "A cloaked ship. Could it be the Romulans?"

Nogura shook his head. "The energy signature is all wrong for a Romulan cloaking device. Besides, the Romulans might be brash and bold, but they're not *that* brash and bold."

"I don't know," Kirk replied, thinking of his past encounters with the reclusive Federation rival. "It's not like they haven't tried unconventional tactics before." He gestured toward the schematic. "As for the energy signature, it could be some new kind of cloaking field they've developed."

Stepping away from the viewscreen, Nogura took a seat in one of the recliners. "Perhaps, but this isn't sniffing around outposts on the border, Jim. We're talking about the heart of the Federation and Starfleet, one of the most heavily trafficked systems in this part of the galaxy. It would be suicide for the Romulans to send a single ship this far. And for what?" He punctuated the question with a derisive snort. "It's not as though they don't have other means of gathering intelligence about what goes on here."

Kirk knew what his friend meant. Romulan spies, surgically altered to appear as Vulcans, humans, or other humanoid races, were a favorite tactic employed by their friends across the Neutral Zone. The practice dated back decades, and though only a handful of these covert agents had been discovered, it was believed that many more still operated undercover within Starfleet and the Federation government. Staff officers like Nogura had taken proactive steps to combat the espionage, and even to play the Romulan Empire's own game against them. According to the reports to which Kirk was privy, those efforts did not enjoy the same success. Of course, he also knew that his clearance did not permit him full access to the details behind such clandestine missions. Matters of that sort were, as both Nogura and Admiral Morrow had told him, "above his pay grade."

"All right," he said, "if not them, then who? The Klingons? Their cloaking technology has never been as good as the Romulans'." He stopped, raising a hand as though to wave away his own suggestion. "No, that doesn't make sense, either, and for the same reasons as the Romulans. Someone new."

"That's what I want you to find out."

It took an extra second for Kirk to glean the true meaning of Nogura's words, and when he did, he looked to see the older admiral staring at him, his expression flat and unreadable.

"Me? Admiral, it's not like you have a shortage of ships to send out there."

Nogura gestured toward the screen. "Ships aren't the problem. If we're dealing with someone or something new, you're the most experienced officer I've got in that department. I want you to go out there, find this thing, and figure out what it or they want."

Despite the anticipation he was already beginning to feel, Kirk kept his tone level. "I'll want to take Captain Spock with me." His friend was detailed to Starfleet Academy as an instructor.

"I'm not stupid enough to break up a winning team,"

Nogura replied. "Take him and anyone else you think
you need."

Kirk nodded. "Understood." It required physical
effort for him not to smile as he added, "We'll need
a ship." The simple statement elicited a chuckle from
Nogura.

"As it happens, there's one available."

Five

She closed the door and engaged the lock, then paused to take one last look through the drape covering the door's window at the departing gentleman.

"You are quite the handful, Mister Clemens."

Unlike her other party guests, Samuel Clemens had by far proven the most fascinating. Rather than filling the air with nonsensical gossip or other mundane conversational claptrap of the day, his intelligence, wit, and opinions regarding politics, religion, and civil rights, just to name a few topics, had set him apart from the other socialites and community leaders who had responded to her invitation for Friday dinner. Whereas she had no real desire to meet again with any of her other guests any time soon, Clemens brought with him enough conversational fuel to ignite many a night's worth of spirited conversation. He had salvaged what otherwise had been doomed to be a tedious evening.

Still, Guinan knew she would have to be careful during any future interactions with the man. His keen eye and inquisitive nature could prove dangerous if she allowed her guard to drop around him.

"I should probably get around to reading some of his books too." Then, rubbing her rib cage, she added, "But after I get out of this corset." She had to wonder who designed such ridiculous fashions for the women of this society, with the layers of heavy clothing and unnecessary accessories that made getting dressed or undressed a chore rivaled only by donning a suit of knight's armor. Were the people responsible for such choices sadists? That was the only logical explanation.

Making her way across the foyer of her town home, Guinan entered her sitting room and crossed to the small rolltop desk sitting in one corner. Inside the desk was a bottle of Aldebaran whiskey, her private stock that she shared with no one. Only after she poured herself a glass of the soothing green liquid did she turn and acknowledge the three aliens standing by her window.

"Are you just going to stand there and stare at me all night?"

To their credit, the trio of aliens—each hairless with pallid yellow skin and wearing garments that were most definitely not in keeping with current fashion trends—appeared sufficiently surprised by her comment. One of them, the group's only female, regarded her with a confused expression.

"You can see us?"

Guinan sipped her whiskey before replying. "If you're wearing a cloaking device, I hope you didn't buy it, and if you did, then you should demand a refund." When it became obvious that none of the aliens understood her choice of words, she decided to switch tacks. "Yes, I can see you, but it was obvious all through dinner that no one else could, so however you pulled it off, congratulations; it works for the most part. Just not on me."

"Because you are not human."

"Look who's talking." Guinan stared at the contents of her glass, pondering this odd meeting. "I'm guessing you're not here to hurt me, or you'd have done it by now. Did my father send you?"

The aliens looked at one another before the female said, "No, we are here of our own volition. Indeed, it is we who are hoping you may be able to assist us."

It took two glasses of the whiskey, but Guinan was able to listen to the story offered by Drevina and her two Iramahl companions, Glorick and Canderon, about how they had landed on Earth five decades earlier, fleeing from the tyrannical rule of another alien race, the Ptaen. They had elected to keep the reasons for their flight to themselves, but Guinan suspected it had something to do with their perceived value to their subjugators and perhaps other members of their own race.

"We limit our interactions with humans to the greatest degree possible," said Canderon, whom Drevina had identified as something of an engineer or technical specialist. "We have no desire to harm anyone, but merely to remain undetected until such time as we are found by our own people."

Guinan could appreciate the desire to keep a low profile. She had been doing much the same thing for many years herself. Defying her father, she had availed herself of the first commercial passenger ship departing her homeworld of El-Auria so that she might "see the galaxy" before settling down into something resembling the sort of traditional role normally expected for a female in her society.

Of all the planets she had visited during her years-long sabbatical from ordinary life, Guinan had taken a particular liking to Earth. Though humans were far less advanced, with respect to technology, she had found much to like about them. They seemed possessed of an indomitable will that pushed them ever forward, and that drive had brought about significant progress on both technological and societal fronts. There was still much to do, and their history was marked by numerous pitfalls and descents into regrettable and even reprehensible behavior toward one another. Still, she saw something, an unrealized potential waiting to be tapped. For this reason among many others, Guinan had opted to remain here for a while longer, just to see how the humans might next surprise her.

Of course, she had not counted on something like this.

"How did you find me?" Guinan asked as she filled her glass for a third time. The whiskey was running low, but there were other bottles in the basement. The alcohol had no debilitating effects on her; she just enjoyed the taste. "Only one person in the universe knows where I am."

Drevina replied, "We have been aware of your presence here for some time. We are unfamiliar with your species, but we first scanned an intermittent communications signal several years ago, one that is far beyond human technological capabilities. Since then, we have been tracking that signal."

Smiling, Guinan swirled the contents of her glass. "That would be me sending messages to my uncle." Only Terkim had supported her decision to defy convention and live life for herself, even going so far as to make sure she had a ticket for the passenger ship departing El-Auria and sufficient money to provide for transportation and other needs. A social outcast from the rest of their family, Terkim had always been the one who best understood her unconventional, even rebellious nature, and it was this similar attitude that had made them such close friends. Guinan had shared all of this with her unexpected guests. It was nice, she admitted, to talk freely about her true identity and travels. Socialite gossip had long ago lost its entertainment value.

Uncle Terkim would love this, she thought.

"We first detected the signal in Europe," added Glorick, whom Drevina had identified as some kind of flight systems operational specialist, a skill for which he had little use here. "We were aboard the steamship that brought you to this country, but we lost you for a time during your visit to New York. Then we detected your signal in Philadelphia and later Chicago. After tracing you to Deadwood, South Dakota, we lost you again until we registered it coming from here."

Drevina said, "You are quite well-traveled."

"You have no idea," replied Guinan. "All right, you found me. Now what?"

"As we said, we came seeking your help. We have never been able to ascertain whether our distress message was received, or if our people know that we survive here. We only request that you help us dispatch a new message."

It was a reasonable request, Guinan conceded, and one she was able to grant. How could she refuse? Assuming their story was true—and she sensed no deception from them—it should be a simple matter for someone from her planet's government to reach out to the Iramahl.

"I can't believe my people wouldn't be willing to help. However, there's a right way to do this, and a lot of wrong ways. For example, once someone from my planet reaches out to yours, the risks of someone else discovering that you're here increase."

The engineer, Canderon, said, "We have lived under that threat since our escape."

"I'm thinking of the people who were *already living* on this planet when you got here. I'd prefer not to endanger them, if possible."

"Understood," said Drevina. "We do not wish the humans any harm, either. Surely there must be a way to send a message that does not raise suspicion or risk?"

Guinan pondered the question. There was one answer, of course. If she wanted to circumvent bureaucracy, she could count on one person to help her do that.

Terkim, you are really *going to love this.*

"Well," she said, studying the glass in her hand that once again was empty, "sending a message and receiving a reply is going to take some time. It's a long way to my planet, after all. You may as well stay here."

Drevina nodded. "That is most gracious."

"Are you kidding? It'll be nice to talk to someone else who's from out of town." She waved toward the window. "Except for that Clemens guy, everybody I run into around here was born here. Hardly any of them have ever left the city, let alone the country. They're boring." She looked through the window, enjoying the view of the city it afforded her. Despite whatever complaints she might have about the people who lived here, San Francisco had become one of her favorite Earth cities.

The city lost a bit of that luster an instant later as the window shattered.

"Move!"

Drevina shouted the warning, but Canderon was the first to react. He grabbed her arm and pulled her out of the way as the first intruder smashed through the window, sending shards of glass and painted wood exploding across the room. Glorick had lunged to protect their mysterious host, Guinan, but the dark-skinned woman was already moving.

Another figure entered through the window and landed with grace on the thick, decorative carpet, by which time Drevina realized the identities of the intruders: Ptaen. As expected, the Consortium had dispatched hunters to find them. How long had they been here, on Earth? How many of them were there?

No time. Move!

The first hunter had already drawn an energy weapon and was bringing it about, aiming it at Drevina, but Canderon spoiled that with an unlit oil lamp swept from a nearby table. It shattered as it struck the Ptaen in the head, giving Glorick an opportunity to move in for another strike. The hunter was faster, lashing out with his free hand and catching Glorick across the face with sufficient force to spin him off his feet and send him tumbling to the floor.

Drevina tried to fire, but the Ptaen was already moving toward her. She dodged to one side, catching sight of Canderon engaging the first hunter. He had disarmed the intruder, and the two were exchanging blows, but the Ptaen was far more skilled in unarmed combat than her friend. It took only seconds for the hunter to drive Canderon to the carpet before he reached to his uniform for a bladed weapon.

Then a red flash filled the room, and Drevina flinched as a harsh ball of energy enveloped the Ptaen. His body racked by spasms, he released a scream that was muffled by the drone of the energy field, and then he vanished.

His companion was turning toward Guinan, who

Drevina now saw was holding a weapon of her own, and as the Ptaen attempted to aim, she fired again. A second ball of roiling energy washed over the hunter, and he disappeared, wiped from existence.

"Friends of yours?" she asked, her expression cold and hard. The object in her hand was compact, looking not at all like a weapon possessing the capability to unleash such power. Drevina watched as she returned the weapon to a pocket of her clothing.

"They are Ptaen. We suspected this might happen, but this is our first encounter with hunters since our arrival." She regarded the mysterious woman who looked so human but quite obviously was much more. "You saved our lives. You may have saved all of my people. Thank you."

"What does that mean? Saved all your people?"

"It is better if you do not know," replied Canderon. "And it would be better if we left you. If the Consortium knows we are here, they will send more hunters."

Glorick added, "We have no way to know how many might already be here. If these two are not alone, they will be missed. We should leave immediately."

"We are sorry, Guinan," said Drevina. "It was not our wish to place you at risk."

"I can take care of myself," replied the El-Aurian. "But your friend's probably right. Staying in any one place too long is a mistake. You should keep moving, for both our sakes."

Canderon asked, "But what of our request?"

"I'll take care of it. I can't promise anything, but I'll

send the message." Then, she offered a small smile. "You know how to find me."

"We appreciate your assistance," Drevina said, "but it is not our intention to endanger you again."

Her destiny, along with that of her friends, lay elsewhere.

Six

U.S.S. Enterprise
Earth Year 2283

"Admiral on the bridge!"

The voice calling out the advisory for the rest of the bridge crew sounded young. Very young, Kirk decided as Captain Spock stepped to one side and allowed him to exit first from the turbolift. Glancing to his right, he saw the Starfleet Academy cadet standing at rigid attention, staring at a point somewhere over Kirk's shoulder, and he forced himself not to smile as the younger man—a human of African descent—swallowed what might well have been a sizable lump in his throat.

"As you were," Kirk said, noting the expression of relief that the cadet was almost able to suppress.

"Thank you, Admiral," replied the cadet. "Welcome aboard the *Enterprise*, sir."

Moving to stand beside him, Spock said, "Midshipman Kenneth Sapp, Admiral, one of our most promising students. He is the current leader of Nova Squadron."

"The name rings a bell," replied Kirk, recalling the name from at least a few of the conversations he had shared with Spock over dinner in recent months. As for Nova Squadron, that unit designation harbored a history going back to the earliest days of the Academy. Only those cadets with the highest grades and who had demonstrated exceptional ability in the areas of leadership, initiative, integrity, and judgment were even considered for placement within that elite cadre, and acceptance into the storied corps almost always guaranteed the qualifying cadet top placement in their graduating class. Many of Starfleet's most celebrated officers had earned postings as cadets with Nova Squadron.

"There are currently eighty-five Nova Squadron members aboard," said Spock, "overseen by the Academy training staff as well as line members of the *Enterprise*'s current crew. Given the time constraints, this was the most effective method of staffing an acceptable complement for our mission."

Upon hearing that a significant portion of the ship's crew would consist of cadets—even the cream of the crop from the Academy's senior class—Kirk had expressed his concerns, both to Spock and Admiral Nogura. However, Spock had countered that the *Enterprise*, being so close to Earth, would benefit from the support actions of other starships as well as the perimeter defense forces charged with safeguarding the Sol system.

Despite his friend's assurances, Kirk could not help the tinge of unease he felt as he beheld the *Enterprise* bridge and noted the crew working at different stations.

The helm position was unoccupied, as were the communications and science stations, but the remaining consoles were overseen by cadets like Midshipman Sapp.

"Is it just me, or are they recruiting them younger and younger these days?"

With an arching of his right eyebrow, Spock replied, "Unless there has been a change in directives, the age requirements for entrance to Starfleet Academy have not been modified for quite some time." The merest ghost of a smile teased one corner of the Vulcan's mouth, punctuating his response. Without saying anything else, he stepped away from Kirk, descending into the bridge's command well and taking his seat in the command chair.

For the briefest of moments, Kirk felt himself moving in that direction as well, before he caught himself and schooled his features to mask his momentary embarrassment.

Where do you think you're going?

This was not his first time aboard the *Enterprise* since the starship's removal from active service and assignment as a training vessel to Starfleet Academy under Spock's command. His friend saw to it that regular opportunities to come aboard presented themselves so that he might conduct "inspection tours" and other similar functions, and Kirk performed similar duties for other starships used by cadets to further their training. Only here, on the bridge of *this* ship, was there no denying the pull of the captain's chair whenever he entered this space. He was unable to just stand to one side, watching its regular crew or a group of cadets going about their duties without recalling the days he had spent here, at the center of it all.

Recalling them, or missing them?

The turbolift doors opened behind him, and Kirk pushed away the unwelcome questions as he turned to see Montgomery Scott, Hikaru Sulu, Nyota Uhura, and Christine Chapel emerging onto the bridge. All four officers smiled in greeting.

"Admiral," Scott said, extending his hand. "No matter the circumstances, it's always a pleasure to have you aboard, sir."

Already feeling better at the sight of his trusted friends and former shipmates, Kirk smiled as he took the engineer's proffered hand. "Good to see you, Scotty." He extended similar greetings to Sulu, Uhura, and Chapel. "We're only missing Doctor McCoy and Mister Chekov to make this a proper reunion."

"I'm sure the good doctor would've come if he were able, sir," replied Scott, "but they're keeping him busy these days."

Uhura made a show of nudging Chapel's shoulder. "That's all right. We've got another of the best doctors in Starfleet, right here."

"Doctor Chapel recently honored my request to serve as the *Enterprise*'s chief medical officer during those training missions when Doctor McCoy is unavailable," Spock said, "or, if he just doesn't feel like it, as he prefers to say. Regardless, we are most fortunate to have her aboard."

Chapel smiled. "Thank you, Captain."

"As for Pavel," Sulu said, "I don't even know where he is, but I know he'd be here if he could."

For a moment, Kirk felt a twinge of regret that the other two members of his former senior *Enterprise* staff could not be here. Leonard McCoy, currently assigned to Starfleet Medical's research facility at Jupiter Station, had been unable to break away from other matters requiring his attention and approval. As for Commander Pavel Chekov, he was not even in the system, having volunteered for a long-duration exploration assignment under the command of Captain Clark Terrell aboard the *U.S.S. Reliant*. Kirk had inquired about that posting as well as the *Reliant*'s mission, but it was one of a handful of starships with duties overseen by Admiral Nogura himself. So tight was the security around the operations of these particular vessels that Kirk would not be informed about the details of those projects until such time as Nogura decided he had a need to know.

"At least you four are here," said Kirk, smiling again. "I'm going to have to find some way to thank Commandant Rouviere for allowing you all to come along."

"The commandant's already figured that out for you, sir," replied Uhura. "He asked us to tell you that you now owe him two lectures next month."

"Done."

There was just enough time for a brief reunion before the *Enterprise* completed the transit from Earth to Neptune.

With the senior officers now at their stations and immersed in their work, only Kirk was left without anything to do, forced by rank and billet to stand and watch as these people with whom he had shared so much fell back into their old roles without missing a beat. He felt like an extra nacelle, as he often did during cruises of this sort. Of everyone on the ship, he was the only one who—for the moment, anyway—served no useful purpose.

Admiral Dunsel, indeed.

"Shields at full strength," reported Commander Sulu from where he sat at the helm console. "Weapons on standby."

Still sitting in the command chair at the center of the bridge, Spock said, "Mister Sapp, sensor report, please."

"No sign of the energy distortion, Captain," replied the midshipman, his attention focused on the data being relayed to the science station from the starship's array of sensors. "So far as I can tell, we're the only ones out here."

Spock replied, "The original reports suggested a form of cloaking technology was responsible for the earlier energy distortions detected by long-range scans." Rising from the center seat, he stepped from the command well and moved to join Sapp at the science station. "The distortion might not be so easy to detect if the vessel—if indeed it is a vessel—is holding station." He looked to Kirk, who was doing his best to remain an observer. "Wouldn't you agree, Admiral?"

"I would." Stepping over to join his friend, he added, "That, and it would be easy to find a hiding place among the moons. We could spend days out here, hunting for the thing, and that's assuming it doesn't give us the slip." He knew that odds were slim for the unidentified craft to elude the *Enterprise* as well as the long-range scans that had detected it in the first place, but Kirk had learned a long time ago never to assume anything. "Beyond a few perimeter outposts, sensor arrays, and early warning systems, there's not much out this far that's worth spying on."

"Covert reconnaissance requires time and patience," replied Spock. "It is possible that anyone attempting to obtain information about our interplanetary defenses would first ascertain our abilities at the perimeter, before attempting to maneuver toward a target of greater perceived value. For a single vessel, acting alone and without support, this would be a prudent and logical course of action."

"It also works if you're just trying to hide," said Kirk.

Spock nodded. "Indeed. Continue scanning, Mister Sapp. Increase scan field to widen your search." Turning to Uhura, he said, "Commander, transmit lingua-code greeting on all frequencies."

Inserting a Feinberg receiver into her left ear, the communications officer replied, "Aye, sir," before setting to work.

"Starfleet's been sending those greetings since that thing first showed up on sensors," Kirk said. "There's been no response."

"And neither do I expect one now. At least, not in the conventional sense."

It took Kirk a moment to realize his friend's meaning, but then the pieces fell into place, and he smiled.

I must be getting old.

"You think they might react to the increased scan
field and our hail, believing we detected them."

"Precisely."

Still hunched over his console, Sapp scowled. "Captain, I'm picking up something, but it's from the
long-range scans." Kirk watched the younger man tap
several controls before leaning once more over the
illuminated sensor viewer. "The energy distortion is
back, but it's not here. I mean, not out here at Neptune,
sir. It's moved farther into the system, and looks to be
heading for Jupiter."

"Are you certain?" asked Spock.

The cadet replied, "Yes, sir. Now that the sensors
know what to look for, the thing is easier to track, even
though the readings are still intermittent. I think I only
caught it because it's moving again."

"Excellent work, Mister Sapp." Turning from the science station, Spock said, "Mister Sulu, lay in a pursuit
course and engage at fastest safe speed."

Kirk said, "Jupiter's a bit more interesting than
Neptune, Spock." In addition to the terraforming efforts that now allowed permanent residents to live and
work on two of the immense planet's larger moons,
Io and Ganymede, Starfleet also had a considerable
presence on or near several of the Jovian satellites.
There was Jupiter Station, orbiting the planet and
containing research and development facilities as well

as Commander Tonia Barrows and the early warning monitoring team that had detected the alien vessel. The moons Europa and Callisto also were home to forward operating bases for perimeter defense of the Sol system's outer planets, as well as training facilities for Academy cadets. As targets went, Jupiter was nothing less than tempting.

"Admiral Kirk," Uhura said, turning in her seat at the communications console, "I'm receiving a message from Jupiter Station. Captain Wyatt reports it and the Starfleet assets there are on full alert, but standing by for your orders, sir."

"Tell them to maintain alert status until further notice. Are any other ships en route to intercept the sensor readings?"

Uhura replied, "The *Endeavour* is the closest starship, but it's also maintaining position in Jupiter orbit, per your instructions."

"Good." Nogura had given Kirk operational command of the entire mission, which included the *Enterprise* and the *Endeavour* as well as whatever assets he thought he might need as the situation continued to evolve. With Spock commanding the *Enterprise*, it left him free to consider the larger picture with respect to the still unidentified craft, along with whatever intentions it might harbor. To Spock, he said, "Right now, we still don't know if this is a threat. I don't want to give the thing any more holes to slip through, but I also don't want to provoke a fight until we know what we're dealing with."

The Vulcan said, "Agreed. The vessel's crew—assuming it possesses a crew—likely knows that we are still able to track its movements despite its attempts at evasion. What is required now is more information about the vessel's capabilities."

Stepping closer to the science station, Spock consulted several of the console's displays. "The energy fluctuations we believe to be related to the craft's stealth technology appear to operate in a manner different from other cloaking devices we have encountered, such as those utilized by the Romulans and Klingons. Those systems are dependent upon energy directed at frequencies similar to those utilized by deflector shield generators in order to mask a vessel's other power emissions. Based on these sensor readings, that does not seem to be the case here."

Sensing motion behind him, Kirk turned to see Uhura crossing the deck from her own station. The look on her face was one of puzzlement.

"Captain," she said, pulling the Feinberg receiver from her ear, "I've detected a very low-level communications signal. It's broadcasting on a wide range, and at a frequency we don't normally track. I only noticed it because I was picking up odd readings along one of the lower bands that we do monitor, and when I tried reconfiguring the communications array to sort it out, this other signal showed up."

Without waiting for a prompt, she stepped closer to the science console and tapped several controls. In response to her instructions, one of the station's smaller display screens flared to life and a string of information began scrolling, almost too fast for Kirk to follow.

"You think it's from the other ship?" he asked.

Uhura replied, "I don't know what else it could be. It's not a spoken message, but more like a continuous data stream, and if I didn't know any better, I'd think it was trying to interface with our sensor array."

"Excuse me."

The voice came from behind Kirk, and he looked to see another of the cadets standing at attention, her body so stiff he was certain she might sprain a muscle. Her nervousness was evident on her face, despite her best efforts to maintain her bearing.

"Cadet . . . ?" prompted Kirk.

"Leah Feeze, Admiral." She swallowed, then stopped herself from saying anything else until she swallowed again. "I'm sorry to interrupt you, sir, but I couldn't help overhearing the discussion, and I . . . I think I might . . . that is . . ."

Spock said, "Midshipman Feeze is preparing to enter the advanced engineering track following her graduation. She has shown remarkable aptitude in starship sensor and tactical systems."

"Something about all of this caught your attention, Mister Feeze?" Kirk asked.

The cadet nodded. "Yes, Admiral. Commander Uhura mentioned the communications signal she detected, and how it's trying to connect with our sensors. What if . . . what if the signal is actually trying to *manipulate* them?"

"Manipulate them how?" asked Uhura.

"It would require a penetration of our sensor array's oversight software, Commander, and it should be impossible with our internal security protocols. However, a focused, pervasive attack at a vulnerable point in our protection schemes might have an impact on our sensor capabilities." Feeze had relaxed a bit now, her confidence no doubt buoyed after not being sent back to her station with a reprimand for daring to insert herself into the conversation.

After crossing his arms, Kirk reached up to rub his chin. "You're talking about affecting what the sensors tell us?"

"Yes!" Feeze's nodding was so animated at this point that Kirk feared for her suffering cranial damage. "That's basically all we're talking about." She gestured toward the viewscreen and the image of Jupiter dominating it. "The ship itself isn't really cloaked at all. It's just fooling our sensors into thinking that. They did the same thing with the long-range sensors from the perimeter defense outposts. It might've even been easier to do that, thanks to the distance involved."

Uhura frowned. "But what about the distortion readings?"

"That may be an artifact of the process," replied Spock. "A result of our security protocols working to correct what they perceive as an incorrect or anomalous reading." He looked to Feeze. "That is a most impressive display of deductive reasoning, Midshipman. Mister Sapp, please assist her in reconfiguring the sensors to account for this new information." Stepping away from the science station, the Vulcan returned to the center of the bridge. "Commander Sulu, if this theory proves correct, we will be in a position to intercept the vessel in rather short order."

Sulu smiled. "I'll be ready, sir."

"Very nicely done, cadets," Kirk said. "Nice to see Starfleet's going to be in good hands when you graduate next year."

"Thank you, Admiral," said Sapp.

Now standing a bit straighter, Feeze could not seem to help her sudden wide smile. "I appreciate that, sir."

Leaving the cadets to their work, Kirk moved to the railing behind the captain's chair. "They're making you look pretty good, Spock."

"They respond according to their gifts, Admiral." His friend once more cocked his eyebrow. "I simply teach them how to harness those capacities."

An alert tone echoed across the bridge, interrupting any reply Kirk might have offered, and Sulu shifted in his seat.

"The sensor mods worked, sir," said the commander. "Readings are still a bit fuzzy, but it's enough to go on. We can get a fix on their general location. A few more minutes, and we should have them locked in."

"Uhura," said Kirk, "relay whatever information you have to the *Endeavour.* I want them to move in, now."

Once again, he found himself feeling out of place as the bridge crew—seasoned veterans and untested cadets alike—turned to their duties. Spock, having retaken his place in the center seat, was dividing his attention between the people under his command and the image of Jupiter, which was growing larger on the viewscreen. Looking past his friend's shoulder, Kirk could see the astrogator and the icons representing the *Enterprise* and the *Endeavour* as the sister vessel closed the distance. Also visible on the scanner was a new indicator, a blue symbol standing in contrast to the red markers signifying the two starships.

"Commander Uhura," said Spock. "Retransmit greeting messages on all frequencies. Mister Sulu, alter our course so that there is no doubt we are moving to intercept the other craft."

Jupiter now filled the viewscreen, and Kirk could see something else: a small object matted against the gas giant's atmospheric maelstrom. "There it is."

"We've finished reconfiguring the sensors, sir," reported Midshipman Sapp. "They can't hide from us anymore."

The vessel was small, thin, and angular, with a bulbous section at its forward end that suggested a cockpit or bridge. To Kirk it resembled a knife's blade. Its hull surface was a striking silver that reflected the feeble light offered by the sun that was five times more distant from Jupiter than it was from Earth. Its very shape suggested speed, Kirk decided.

Spock replied, "Excellent work, Mister Sapp. You as well, Mister Feeze."

"They're making a run for it," Sulu reported, pointing to the viewscreen.

"Maintain pursuit course."

Kirk said, "After all of this, they're not going to stand and fight?"

"They can't, sir," reported Sapp. "They're unarmed. Sensors aren't detecting anything that might be an external weapons port."

"Life signs?" asked Spock.

The cadet shook his head. "Inconclusive, sir. The ship's hull is reflecting our scans, so we can't get a look inside."

"Captain," Uhura called out, "I'm picking up an incoming transmission. It's on a low frequency, like their other broadcast." Her attention still fixed on her console, she moved one hand across the clusters of controls while her other hand held her receiver to her ear. "It seems to be a repeating message, audio only. There's not a lot here, but I'm feeding it through the universal translator." As Kirk moved to stand next to her, the communications officer tapped additional keys before looking up and nodding. "I think I've got it, Admiral. It's a greeting, and . . . something else."

Kirk replied, "Let's hear it."

A moment later, the bridge's intercom system flared to life, and a high-pitched, almost childlike voice said, *"Greetings. We apologize for our secretive transit of your star system. We are travelers, searching for a spacecraft that went missing in this area of space some time ago, and we request your assistance. It is our belief that this vessel crashed on your system's third planet."*

Seven

"Energize."

Along with Spock, Kirk stood before the transporter room's shielded console, facing the pad as Montgomery Scott manned the station itself. The chamber flared to life in response to the engineer's commands, and two columns of sparkling light appeared. They solidified into a pair of humanoid shapes as the transport process completed, and both figures looked first at each other before glancing around the room, and Kirk forced himself not to smile as both new arrivals patted themselves as though to verify that their entire bodies had made the transit.

"I'm Admiral Kirk," he said, stepping forward and offering a small, formal bow. "Welcome aboard the *Enterprise*. On behalf of the United Federation of Planets, I extend you our warmest greetings."

Both of the aliens—a female and a male, as far as Kirk had been able to determine during their earlier communication in preparation for this meeting—nodded in return, and it was the female who spoke first.

"Thank you, Admiral. I am Jepolin, and I stand before you as a representative of all the Iramahl people.

Once again, please accept my apologies for our furtive entry into your star system. It was a precautionary measure on our part, and one I am happy to see was unwarranted." She held out her hands, which were long, thin, and possessed three fingers and a longer digit on the outside of the hand that resembled an opposable thumb. Neither of the Iramahl possessed any hair on their heads or narrow faces, and pale yellow skin accented by bright gold eyes flanked a thin, angular nose. Each was dressed in a single robe-like garment covering them from the neck down, leaving only their heads and hands visible, and appeared tailored to minimize any gender-specific physical attributes. Jepolin's garment was deep blue with an intricate gold pattern woven into the shiny fabric, while her male companion's ensemble was emerald green and featured similar embroidery.

As introductions were made, Jepolin eyed Spock with an expression of curiosity.

"Captain," she said.

Spock nodded. "Envoy."

"We have heard of the Vulcan people, and your long history of embracing logic over emotion. It is a subject I have always found most interesting." Then, Jepolin brought herself up. "But I digress from matters of greater importance. Perhaps once we have addressed the reasons that have brought us to your system, we might spend time pursuing less urgent topics of conversation."

"I welcome the opportunity," replied the Vulcan.

After dismissing Scott—and once Spock had contacted the bridge and ordered Commander Sulu to proceed with the *Enterprise* escorting the Iramahl vessel to Jupiter Station—Kirk led Jepolin and her companion, Opirsa, from the transporter room. Waiting in the passageway were two security officers, whom Spock directed to maintain a discreet distance behind the group as they made their way through the corridor. Arriving at the conference room that had been prepared for use by him and the *Enterprise* senior officers as well as their guests, Kirk nodded to another pair of guards who stood flanking the entrance. When the door opened at his approach, he paused at the threshold, gesturing to Jepolin and Opirsa.

"After you, please." When Jepolin paused to eye the security officers, Kirk added, "Don't be alarmed. A security detail is standard procedure aboard a starship when guests and other non-crewmembers are brought aboard."

Jepolin nodded, and when she smiled, it was almost as though her thin mouth might threaten to stretch her face. "I understand, Admiral Kirk. Given the circumstances of our arrival, it makes perfect sense for you to treat us with a degree of caution."

"It's a formality, madam," Kirk said, following Jepolin and Opirsa into the room. The curved table had been prepared with a selection of food and beverages, both from the *Enterprise*'s galley as well as the Iramahl vessel. As part of his duties, Spock's yeoman had inquired about dietary requirements and provided food and beverages for their guests.

After directing everyone to seats, Kirk took his own place at the head of the conference table. "All right, Jepolin, I think it's safe to say that my crew and I are very interested in what you have to say."

"Indeed," Spock added. "Your insistence on secrecy for this discussion has also aroused our curiosity."

Kirk had already apprised Admiral Nogura regarding the startling revelation of an Iramahl ship's crash-landing on Earth. According to Spock's calculations based on information provided by Jepolin, the craft had arrived at some point in the mid to late nineteenth century. There was no way to know where to even begin looking, but sensors were already being brought to bear in order to search for signs of the alien vessel as well as any remains of its crew.

Jepolin replied, "I apologize for what must seem like undue caution on my part, gentlemen, but please understand that trusting anyone from another species is not something that comes easily to us. I am afraid that is a consequence of the existence my people have endured for generations."

"Captain Spock has enlightened us on that," replied Kirk. "I must admit that I'd not heard of your people before today, or the plight you've faced."

"That is understandable," said Opirsa. He glanced to Jepolin, who nodded, before he continued. "Our star system is located beyond the far boundaries of one of your interstellar rivals, the Klingon Empire. Given the attention they command, as well as the other concerns you face with other adversarial powers, it is understandable how our world might be overlooked."

The words stung, but Kirk tried not to take them as any sort of personal accusation or attack. "It wasn't by design, I assure you. However, you're here now. How can we help you?"

Opirsa said, "Our people have only recently emerged from under the oppressive rule of another civilization, the Ptaen, who control a small area of the space beyond the Klingon border. In fact, the Ptaen Consortium and the Klingons have had some dealings, including the transfer of Iramahl subjects to Klingon rule after the Empire began encroaching on Ptaen territory."

Holding his hands clasped before him as he sat straight in his chair, Spock replied, "I have only briefly examined the data Jepolin provided, Admiral, but I learned that these interactions occurred approximately fifty years ago and were limited in scope and duration. Apparently, the Klingons and the Ptaen Consortium were able to reach an agreement whereby the Empire respected Ptaen territorial claims in exchange for crossing privileges through their space." He cocked his eyebrow. "For the Klingons, it was a most magnanimous gesture, given their usual methods of expansion and conquest."

"The Ptaen, despite their size relative to the Klingon Empire," said Jepolin, "possess the armaments and wherewithal to defend their interests. We suspect that if the Klingons were not occupied with other concerns—such as the Federation—they would have more than sufficient resources to send against the Ptaen." She cast her gaze toward the conference table. "However, the Consortium was still powerful enough to enslave my people."

Kirk said, "But you were able to fight back against them."

"After a time, and after the loss of so many of our people," replied Opirsa.

"The resistance effort that began hundreds of years ago has only come to fruition within the last twenty years. My people initially declared our independence from the Ptaen more than seven centuries ago. What followed was a series of revolts interspersed by periods when the Ptaen reasserted control, only to be thrown off by renewed insurrection."

Jepolin said, "It took us some time to organize and formalize our resistance strategies, which took a number of forms. In addition to direct action through sabotage and other guerilla tactics, we also used spies, both Iramahl as well as Ptaen who were sympathetic to our cause, to gather information and relay it to contacts within the resistance movement. It was through such methods that we learned the Ptaen were controlling us through an extended campaign of genetic modification."

"Eugenics?" asked Spock.

Opirsa nodded. "That is correct, Captain. Ptaen scientists discovered a way to alter our genetic structure so that our life spans were artificially shortened. Instead of living for the equivalent of several of your centuries, our people would live just a fraction of that time. This was the primary means of controlling our population. In the beginning, the genetic manipulation was introduced to all living Iramahl, or at least the vast majority, including our pregnant females. Over time, the process evolved both on its own and with the help of Ptaen scientists who seemed to take great joy in finding more effective ways to forward these modifications. For generations, we passed along the very chains used to enslave us. The chains were not metal, but instead the strands of our own genetic code."

"Genetic engineering," said Kirk, shaking his head. "We have dark chapters in our own history on that subject."

Jepolin replied, "When we first learned what the Ptaen had done to us, there was no way to reverse or repair the condition. However, groups of scientists within our own community—working with understanding Ptaen dissenters—began to develop a way to combat the process. At first, the goal was simply to extend the average Iramahl life span, which at the time was limited to a few decades, as you measure time, but discoveries soon were made that gave us hope that the condition afflicting us could be reversed altogether."

Kirk sighed. "I can't imagine the Ptaen would react well to such news, once they found out about it." His mind conjured images of spacecraft in high orbit, showering Iramahl cities with hellish retribution.

"You are quite correct, Admiral," said Opirsa. "Once the Consortium realized we were close to discovering a means of fighting one of their key strangleholds on us, they increased their efforts to defeat the resistance. This was only exacerbated when our resistance began distributing information via subversive broadcasts, electronic media, and every other avenue available to us, making it known the resistance's intention was to see that every living Iramahl received the cure by any means necessary. A number of threats were disseminated, warning of airborne chemical assaults in order to deliver the agent to large population centers." The Iramahl smiled. "In truth, Admiral, the research never advanced to the point where such a bold action was feasible, but it made for good propaganda and kept Ptaen hunter squads busy as they investigated threats while resistance cells carried out other, actual attacks."

Jepolin said, "Anyone with knowledge of this possible cure became enemies of the state. Rewards were posted for anyone, Ptaen or Iramahl, who could provide information leading to the capture or killing of such fugitives. I am ashamed to say that many Iramahl were betrayed by our own people, as often as not through false accusations. Ptaen officials and the squads they dispatched were indiscriminate, and if an innocent Iramahl fell victim to their overzealous methods, then that was simply a cost of waging the larger battle."

Such deception and disloyalty were common in conflicts throughout history, Kirk knew. War never boiled down to a simple division between sides, let alone singular devotion to a shared ideology within one sect. Allegiances were challenged or changed as battles raged on, chewing up lives, resources, and resolve. In many cases, simple survival motivated a person to turn on a comrade, or even a friend or family member, in order to avoid being consumed by the seemingly unending war machine. Kirk had no doubts that such scenarios along with countless others colored the Iramahl's history and their struggles with their Ptaen oppressors.

Swiveling in his seat so that he faced Jepolin, Spock asked, "What happened to the scientists and others who possessed knowledge of this cure?"

"Out of necessity," replied the Iramahl envoy, "the number of people with access to the information was limited, and once we realized the Ptaen were aware of our efforts, those specialists and others who were helping them were scattered. Many of them went into hiding, either on their own or with help and protection from different resistance cells. Please understand, Admiral, that at this point, the cure had not yet even been proven to work; the Consortium was acting out of simple fear." She offered another smile, though Kirk could see that the expression was not meant to convey humor.

"The propaganda was quite successful in that regard," Jepolin continued, "as it served to incite the Ptaen to even greater action. Though it took considerable time and effort on their part, they managed to hunt down almost everyone involved with the initial efforts to develop the cure. Only a handful escaped, and for years they avoided capture, thanks to the ongoing efforts of the resistance. Even while evading the hunter squads, they continued their work to develop the cure, and for a time many Iramahl believed the fugitives would reach the end of their own curtailed life spans before achieving the success they sought. Then resistance leaders began to receive messages: the cure had been found."

Jepolin paused, drinking from the water Spock poured for her from one of the carafes on the table. Kirk sensed her discomfort and empathized. Being the representative of an entire race carried a weight that could test even the hardiest of individuals, and that stress had to be worse given the Iramahl's recent escape from Ptaen rule.

"As word of the cure began to spread," said Opirsa, "our people renewed their fight. Soon, skirmishes were taking place all across Consortium territory as more and more Iramahl rose up in resistance. Something else had begun to work in our favor as years passed. A small yet growing number of our people were being born out of Ptaen control; they were not being subjected to the genetic modifications. It took some few generations, but eventually we began to see increases in average life span. At first, it was only a handful of years, but rates have been rising—slowly, but steadily—as time has passed. While it is not enough to give us the salvation we have long sought, it is something."

Kirk frowned. "But what about the cure?"

"The group of scientists who made the reported break-through apparently tested it on themselves, and the data they were able to send corroborated their claims. This was a call to arms for our people, Admiral, and every effort was made to affect the transfer of the scientists to a safe haven. What was not realized at the time was just how far they had traveled to avoid Ptaen pursuit."

Of course. A twinge of regret surged through Kirk's gut as he realized where this was going. "They came all this way?"

Jepolin replied, "It seems so. The coordinates included in the encrypted distress message match the astral maps we have at our disposal. We received a later message through . . . a most unconventional means, but it was enough to inform us that they had at least survived the crash and lived for a time on Earth."

"And you have come in search of them," Spock said. "Do you believe they may still be alive?"

The Iramahl shook her head. "No, Captain. According to the most recent hypotheses put forth by our scientific community, we do not believe that Iramahl life spans, even without the effects of genetic manipulation, would allow them to have survived this long. Since other scientists, despite their best efforts, have so far been unable to duplicate the breakthrough they apparently made, it is our hope that they may have found a way to preserve and protect something from their work. Ideally, there might be offspring as well."

"Even if none of their research survived," Spock said, "if you are correct and these Iramahl tested their cure on themselves, then their blood would carry the basic components needed to reconstruct the cure. Their remains could provide genetic material sufficient to accomplish this."

Opirsa replied, "That is our hope, Captain. Even though we have seen a marked increase in our overall life spans over the past few generations, the truth is that we continue to pass the genetic tampering to our offspring. Further, the original condition has also given way to other impacts on our health, in the form of various physical and mental aberrations. While it is possible, even likely, that we eventually will rid ourselves of this affliction, we fear it will come too late to save the Iramahl as a species. The consensus is that drastic action is required, which is why we are here."

"It's possible we can do something to help you," Kirk offered. "We've got some of the best medical and scientific minds in the Federation at our disposal. I can't imagine them not being able to find some kind of workable solution."

"That is very generous of you, Admiral," said Jepolin.

Spock said, "Given your distinct physiological differences from humans, it is logical to presume these Iramahl fugitives would have needed to avoid contact with the planet's indigenous population."

Jepolin replied, "That may be due to one of those health abnormalities I mentioned earlier. It is an ability that is measurable in only a small percentage of our people, though at least one of the refugees we seek possessed it, just as I do."

When she said nothing else, Kirk looked to Spock, hoping his friend might be able to help him understand what he had to be missing. When the Vulcan merely regarded him with his usual placid expression, Kirk returned his attention to Jepolin.

The Iramahl's seat was empty.

"What the hell?" he asked, eying the vacated chair. "Where did she go?" He looked again to Spock, who now was looking toward the seat.

"Fascinating."

Kirk scowled. "What?" Then, before his eyes, Jepolin coalesced into existence, still sitting in the chair as though she had never moved. There had been no whine of energy or other indication that a transporter or even a cloaking device had been used. Jepolin was just there, staring at him. "You can make yourself invisible?"

"Nothing so astonishing, Admiral, I assure you." Jepolin leaned forward in her seat. "Generations ago, some of us learned we possessed the ability to influence the thoughts and perceptions of others. Mostly it can be used to make someone believe or continue to believe that they are alone. In some rare instances, those with the gift are able to appear to others as someone else entirely. I do not possess that ability myself, but I have experienced its effects. Our people are susceptible, of course, as are the Ptaen. Naturally, it was an ability we strove to keep the Consortium from discovering, and so far as I understand, they still do not know about it."

"That's incredible," Kirk said. "We've encountered species who exhibit comparable abilities, along with telepathy, telekinesis, and other similar traits."

Opirsa said, "We do not possess the ability to read minds, Admiral, and neither are we able to coerce another being into doing something against their will. It seems the limit of this gift is simply to allow those who possess it to hide their presence from those who can be affected by the influence."

"In truth," added Jepolin, her eyes widening, "I had no idea it would even work on humans." She turned to Spock. "Though Vulcans evidently are not affected."

Nodding, Spock replied, "It appears so."

The intercom whistled, followed by the voice of Commander Uhura. *"Bridge to Captain Spock. We have arrived at Jupiter Station, sir. Mister Sulu has entered us into a parking orbit, and the Iramahl vessel is maintaining station off our starboard bow. The station's commander has already contacted us, asking if we need anything."*

Pressing a control set into the table near his left hand, Spock replied, "Thank you, Commander. Please alert Captain Wyatt that we will be requesting Doctor McCoy's assistance."

"Aye, sir. Admiral Kirk, we've also received an update from Starfleet Command. Initial sensor sweeps of Earth show no indications of Iramahl life-forms or technology, though Admiral Nogura stresses that the effort is less than half completed."

Kirk said, "Please give the admiral my thanks, Uhura."

As the connection was severed, Spock clasped his hands atop the conference table. "The logical conclusion is that the Iramahl died either of natural causes from some other event, or else they found a way to leave the planet. The first scenario would not explain the failure to detect any sign of their vessel, however."

"Assuming Nogura's report holds up," replied Kirk.

"Given estimated Iramahl life spans," Spock said, "they could have survived for nearly three hundred years after their arrival. This would depend on a number of factors, of course. They could have been discovered or killed, though there likely is no way to corroborate this theory, given the fragmentary nature of historical records prior to the twenty-first century."

"There is another possibility," said Jepolin, her expression one of sadness. "The Ptaen could have found them."

Eight

Closing his notebook, Captain James Wainwright returned it and his pen to his briefcase before looking once more to the elderly couple sitting across from him on their living room couch. Their expressions were near mirrors of each other's, regarding him with interest as well as skepticism.

"I want to thank you again for your time," Wainwright said, lowering the lid of the briefcase, which sat on the small oval coffee table between his chair and the couch. "It's very much appreciated, I assure you."

The man, Henry Clarke, released a grunt that Wainwright took to be an offering of amused disbelief. His wife, Martha, seemed content to say nothing else. She had been quiet during most of the interview, allowing her husband to answer each of the questions posed by Wainwright and only providing occasional commentary when prompted. It ended up not being much, as she apparently had not been witness to the strange craft that had captured the attention of so many people in this area.

"What do you all do with these reports you collect?" asked Clarke, gesturing toward the briefcase. He had the large, callused hands befitting a farmer, something Wainwright had noticed upon their initial handshake. They were the hands of a working man, someone who had little time or patience for anyone in a suit, even if that suit belonged to a military officer. The interview had taken the better part of two hours, time Henry Clarke likely would have spent finishing up whatever chores he had set out to complete this day. It was getting dark, and for the Clarkes it also was getting late. Mrs. Clarke had already made subtle hints about needing to get on with feeding her husband, and her more recent suggestive nod toward the closed door leading to the kitchen had not even been that understated. In fact, Wainwright had harbored a faint yet still perceptible sensation since arriving here that he was not welcome. The Clarkes had been polite, of course, but there remained the odd feeling that he was not wanted there. It was a suspicion strengthened by Mrs. Clarke not inviting him to join them for their evening meal. Not that he was hungry, but the obvious lack of hospitality seemed unusual for a traditional rural couple.

You're imagining things, but that doesn't mean they want you here all night. Finish up and leave them to their supper.

"The reports I'll be writing about my visits with you and your neighbors and officials from Fort Monmouth will go into a case file we've created for this incident. We'll continue to update the file as we get more information, and after a time, a final determination will be made as to what we think really happened here."

Grunting again, Clarke stared at him, his eyes narrowing. "And what do you think happened here, Captain?"

"It's not my job to speculate, sir." Wainwright patted his briefcase. "I conduct interviews, take statements, organize facts and other information I'm given or find on my own, and then organize it so that someone with stars on their shoulders can make a decision. By the time they get around to doing that, I may well be on the other side of the country, talking to another couple just like you about what they think they saw."

Damn it.

The phrasing was bad, and he knew it. Henry Clarke knew it too, as was evident by his hardening expression.

"You don't believe I saw what I saw? You're the one who came looking to ask a bunch of questions, and you obviously know more about this thing than I do, so why'd you bother coming here at all?"

Holding up a hand, Wainwright said, "I'm sorry. I didn't mean for that to sound the way it did, sir. I truly believe you saw something. You don't know what it was, and I certainly don't because I wasn't here to see it." He patted the briefcase again. "My job is to gather information from you and the other witnesses, try to make sense of everything said by everyone, and submit a report. People smarter than me will figure out what to do after that."

That seemed to mollify the farmer, at least enough to reduce the tension that had suddenly filled the room. It was a practiced answer, and one he had developed for dealing with situations just like this one. He already had lost count of the number of times he had delivered some variation of it to people just like the Clarkes. Sometimes offering such a rehearsed response bothered him, because the truth was that Wainwright wanted to believe them and everyone else with whom he had spoken over the past four years.

Where the hell did the time go?

Was it not only yesterday that he was sitting in a drab office at Wright-Patterson Air Force Base, which at the time was still called Wright Field before that installation was merged with neighboring Patterson Field, when his world changed around him? In actuality, his perceptions had already been shifted just months earlier, while he was stationed at Roswell Army Air Field in New Mexico and had come face-to-face with actual aliens from another planet. At the time, Wainwright had been of two minds about the incident. First, he was worried that these aliens, *Ferengi*, as they had called themselves, were but the first of uncounted invaders who would soon be coming to conquer Earth. At the same time, he had been fascinated with the technology they seemed to possess. Could humans develop such things? Spaceships? Machines to create almost anything a person needed from nothing? Traveling to other worlds the way humans drove between cities? It was the stuff of stories he had enjoyed since childhood.

He was not alone with such feelings. Another person with similar thoughts was Jeffrey Carlson, a civilian professor Wainwright had first met just a few months earlier at Roswell. It was Carlson who, in September 1947, had invited him to join a top-secret government organization, Majestic 12, with a single mission: search for evidence of extraterrestrial activity on Earth, and develop strategies to combat any aliens who were proven to pose a threat. As part of that, Wainwright, along with a handful of air force officers, had been detailed to another initiative, Project Sign, which was tasked with investigating the growing number of people coming forward to report seeing unidentified flying objects, or UFOs. Were they flying saucers, rockets from Mars, or other alien invaders from distant galaxies? It was Wainwright's job to determine the veracity of such sightings.

And here we are.

"So you don't think we're crazy," said Clarke, still eyeing him with suspicion, and Wainwright again felt that odd sensation of unease. It seemed to lurk at the edges of his subconscious, like someone standing just beyond the limit of his peripheral vision but whose shadow could still be seen. Despite his best efforts, he could not shake the odd feeling.

Instead, he forced a smile. "Of course not. It certainly helps that so many people saw the same thing. Even soldiers over at Fort Monmouth have made reports." That much was true, and two more Project Sign case officers were at this moment conducting interviews with officers and enlisted personnel assigned to the small army base not too far south from the Clarke farm.

What had separated the sightings of the strange, unexplained craft in the skies above the New Jersey coast from the number of "eyewitness accounts" Wainwright had investigated since joining Carlson, MJ-12, and Project Sign? In this case, it was the sheer number of people who had called the local police as well as radio and television stations to report on the mysterious lights in the sky to the east. There was also the wrinkle of this craft having been detected by military radar, in the person of a young soldier undergoing Army Signal Corps training at nearby Fort Monmouth. According to the account provided by the man, he had picked up a low-flying target while manning a radar set, all while several officers stood dumbstruck and watched him attempt to track the source of the radar return, which had been clocked at speeds in excess of seven hundred miles per hour. The object quickly disappeared from the soldier's screen, but a military pilot on a training flight later spotted the thing while conducting his final approach to Mitchel Air Force Base in New York.

The army angle already elevated this incident above most of the others Wainwright had investigated just during this past year. Reports of sightings of strange ships, along with the occasional encounter with mysterious, inhuman beings, were on the rise. Many of these could be explained as confusion with legitimate aircraft or other mundane phenomena, or simply the blathering of attention seekers. This one, however, with so many credible eyewitnesses, begged for greater scrutiny, which made Henry and Martha Clarke's reluctance to be interviewed so intriguing.

During his canvassing of the area that included the small Clarke farm, Wainwright had noted that while most of the people from the surrounding homes and properties had called the police or someone else to report what they had seen, no such call had come from here. When he had knocked on the door and introduced himself, Wainwright was somewhat surprised by how disinclined the Clarkes had been to answer his questions. They had relented after a few moments' resistance, but during the entire interview had acted as though they would rather talk about anyone or anything else. Their answers to his questions were adequate but not remarkable, as Henry Clarke claimed to have seen the mysterious object for only a couple of moments before it flew away. Of course, Henry Clarke was a working-class man, with things to do and an earning to make. Since he was the lone laborer on the farm that he had taken over from his father, who in turn had inherited it from his grandfather, daylight was valuable, and Wainwright's presence and questions had wasted part of that precious commodity.

He glanced first at his wristwatch and then a clock on the mantel over the living room's fireplace. Both timepieces told him the same thing: it was late.

Just past nineteen hundred hours on a Friday. You sure know how to have a good time, don't you? It was getting dark earlier now, as the end of Daylight Saving

Time for the year approached with month's end. At this point, he had lost whatever hope there might have been to catch a flight out of McGuire Air Force Base and back to Wright-Patterson. Instead, he would have to spend one more night in the visiting officer's quarters. How many similar evenings had he experienced? More than a hundred in the past nine months, if his memory served him, but in reality he had given up keeping count. He was sure his wife, Deborah, knew the exact number. It had been the subject of yet another in an increasing string of conversations regarding his job and the long hours and separation it required. The latest such animated discussion had occurred earlier that afternoon, which he had washed away with a drink at the officer's club before the drive to Oceanport and the day's interviews. Both the bourbon and the argument had left a bad taste in his mouth.

Don't start with that.

Clearing his throat, Wainwright said, "I've taken far too much of your time, and I apologize again for calling on you unannounced." He rose from his chair, reaching for the briefcase and his service cap. Mr. Clarke stood, extending his hand.

"Good luck with your reports," he said. "I don't know that I'd wish those things on my worst enemy."

The deadpan delivery was enough to make Wainwright chuckle, and he was thankful for the sudden lightening of what was becoming an awkward moment. He took the proffered hand and shook it, just before he heard the sound of the kitchen door opening behind him and saw Henry Clarke's eyes widen in surprise.

Wainwright felt himself pulled off his feet, across the coffee table and onto the couch, which the Clarkes had vacated. Both of them were lunging around the table and away from him, much faster than any couple in their fifties had any right to be moving. Rolling onto his side, he was in time to see them crossing the living room toward the kitchen, where in the doorway stood . . .

. . . *something.*

Two figures crowded the doorway, both of them garbed in dark clothing that covered them from neck to feet. Their heads were elongated, with light violet skin, protruding chins, and broad foreheads atop which sat long, dark hair that reminded him of a horse's mane. Pronounced brows featured odd, narrow ridges or creases extending from the top of their thin noses up and over the top of their skulls. As Wainwright tried to process all of this in the few seconds afforded to him, one thought overrode everything.

Not human.

The Clarkes threw themselves at these new arrivals, but even as they moved, Wainwright saw their bodies changing. Clothing and flesh seemed to shift and blur together. Skin turned yellow, arms and legs stretched, and then four unrecognizable beings were fighting one another. The thing that had been Henry Clarke slammed into the first intruder, driving them both back into the kitchen, where they crashed past a wooden chair and onto the floor. Wainwright heard plates or glasses shattering on the tile even as the second intruder lunged toward whatever had been Martha Clarke. She—or it—lashed out at the opponent, landing strikes at the throat and face almost too fast for Wainwright to follow. The intruder also got in one or two hits, but it was obviously outmatched.

From the kitchen came the figure that had been Henry Clarke, and Wainwright saw that it now held in its hand a long carving knife. Without breaking stride as it reentered the living room, the creature moved in behind the remaining intruder and plunged the knife into the back of its neck. The creature's body went limp and it fell forward, toppling to the floor and just missing the coffee table.

Then the things that had been the Clarkes turned to look at Wainwright.

"What the hell are you?"

It was all Wainwright could say before one of the creatures, holding something he did not recognize, stepped closer and aimed the strange object at his face.

Nine

Wainwright's eyes opened at the sound of someone knocking on a nearby door, and he jerked himself upright, immediately regretting the sudden movement. He looked around, seeing the familiar surroundings of the room in which he had been staying for the past three days. Or was it four?

What the hell day is it? Where the hell am I?

"Captain Wainwright?" said a muffled male voice through the door. "Sir, are you all right?"

"Yeah," he called out, his voice raspy. "Yeah, I'm fine. What is it?"

"You've got a call at the front desk, sir," replied the man on the other side of the door, who Wainwright realized was probably the enlisted airman on duty at the VOQ's front office.

Visiting officer's quarters, he reminded himself. McGuire. That much made sense, at least.

"Tell whoever it is I can't come to the phone," Wainwright said. "Please take a message and let them know I'll return their call in thirty minutes."

"Yes, sir. Right away, sir." Footsteps moved away from the door, growing distant before fading altogether and leaving Wainwright in relative peace.

His head hurt. His *hair* hurt. What was wrong with him?

Then he saw the half-empty bottle of bourbon on the table by the door. When had he bought that? The only drinks he had consumed during his stay at McGuire had been with dinner in the officer's club, and only one with each meal. He tried to remember the events of the previous evening, which had to have included a stop at the Base Exchange or an off-post liquor store, but he had no recollection of that. Indeed, his memory seemed like a jumbled mess this morning. What the hell had happened?

His gaze fell upon the briefcase sitting on the credenza along the room's far wall, and bits and pieces of half-recalled details began to coalesce in his alcohol-addled mind. Interviews, in town. Not here, though, but rather Oceanport, and Fort Monmouth Army Base. The sighting. The UFO. A number of people had seen the thing, and he had been tasked with obtaining statements from military personnel and civilians. That was it.

But where had the booze come from?

There was something else, some half-forgotten thought that seemed to tickle the edges of his mind, but Wainwright could not pull it into focus. Grunting in irritation with himself, he eyed the bourbon with disdain. Had he really drunk himself into a total stupor? Why?

Deborah. Their last phone conversation. No, their last argument.

Oh, you are such an idiot.

Standing in the far corner of the small, sparsely furnished room, Drevina and Glorick waited in silence until the human military officer finished dressing and exited the quarters, closing the door behind him. Only then did Drevina allow herself a moment to relax in relief.

"Your skills are improving," offered Glorick.

"I have had more than sufficient time to practice."

"He suspects nothing," said Glorick, gesturing toward the door. "You did well."

Drevina nodded. "I am just grateful he escaped injury." The altercation with the Ptaen hunters had been as sudden as it was vicious. There had been no warning, even though she and Glorick had detected the arrival of the Ptaen scout craft days earlier. They had been unable to track its point of origin with the equipment at their disposal, which only served to reinforce their friend Canderon's opinion that the time had come to set up a more permanent base of operations from which they could better protect themselves and avoid these sorts of surprise confrontations. He had left several days earlier from the farm that had served as their home for more than a decade, scouting locations that might serve as a suitable hiding place.

"We should go," she said after a moment. "There is much to do." She and Glorick had spent the past hours disposing of the two Ptaen hunters who had attacked them the previous evening, and ridding the farmhouse of all traces of their presence. Then there was the matter of seeing Captain Wainwright safely back to his quarters here on the air force base. The neural scanner from their sparse medical kit had been useful in wiping the man's short-term memory, though Drevina disliked using the device due to the blunt manner in which it operated. Individual memories could not be removed, forcing Drevina to erase everything dating back several hours, to provide a gap of time that could be explained in some other fashion. It had taken her several decades to modify the device to work on human neural pathways without causing undue harm or wiping away greater portions of a person's memory than necessary.

"Do you think there will be others?" asked Glorick.

"We must assume as much." It was the first time they had seen any sign of Ptaen pursuit in many years, and Drevina had wondered if the Consortium might well have abandoned their hopes of finding her and her companions. She had lain awake on many nights, wondering how Ptaen and Iramahl civilization had fared since their flight into deep, uncharted space. Had her people overthrown their oppressors, or had the Ptaen only strengthened their tyrannical grip? The few Ptaen hunters she had been able to question had offered no useful information, leading her to theorize that they also were uninformed as to current events on their homeworld.

What Drevina and the others had never been able

to determine with certainty was whether the Ptaen who had been chasing them all these years on Earth were part of the same group, or if the Consortium had sent more than one team of hunters. Her suspicions about there having been more than one attempt were strengthened with the sighting of the unidentified craft five nights earlier in the skies above New Jersey. There had been no way to verify that the spaceship—if indeed it was such a vessel—had been of Ptaen origin, but the subsequent arrival of the hunter team could not be coincidental. Had the ship just arrived at Earth? It was also possible that the craft had been here for some time, with the hunters only using it when they discovered some clue as to their quarry's whereabouts.

"People will wonder about the Clarkes." As he spoke, Glorick's expression turned somber. "That is unfortunate, though unavoidable."

Drevina nodded in agreement. The couple who once had lived on the farm she and her friends had used as a temporary home were two of a very limited number of humans the Iramahl had been able to trust with the truth of their identities. The male, Henry Clarke, had discovered Drevina, Glorick, and Canderon taking refuge in his barn during a fierce rainstorm, finding them before Drevina had been able to use her abilities to prevent him from seeing them. Though the first moments of that meeting had been tense, Glorick had succeeded in convincing the human that he was in no danger. Clarke, who described himself as "a man of faith," had admitted to having those beliefs shaken as his eyes fell upon beings from another world, but in short order his gentle, compassionate nature asserted itself.

Both he and his mate, Martha, had treated Drevina and her companions with kindness and respect from that first day. Many nights were spent in that barn, with the Iramahl sharing stories from their long journey into exile, their arrival here on Earth, and the decades that had passed with them hiding from Ptaen hunters. The farm's remote location afforded a high degree of isolation, allowing Drevina and the others relative freedom of movement, though they quickly fell into a habit of leaving the barn only at night. It had taken months of work, but Glorick and Canderon eventually succeeded in excavating a tunnel connecting the barn with the Clarkes' house, allowing transit back and forth with no risk of observation by casual passersby or—as the Iramahl feared—Ptaen search teams.

Drevina and the others had been saddened when Henry Clarke fell victim two years earlier to a heart attack. Despite her best efforts and the medical equipment at their disposal, she had been unable to resuscitate him. Martha had been devastated, falling into a spiral of depression from which she would never emerge. The three Iramahl had elected to stay and care for her, which made it all the worse when they found her one morning in her bed, having died in her sleep after taking a large dose of medication. In the months since then, Drevina and her companions had stayed at the farm, using for cover Drevina's growing ability not just to mask their presence but also to make others think they were seeing someone else. When necessary, Drevina and Glorick adopted the Clarkes' personas, but it was a short-term measure at best.

The farm was already falling to neglect, as the Iramahl were unable to tend to it as Henry Clarke had done. Martha Clarke's passing had not been reported to the proper authorities, though Drevina and Glorick had seen to it that her remains were placed secretly with those of her husband in the local cemetery. Sooner or later, someone familiar with the Clarkes would get suspicious, and that would attract attention the Iramahl fugitives did not need.

"We will leave things as well as we are able," said Drevina, "but it is again time to move." How many times had they been forced to take this same action over the course of the century they had lived in hiding here on Earth? Too many, Drevina conceded, but what other choice did they have? Canderon had become convinced that their original distress message had not been received and help was never coming. Glorick was the first one to discuss the possibility of finding another way off the planet and attempting to return to their home planet, but even he knew that to be an implausible notion. The humans had only possessed aeronautical technology for less than fifty years, and the very idea of venturing beyond the confines of this world was constrained to works of fiction. That left using a Ptaen craft if one could be found, and the hunters had been very careful not to leave them at known locations on the occasions teams managed to find their targets.

They had heard and read stories about sightings of unidentified flying objects in locations around the world, but none of these reports had seemed credible. Legends seemed to have been spun about one craft in particular, which many people believed to have crash-landed in the deserts of New Mexico just a few years earlier. Though that event appeared to be the starting point for most people's awareness of such unexplained craft, stories of mysterious objects hovering over cities and towns went back much further. Drevina and her companions had even investigated one such incident alleged to have occurred in the small village of Aurora, Texas, more than fifty years earlier, but they had found no evidence to substantiate the claims.

As for the event at Roswell and sightings reported after that crash, the refugees had come to learn that the government of this society was actively searching for confirmation that such craft existed and that they were piloted by extraterrestrial beings. They sent agents to investigate, such as the one Drevina and Glorick had just encountered. There would be more like this man, she knew, but they were a lesser problem than the Ptaen hunters, at least for now.

"After all this time, they still chase us," Glorick said, shaking his head. "One would think the pursuit would be viewed as fruitless."

"If they are still hunting us, that means we remain valuable to our own people as well as the Consortium. And that means our own people still seek us as well.

We must therefore find a new home, some place to hide and prepare, for we must keep up with our portion of the fight."

Drevina saw the doubt on Glorick's face as he asked, "For how long?"

"Until the fight is over, one way or another."

Ten

Nogura looked tired, Kirk decided. Had the admiral even slept since dispatching the *Enterprise*? Between the hunt for the Iramahl ship and the subsequent discussion with Jepolin and Opirsa, it had been nearly one full Earth day. Even Kirk had only managed a couple of brief naps, and he was beginning to feel fatigue taking hold. How did Nogura manage to keep exhaustion at bay?

If the admiral was operating at less than peak efficiency, it was not apparent by his voice. *"According to the latest reports, Jim, there's no sign of any living Iramahl anywhere on the planet, or anything that might be the remains of an Iramahl, or any indications of a ship matching the description and specifications you sent. There are still some areas to be checked, but I'm not holding out much hope."*

"How much time do you think it'll be before an initial sweep is completed, sir?" asked Kirk, sitting at his desk and staring at the admiral's visage on the viewscreen occupying the rear wall of his guest quarters.

The suite had been assigned to him for the duration of his stay aboard the *Enterprise*, which made sense given that Spock occupied the rooms designated for the ship's captain. Still, it was an odd feeling for Kirk, being a guest on what once had been his vessel.

Looking at something off screen, Nogura replied, "*Approximately five hours. Most of the places that are left are those that present problems for sensors. Deep ocean trenches and things of that sort. There are some areas that have been marked for a closer look, and we're dispatching teams to those locations now, just to be thorough. What do you plan to tell your guests?*"

"That's a good question."

From where he stood behind Kirk, Spock said, "It is possible that the Iramahl fugitives, assuming they made successful planetfall, took steps to mask the presence of themselves and their vessel. They may very well have destroyed the ship, or found a place to scuttle it so that it remained undetectable."

"It's hard to believe that there's any place on Earth that might prove a suitable hiding place from state-of-the-art sensor technology," said Kirk.

Nogura leaned back in his chair. "*Let's say you're right about them having found a place to hide their ship. What about the Iramahl themselves? If your estimates are correct and they managed to live to the late twenty-first or early twenty-second centuries, we should still be able to detect some residual bio-scan readings.*"

"That presupposes the Iramahl did not take steps to eliminate evidence of their own passing, Admiral."

"*So you think they may have . . . what? Disintegrated themselves at the point of death or near-death?*"

"I accept that as a rather extreme scenario, sir, but it's not beyond the realm of possibility."

Nogura made a show of covering his face with one hand. "*One of these days, I'll learn to just smile and nod whenever I discuss anything with a Vulcan. It'd just be easier for everyone.*" Returning his hand to his lap, he regarded Kirk through the screen. "*The Federation Council is preparing to dispatch a diplomatic envoy to the Iramahl homeworld. My gut tells me that the Ptaen Consortium will have something to say about that once they get wind of it.*"

"We've never dealt with either of these governments before," Kirk said. "The Ptaen are likely to be unhappy with any perception that we're taking the Iramahl's side in whatever ongoing dispute they have."

"*That's for the diplomats to figure out. Speaking of which, a couple will be on their way out to you. Until then, you're our point person with our guests. We'll keep you apprised of the sensor sweeps here. Nogura out.*"

The communication link was severed and Nogura's face disappeared, replaced by an image of the Federation seal. Kirk swiveled his chair away from his desk to face Spock, who remained standing a few paces behind him with his hands clasped behind his back.

"How is it that we've never encountered either of these two races before?"

Spock's right eyebrow rose. "It is not surprising, given the location of their respective star systems on the far side of Klingon territory. We are not even fully aware of all the different civilizations the Empire has subjugated, let alone any worlds in that area of space that remains unaligned or unconquered by the Klingons."

His door chime sounded, and Kirk ordered the door to open. It slid aside to reveal the lanky form of Leonard McCoy, who sauntered into the room and moved to the couch along the wall in the office section of Kirk's quarters. Without waiting for an invitation, McCoy dropped onto the couch.

"Got anything to drink in this place?" the doctor asked by way of greeting.

"And hello to you, too, Doctor," said Kirk, stifling a smile.

McCoy sighed. "I've seen a lot of strange things in my time, Jim, but those people are something else."

Spock said, "You are of course referring to our Iramahl guests."

"No, Spock. I mean the two crewmen sweeping the hangar deck." Grunting something Kirk could not hear, the doctor shifted his position on the couch and crossed his legs. "We've seen our share of genetic engineering in our day, but never like this. Usually, the goal of such manipulation is to make enhancements— address deficiencies, improve quality of life, that sort of thing—but this is completely different. The changes made by the Ptaen to artificially and deliberately shorten the life span of an entire race? And for the sole purpose of maximizing their ability to control them?" His expression grew contemptuous. "It's disgusting."

Kirk eyed his friend with sympathy. Among Leonard McCoy's many qualities was his unfailing humanity when it came to anyone who might be even tangentially in his care. Just a brief visit with Jepolin and Opirsa in the *Enterprise*'s sickbay, conducted immediately following the doctor's arrival from Jupiter Station, had been enough to ignite within him the same fiery passion he had displayed as a physician for all the years Kirk had known him.

"Bones, is there anything we can do to help them?" asked Kirk.

Blowing out his breath, McCoy replied, "I don't know, Jim. At least, I don't know yet. Christine and I discussed a few tests we can run. Jepolin and Opirsa have agreed to provide some blood samples we can use for further study. Given time, we may be able to come up with something similar to what their own scientists created."

Spock said, "The cure apparently developed by the Iramahl scientists resulted from years of research, about which we have no details."

"You're right," said McCoy. "We'd be starting from scratch, but they're here and they've asked for our help, and you know how much I hate standing around and trying to behave myself while the diplomats and other grown-ups are talking." He looked to Kirk. "I honestly don't know if we can help them, or how long it'll take, but we have to try. What else are we going to do?"

"For now, just do what you've been doing, Bones. Get started on your tests. I'll clear it with Nogura to make sure you get whatever help and resources you need." Turning his chair, he looked up to Spock. "If those Iramahl landed on Earth four hundred years ago, there has to be some evidence; something they left behind. They somehow sent a distress call, so they were hoping someone would find them. It makes sense that they'd plan for that." He had only been mildly surprised to learn that the message Jepolin mentioned had come from yet another extraterrestrial being living on Earth during the nineteenth century. The Iramahl envoy had not shared the identity of that individual, which only served to make Kirk wonder just how many aliens had decided to call Earth home in the centuries before humanity left their world and found other civilizations living among the stars.

It seems we're the galaxy's preferred vacation destination.

Spock said, "Now that Doctor McCoy and Doctor Chapel have completed an initial examination of our guests, and Mister Scott has conducted a survey of their vessel, I believe I may be able to provide Admiral Nogura with additional information that can be used to refine the sensor sweeps currently being conducted. However, given the span of time that has passed, we must entertain the possibility that the Iramahl and their ship were somehow lost."

"He's right, Jim," added McCoy. "Suppose they survived to the twenty-first century. World War III wiped out whole sections of the planet. They could easily have been caught up in that, or one of the earlier wars, or some natural disaster. They could've been found by someone and imprisoned or dissected, or stuffed in a vault somewhere. We already know people of that era managed to find more than a few examples of alien technology. Hell, some of that was probably even our fault. Remember how paranoid humanity was in the twentieth century? How we were always pointing missiles at each other and ready to end it all with the push of a button? Imagine living during that time and finding aliens from another planet."

Kirk did not have to imagine such a scenario, having already observed it firsthand on more than one occasion. Indeed, he and Spock . . .

Indeed, we have.

"Spock," he said, surprised at himself for the idea beginning to take form in his mind, "what if we had a way to determine their whereabouts and activities during an earlier point in time."

It seemed to Kirk that his friend took an extra moment to gather his apparent meaning, but when he did, both eyebrows rose.

"Admiral, may I remind you that the risks which come with traveling through time are not to be underestimated. Undertaking such a task, with no means of determining a logical destination point in the past, would only exacerbate those dangers."

McCoy added, "And let's not forget that it's just a plain crazy idea, all by itself." He hooked a thumb over his shoulder. "Besides, can't you just hear what Nogura and the other admirals at Starfleet Command would say once you even suggest this? Nogura might have a heart attack just on general principle."

"I'm not suggesting we travel anywhere," Kirk said, holding up his hand. "We've done it enough times to know it's not to be done lightly." He paused, studying the contrasting expressions on the faces of his two closest friends.

"What I'm suggesting is that we find a way to get some . . . *specialized* help."

Eleven

Roberta Lincoln loved this town.

Looking down from her twelfth-floor vantage point as she stood in her employer's office, she could not help but be taken in by the sprawling metropolis that was her home. It was at night that the city truly came alive, pulsing with an energy that made it seem like a living thing. The Empire State Building, towering above everything around it, was aglow with lights on every floor. Though it had stood as the world's tallest structure for nearly forty years, Roberta had but to turn her head to see the buildings that would surpass it: the Twin Towers of the World Trade Center. The construction of the first tower was nearing completion, with its counterpart due to finish next summer. Both towers and their attending buildings would be a hub for business, financial, and retail interests with an eye toward reinvigorating the Lower Manhattan area. The construction effort had been a massive undertaking, which Roberta had watched first from the N train as she went into the city, and later when she came to work as a secretary for what she thought was a research firm tasked with writing a new encyclopedia.

Then had come the day Roberta learned the truth about her employers and their supervisor, the enigmatic man known as Gary Seven, signaling the end of her life as she knew it.

After traveling around the world with Seven—as well as to one or two other exotic locales—and beholding such sites as Chicago, San Francisco, London, Vienna, Paris, Hong Kong, and Tokyo, just to name some of her favorites, there just was no comparing any of those destinations to the city of her birth. It was something to which she would not have given much thought even a year ago, but those intervening months had given her much cause to appreciate the vibrant metropolis that was New York City. Roberta could never imagine living anywhere else, on this planet or any other.

Although that Risa has a few things going for it.

Staring at the Empire State Building, she imagined for a moment a dirigible moored to the spire atop the mammoth structure, in keeping with some designer's crazy idea back when the building was still under construction. She pictured well-to-do socialites boarding and disembarking the airship as it floated more than a hundred stories above the city. Such a scene had never come to pass, of course. Still, Roberta thought the idea made for an exhilarating, adventurous means of travel from this, the grandest city in the world.

"When did I become such a romantic?" she asked aloud, for no real reason. It was not as though anyone could hear her. Seven and his cat that was more than just a cat, Isis, were away "on business," as he preferred to put it, employing the unremarkable term to describe most of their travel, which often was anything but mundane. Two years ago, the idea of Seven—let alone her—venturing away from Earth to a distant planet was absurd, and yet here she was, minding the store while her mysterious employer and his equally baffling feline companion were on a planet billions of miles away.

And my college advisor thought I'd only make a decent secretary. Guess she owes me an apology.

A mechanical tone sounded from behind her, and Roberta turned to the window to see the translucent green cube, ostensibly a stylish paperweight, pulsing with light from where it sat at the head of Seven's oversized walnut desk. Like many other items in this office, the cube presented a facade to the unknowing observer while masking its true purpose. In this case, it was an interface to yet another of the room's hidden treasures.

"Computer on," called Roberta, shifting her attention to the inset bookcases near the door leading from Seven's office. The entire set of shelves swung outward, away from the door, to reveal the sophisticated workstation and interface to the Beta 5, the advanced computer that was in more ways than one another member of Gary Seven's team. Moving from behind the desk, Roberta crossed the office to the newly revealed mechanism.

As the computer completed its activation, a stilted, feminine voice said, *"Computer on."*

"You rang?" asked Roberta. Though the Beta 5's ability to act based on voice commands was impressive, it had been lacking as far as understanding casual terminology and slang. Gary Seven tended to be clipped and formal when issuing instructions to the computer, whereas Roberta had been trying to expand its vocabulary and ability to parse orders she gave it using everyday speech. So far, the results were mixed, but she vowed she one day would win over the feisty, even smug contraption.

"*Occurrence,*" replied the computer. "*Military satellite has detected an object beyond planet atmosphere.*"

Roberta frowned. "What? Are you sure?"

"*Affirmative, Miss Lincoln. I am intercepting and interpreting satellite telemetry.*"

"Please don't tell me we're being invaded by aliens."

"*Insufficient data to render informed judgment.*"

Crossing her arms, Roberta eyed the large round display screen that was the Beta 5's primary means of visually communicating information. "How long before you have whatever *sufficient data* you need to make a judgment?"

"*Object is approximately three meters in length and contains a warp-based propulsion system. I detect no weapons.*"

"Warp-based? That rules out anything launched from this planet." According to what little nuggets Gary Seven had provided about the future of her homeworld, faster-than-light travel was an advancement humans would not achieve for another century. It was the humans of the 1970s who concerned her at the moment. "Can you interrupt any signals sent from the military satellite back to Earth?"

"Affirmative. I am already doing so, in accordance with Supervisor 194's directives on such matters."

"Great. Make sure you record a copy of anything the other . . . whatever it is . . . might transmit." She rolled her eyes. "Of course, you're probably already doing that too."

"Affirmative."

According to Seven, it would also be a century before any warp-capable species were due to visit Earth, at least officially. Roberta wondered if that event and humanity's own discovery of faster-than-light travel might be related, but so far, her inscrutable employer had not deigned to share such information with her. To this point, he had been quite guarded with what he knew about Earth's future history. Roberta suspected he was taking steps to make sure she was not confronted with too much knowledge too quickly, perhaps in a bid to make sure she did not become overwhelmed with the reality of the path her people would be traveling in the years to come. To that end, Seven also had taken a very protective stance as far as the detection of any alien signals or vessels was concerned and had instructed her and the Beta 5 to do the same.

"Where is this thing, anyway?"

"Currently on approach course to Earth. Trajectory suggests it has made a transit of the sun."

Pondering this, Roberta asked, "If that's the case,

then where did it come from?" Her grasp of the intricacies of space travel was growing thanks to her association with Seven and the Beta 5, but there was still a great deal for her to learn. However, even she was aware that a craft approaching them from the sun, assuming it arrived from outside the solar system, likely had to have been hanging around out there for quite some time. From where had it traveled, and more importantly, who had sent it? "And only three meters long? That's not big enough for anyone to be inside it, right?"

"*Such diminutive size would preclude most humanoid life-forms.*" A string of chattering and other noises sounded from somewhere within the computer's depths, and the multicolored displays moved faster and with greater intensity, illustrating the Beta 5's increased processing efforts as it continued to examine and collect information about the mysterious object it had detected. "*I am detecting an encoded transmission.*" The advanced mechanism said nothing else, though Roberta watched and heard signs of its focused activity as it chewed on this revelation before it added, "*It is a message directed to Supervisor 194.*"

"What? Are you sure?"

"*I am capable of analyzing and interpreting information to which I am exposed, Miss Lincoln,*" replied the Beta 5, its mannered delivery sounding to Roberta a bit haughtier than usual. Though she sometimes liked to see if she could tweak the computer into such responses, now was not one of those times.

"Okay, fine. Seven's not here. Can you still play the message?"

"Affirmative. The message is intended for you, as well."

"Couldn't you have just said that to begin with?" Roberta shook her head, waving her hand toward the machine even though she knew it did not see her movements. "Never mind. Just play the message."

The computer's circular display screen flared to life, and the image of a human male coalesced into view. Though he appeared older than the last time Roberta had seen him, there was no denying the identity of the man now staring at her.

"Mister Seven and Miss Lincoln, this is Admiral James Kirk. It's been some time since we last spoke, and I hope this message finds you well. I apologize for the unconventional nature of this communication, which is being transmitted to you via an unmanned survey probe we sent to the twentieth century using the light-speed breakaway factor or 'slingshot effect' we've used before to travel through time. We thought this was the least risky method of making contact with you. Why go to all of this trouble?" His expression softened. *"I need your help."*

Roberta listened with rapt fascination as *Admiral* Kirk recounted the plight of an alien race known as the Iramahl and their fight to overthrow the tyrannical rule of another civilization, the Ptaen. Her eyes grew wider when the admiral explained how the Iramahl believed a small group of their citizens had somehow found their way to Earth during the nineteenth century, and that they may have survived an apparent crash landing and could even now be living in seclusion somewhere on the planet.

"Pause the playback," she said after Kirk had reported this bombshell. Reaching up, she rubbed her forehead. "I feel another migraine coming on."

"There are a number of remedies I can prescribe for your discomfort, Miss Lincoln," offered the Beta 5, and for a second Roberta thought the computer almost sounded sympathetic.

"It's just an expression," she said. Then, before the computer could hone in on that, she added, "Continue playback."

Without replying, the Beta 5 complied with her instructions, and Kirk's halted image once more began speaking. *"We believe, based on what the Iramahl have told us, that even with their modified or restored life spans, the Iramahl who found their way to Earth would not have lived to the twenty-third century. In fact, we have no way of knowing if they even survived their ship's crash, or if they died from some unknown reason at some point before old age claimed them. Our efforts to locate any remains of them or their technology have been unsuccessful."*

He stopped, and a small wry grin appeared on his face. *"Then we got the bright idea of searching for them in another time period. Naturally, your names came up during the discussion. The Iramahl feel that finding these people, or at least some record of the knowledge they possessed, is one of the few means of helping their civilization.*

We're talking about an entire race here. There has to be something we can do, and I'm hoping you can help us."

Despite the difference in years and rank and even the uniform he now wore, Kirk's eyes—those hazel eyes of his—still burned with the passion and determination she had seen during her previous encounters with him. That he had opted for this irregular means of making contact with her and Seven only spoke to the lengths he would go to find a solution to the problem he now faced.

"Mister Spock has included in the message files carried by this probe information about Iramahl physiology and technology. It's our hope that you can use them to assist in any search you make for the Iramahl. He's also included similar information pertaining to the Ptaen, who may have sent their own people to Earth in a bid to find and kill the Iramahl. As for the probe carrying the message, it's been programmed to head into the sun once it confirms you've received this message. One less thing for you to worry about." Kirk's expression grew somber. *"I know this is asking a lot, but I wouldn't be asking if I didn't think you were the best chance of helping the Iramahl. Given the risks involved with time travel, we won't be repeating this stunt to contact you again. Instead, we've included our current date and time information from the point the probe was sent back to you, and I'm hoping you can reach out to us, if and when you're able to tell us anything. Thank you, my friends."*

Kirk's image faded, leaving the display screen blank, though the rest of the Beta 5's status indicators had once more ramped up. The computer was deep into processing whatever information it was receiving from the probe.

"Aliens hiding on Earth," Roberta said, again to no one. "Gee, that's new." The sarcasm rang in her ears as she considered Kirk's message. After all, the idea of extraterrestrials living and lurking among humans was not a novel concept; it had been a staple of science fiction stories for decades. Beyond that and thanks to her association with Gary Seven, she had met actual aliens who really had been living here, for one reason or another, and not all of them peaceful. It had been less than a year since her last such encounter, which— interestingly enough—had also involved Kirk.

"When did he get promoted, anyway?" The last time she had seen James Kirk, he had been a younger man, captain of a starship three hundred years in the future. So, here it was just a year later for her and he looked fifteen years older than during their last meeting, which had ended up requiring her to travel with him a year back in her time to deal with another set of aliens on the run. Only then, it had been a pair of Certoss agents from the future, doing their level best to destroy Earth so that humans could not subjugate their own race at some distant point in time.

Too bad I'll never be able to tell anyone about any of this. It'd look great on my resume. Of course, my brain will have exploded from all the headaches this stuff gives me, but that should make me perfect for upper management or politics.

After more than a minute of work on its part, the Beta 5 emitted a sharp beep that echoed across the office as the computer's banks of indicators began to subside.

"I have added the probe's data to my files, Miss Lincoln."

"Is there anything in there that might help you with finding these Iramahl characters?"

"Affirmative, though the process will take time. Shall I begin?"

Though Roberta did not expect the computer to find anything right away, its ability to sift through scores of recorded information was formidable. Television and radio news broadcasts, data transmitted via satellites and other government and military computers, telegrams and telephone conversations, all of it was available to the Beta 5, provided it could navigate a path into whatever network, line, or other medium was being used to route the information. She did not understand the complexities of the process, though she had learned enough during the past two years to appreciate just what the advanced mechanism could do once unleashed. It did not require rest, for one thing, and it could work on multiple problems at the same time, making it the ideal tool for a task like this.

"Yeah, knock yourself out. In fact, expand your search parameters to include any reports about sightings of unidentified craft, claims made to local papers or news stations about people seeing aliens, that sort of thing. Order anything you find based on whether the reports were confirmed or refuted, and cross-check everything against any government records you can access." Much of that information was not available in electronic form, she knew, in particular almost anything of a sensitive or even classified nature. At least, that was the case at present. As the influence of computers continued to grow in the private sector as well as government and military circles, the amount of information being transcribed from paper to data storage was growing by the day. Soon, there would be a time when almost all information—entire libraries—would be stored in such a manner, which would make a task like the one the Beta 5 was undertaking that much easier. For now, though, there would be a lot of fruitless searching and dead ends as the computer hopscotched its way through whatever resources it could find and penetrate.

More to herself than the Beta 5, she said, "Seven's going to pop his cork when he finds out about this." In truth, she did not think her employer would react in too negative a fashion once she informed him about this latest odd development. So far, the only thing she had done in response to Kirk's request was order the computer to begin the arduous process of sifting through untold volumes of data, a process that could take days, if not weeks or even longer, depending on what information the Beta 5 was able to access. All of that was in addition to the work she and Seven already were doing, and no doubt would be doing in the weeks, months, and even years that lay ahead. Of course, she realized there was no rush. Time, in an odd sense, was on her side, at least to a certain extent. If they did manage to find anything about these Iramahl, Admiral

Kirk would still be waiting three hundred years in the future.

And there's my time travel headache coming back again.

Pondering her next steps, Roberta decided that perhaps a little more help might be useful for this task. "Computer, send a message to Mestral. Let him know we'd like to have him pay us a visit."

A Vulcan, Mestral had been living among humans for more than a decade after his own survey craft with a small crew had crash-landed in rural Pennsylvania in the fall of 1957. When a rescue ship arrived at Earth in search of him and his companions, Mestral had elected to remain behind, seeing his time on Earth as an unparalleled opportunity to observe a civilization on the cusp of major technological and sociological advancements. After he had convinced the two Vulcans who had survived with him of his desire to stay, they reported to their rescuers that he had died in the crash.

Mestral had maintained a low profile since then, concealing his true nature from those humans with whom he interacted, though he had revealed his identity to a pair of human military officers who at the time were investigating the presence of alien activity on Earth, which in turn eventually brought him to the attention of Seven and Roberta.

And of course, Mestral and the Certoss ended up involving Kirk. How does that man keep finding this sort of trouble?

"That was your own fault," Roberta said, replying to

her own thought. "You're the one who got him to help you, remember?" She had traveled to the twenty-third century and found that Mestral, along with one of the Certoss, had transported through time to the *Enterprise*, using the transporter equipment hidden inside Seven's office. With Kirk's help along with that of his first officer, Spock, Roberta had managed to find the Certoss agent's companion, who for decades had been working toward that whole destruction of Earth and humanity thing.

"It's all just one big ball of crazy, isn't it?"

"Insufficient query," said the Beta 5. *"Please restate your request."*

"Never mind." Roberta tossed a dismissive wave toward the computer. "Have you found Mestral?"

"Negative. The servo given to him by Supervisor 194 is not responding to my signal."

Frowning, Roberta stepped closer to the workstation. "What? Can you locate it?" Seven had provided Mestral with a servo pen similar to the ones carried by him and Roberta. Though it lacked most of the functionality built into the tools at their disposal, the servo still allowed him to communicate with them as well as make use of the transporter system or *Blue Smoke Express*, as Roberta had taken to calling it.

"I am unable to locate the servo," reported the computer. *"Mestral's current location is unknown."*

"Wait. You're saying he disappeared?"

Where the hell had he gone?

Twelve

Marine Corps Air Station—El Palomar, California
May 21, 1971

Everything, as always, was gray.

The cinderblock walls forming the windowless room were painted gray. Scratched and scuffed, the metal table at the room's center, and to which his hands were cuffed, was a lighter shade of gray. The chair in which he sat, along with its counterpart on the table's opposite side, displayed equal neglect and featured paint that approximated the table's hue. A single bulb hung from the center of the ceiling, providing the sole source of illumination, though its success was marginal when considering the amount of the room that still lay in shadow. It was a deliberate effect, he knew, a concerted effort on the part of his hosts to elicit an emotional response in those brought here, in particular an impression of isolation if not outright sensory deprivation.

The tactic had not worked on him during any of his previous visits to this room, and Mestral doubted it would prove successful anytime soon.

How long had he been here? In this room, twelve minutes and forty-seven seconds as humans measured the passage of time. In the facility where this austere, uninviting chamber was located? Despite the lack of visible timekeeping devices and any view of the outside world, Mestral knew that he had been here for eight months, two weeks, and three days. Though he had been moved from room to room, and often spent prolonged periods locked in what his guards called "solitary confinement," he had been able to keep track of the days as they added up to weeks and then months. Those intervals of enforced solitude had been interspersed with periods of prolonged questioning. Some of those conversations had been enlightening, even fascinating, as he spoke with a small number of military officers and the occasional civilian scientist, each of them at once eager and at first apprehensive about the answers he would provide for their many questions. The fear seemed to have ebbed over time, and now Mestral found he actually looked forward to the sessions. On the other hand, the intervals at which they occurred had become predictable, taking place once every seven days and at approximately the same time of day on each occasion.

Mestral heard the footsteps a full thirty-six seconds before a key was inserted into the lock on the other side of the heavy gray door. Metal turned against metal, and the door swung outward to reveal a human male wearing the blue uniform of an officer in the United States Air Force. The single star on each shoulder indicated his rank as that of a brigadier general, making him the most senior military official he had yet met. A collection of multicolored ribbons over his left breast pocket signified a lengthy and distinguished career, and the black name tag over his other pocket was labeled OLSON. Mestral recognized the name, though until this moment he had not had occasion to mention this to anyone.

A guard outside the room closed the door behind the man as he stepped into the room, and Mestral heard the door's lock turn back into place. The new arrival, holding a black portfolio, stood silent for a moment, brown eyes staring at Mestral. The man's blond hair was receding and had gone gray at the temples, and lines creased his forehead and around his eyes.

"Good morning, Mestral. My name is General Stephen Olson," the man said after a few more seconds. "I represent a group with which you're familiar, Majestic 12."

Mestral reacted to the statement with the raising of his left eyebrow. Though he had suspected the organization's involvement in his capture and incarceration, and he had mentioned his knowledge of the top-secret program during several of his past discussions with other military officers, today was the first time anyone had admitted to any association with it.

"I am familiar with Majestic 12, General, just as I am familiar with you, though at the time you were a colonel."

Nodding in approval, Olson moved to the empty chair across from Mestral and sat. He laid the portfolio on the table but did not open it.

"You're also familiar with Project Blue Book," he said, the fingers of his right hand resting atop the portfolio. "Not just familiar, but very conversant in its activities, at least until the project was deactivated."

"That is correct." Mestral returned Olson's stern gaze, though his own expression remained composed. All of this had been covered during previous conversations, the details of which he was certain the general knew.

"You worked extensively with two of Blue Book's case officers, James Wainwright and Allison Marshall." As he spoke, Olson began tapping his fingers on the portfolio.

"General, I believe I have demonstrated cooperation and honesty in all of my previous interviews, and I find it difficult to believe that you are not aware of my responses to such questions during those conversations. However, to answer your question, I did know Mister Wainwright and Miss Marshall, and I did assist them on some of the cases they investigated for your military."

He had come to know Wainwright and Marshall after learning about the existence of Certoss agents on Earth. He had brought this information to the officers, who were part of a group tasked with investigating reports of extraterrestrial activity on Earth and whether such activity posed a threat to the planet. The project had been active for many years, beginning in the late 1940s, after an alien vessel landed in the southwestern United States, and continuing through the previous decade.

Despite its outreach to the public in its quest to learn the truth about alien activity, Wainwright told him that Blue Book had in effect become something of a disinformation campaign before its ignominious end. It was the human's belief that the project was little more than a distraction for the citizenry while Majestic 12 carried on with the real work of investigating and analyzing such reports, along with any actual extraterrestrials they might discover.

However, that had not always been the case. At its inception, Blue Book and the projects from which it had evolved had attempted a serious examination of such sightings and other reports. Indeed, Wainwright and Marshall had been dispatched to Pennsylvania in 1957 to investigate sightings of an unidentified craft: his own. Mestral later learned that their efforts to understand the truth of the crash were thwarted by the actions of human agents working for alien benefactors—the Aegis—with an interest in seeing Earth survive what they knew would be chaotic times in the years ahead. Though Mestral had shared his relationship with Wainwright and Marshall, the questions put to him had been phrased in such a manner that he was able to navigate them while still maintaining the secrecy of the Aegis agents and their successors, who continued to work "behind the scenes" for Earth's benefit.

Olson nodded. "Yes, you've been very cooperative. I, for one, appreciate it, but I've wondered why you've been so accommodating."

"There is nothing to be gained by deception." Within

the first days of his capture, Mestral had come to realize that lying to his hosts—even without the cultural prohibitions that normally required him to abstain from such actions—would be a fruitless gesture. His initial decision had been motivated in large part due to his treatment while in custody, which to this point had been civilized, all things considered.

He had not endured physical mistreatment or abuse, and though a team of doctors had examined him at length, their most invasive procedures had been taking blood samples and subjecting him to a series of X-rays. The primitive means of examining a patient's internal organs was as advanced as the humans' current medical technology, and Mestral had found the exercise quaint as well as educational. His blood had been of particular interest to the doctors studying him, and there had been several discussions about his physiology as well as how it differed from humans.

It had been his blood that had led to his capture. At least, that was story given to him by one of the military officers who had conducted his first interrogation. He had cut himself in the kitchen of his apartment while working there as a construction engineer in San Diego, and his accident had been observed by a neighbor. Though he was never given the details, Mestral suspected that person had contacted authorities, and the military had then become aware of the incident.

As part of the overall treatment he had received, his dietary requests had been honored, and he even had been allowed the occasional respite from his cell, though never to an outside area. Still, that gesture had been enough to provide him with some information as to his location, with stone walls and tunnels leading him to believe he was being held in some form of underground facility. Mestral had not bothered to ask for confirmation of his suspicions, and his hosts had not deemed it necessary to offer such information.

"As I've told others who've questioned me on this matter," he continued, "my people prefer not to lie, except in the most extreme circumstances where lives may be at risk. Besides, you have nothing to fear from me, General. I intend no harm toward you or anyone else. Though my arrival here was to a degree accidental, my decision to remain here was motivated by a sincere desire to observe your people."

"Not to learn from us?"

Mestral once more allowed an arched eyebrow. "Observation implies education, General. If you mean do I seek to discover some weakness or other vulnerability that might be exploited, then no. As I have previously stated, and as Mister Wainwright and Miss Marshall have doubtless testified, my intentions here are nothing but peaceful."

"They both spoke highly of you," Olson replied, "as has Professor Carlson."

Jeffrey Carlson, the older human male whom Mestral knew to be one of the founding members of Majestic 12, had also been an overseer of Project Blue Book and Wainwright and Marshall. The name was one Mestral had not heard in all the time he had been here.

"I trust the professor is well."

Olson said, "We're keeping him busy, but yes, he's doing fine."

During their first meeting, Mestral had been struck by Carlson's welcoming nature and genuine desire for friendship. A compassionate, humble man, the professor had wanted to forge an understanding between humans and the extraterrestrials who had chosen to visit Earth. He believed there was much to be learned on both sides from such a meeting, and Mestral also knew that Carlson for some time had been involved in an effort to reverse engineer retrieved alien technology in the hopes of one day replicating it.

"And Mister Wainwright?" No information as to the status of Wainwright or Marshall had been provided during previous interviews.

"I'm afraid I'm not at liberty to divulge that information."

Mestral nodded. "I understand. It is my hope that he also is well."

The general said nothing else for a moment, and Mestral at first thought this might be some new interrogation tactic Olson was employing. With his hand still resting atop the portfolio, the man seemed to want to ask something else, though perhaps he was conflicted about how to give voice to his thoughts. Was he wrestling with doubt, or fear?

"I'll level with you, Mestral," Olson said. "There are several thousand scientists who would love to be sitting here talking to you. Of course, they don't know about you and probably never will." For the first time, he smiled. "We prefer to keep you to ourselves. There's a reason you've been well treated, as opposed to being dissected or something. You see, there's been much discussion about how you might be able to demonstrate your peaceful intentions toward us."

Leaning forward in his chair, Olson opened his portfolio. The first thing Mestral saw was what looked to be a technical diagram printed on a piece of white paper. Typed and handwritten notes surrounded the object at its center.

"We have a team of people," the general continued, "led by Professor Carlson, as a matter of fact, who are working to build something like this for us." He lifted the paper and laid it at the center of the table, orienting it so that Mestral could read the notes. It was a spacecraft, though as far as he knew it was unlike anything currently in existence anywhere on the planet. Even the drawings he had seen in magazines about proposed future generations of space vessels looked nothing like what now lay before him. Instead, this resembled something he might see in a film or on the cover of a fiction book or magazine at the library.

"Interesting," he said. One set of letters, handwritten near what was labeled as the vessel's rear section, caught his attention: FTL. He was just able to reach it before the chain connecting his handcuffs to the table went taut. "What does this term mean?"

Olson leaned over the table to see. "Faster than light."

"Indeed. I was not aware that your space-travel capabilities had advanced to such a degree."

"It hasn't. Not yet, anyway." The general shrugged. "To be honest, we're nowhere near anything like that. This is just somebody's wishful thinking, but it could be more than that, with your help."

Mestral regarded the drawing for another moment. "You're proposing that I assist you in realizing this concept."

"I won't lie," replied Olson, reaching out to tap the paper with one finger. "There are a bunch of people who are a lot smarter than I am who think there are several thousand different ways to better spend the money this'll cost, but they have the luxury of living in ignorance. Now that we know—really know—that there are people like you out there, and they can travel faster than light to get here from wherever they live, it makes sense for us to have the same capability."

It took Mestral but a moment to infer the general's unspoken meaning. "You mean for military use."

"Protecting the planet is the name of the game." Olson retrieved the drawing and returned it to his portfolio. "Personally, I'd be happy if everybody else in the universe would just leave us alone, but we have to be ready to defend ourselves in the event somebody comes calling." He shrugged. "And let's face it: Without that sort of propulsion capability, we're stuck in our own solar system. It takes months or years just to get to the other planets. Even if we just want to go out and have a look around, we need something like this."

He was right, of course. Mestral could concede that much, at least so far as the logistics and reality of space travel were concerned. However, the human race, at this point in its growth as a civilization, was very much a captive of ideological and sociopolitical chaos. They still waged war on one another for all manner of reasons ranging from resource control to religious and political differences and everything in between. Until they learned to live in peace amongst themselves and celebrate rather than fear their diversity, it was logical to assume they would carry their aggression to the stars. So long as that was a possibility, Mestral knew he could not assist them.

Before he could say anything else, he was interrupted by the sound of the door unlocking. Olson's expression told Mestral that he also was surprised by this, and he shifted in his seat to face the door just as it opened. Standing in the entryway was not the guard or another officer, but instead a blond woman wearing dark, nondescript civilian clothes.

"Who the hell are you?" Olson snapped, rising from his chair.

Without saying a word, Roberta Lincoln raised her right hand and aimed a slim, silver object at the general. Her servo made a small metallic sound and Olson's body went rigid. He settled back into his chair, his body limp. Lincoln stepped forward, grasping his shoulders and lowering his head to the table.

"Miss Lincoln," Mestral said. "It is agreeable to see you again."

"Same here," the woman replied, aiming her servo at Mestral's handcuffs. The device hummed again and the cuffs opened, falling from his wrists. Satisfied with her work, Lincoln smiled.

"You're a hard man to find, you know that?"

Thirteen

Despite James Wainwright's best efforts to ignore him, the orderly was still there.

"You need to start getting ready for your next session, sir," said Robert from where he stood just inside the doorway, and Wainwright heard the note of annoyance in the other man's voice.

"I'm ready," he replied, without looking up from the paperback novel he was only half reading. Wainwright had found the dog-eared book in the day room's lending library. It was labeled as an action-adventure thriller, the fourth in a series about which he knew nothing, and focused on a Vietnam veteran fighting organized crime elements in various cities around the country. This book had brought the character to Miami, and every other page seemed to be filled with vivid descriptions of gunplay and other violence meted out against what Wainwright supposed were deserving individuals. Though not terribly deep, the story was entertaining enough, and certainly more enjoyable than the orderly at the door or the upcoming therapy session.

"You planning to go like that?" asked Robert.

Looking down, Wainwright surveyed his current attire, which consisted of the same light blue pajamas issued to all patients, a dark blue terry cloth robe, and slippers. With one hand, he reached up to rub his chin and felt stubble. His hair, which was longer than he would have preferred and definitely out of air force regulation, had to be disheveled, as he had done nothing about his appearance since rising from bed two hours earlier.

"Yeah," he said. "I think I am."

Robert released an audible sigh. "Doctor Silverman's not going to like that." He stood in the doorway to Wainwright's room with his muscled arms folded across his chest. The man possessed an athletic build, more of a gymnast or wrestler than a weightlifter, and Wainwright had seen him handle himself when confronting unruly patients who decided to get physical with him. He harbored no illusions about being able to take the other man in a similar situation.

"What's he going to do?" Wainwright asked. "Shave my head and ship me overseas? I'm twice his age, for crying out loud. Does his mother even know he's down here playing doctor?"

"They might shave your head and send you to clean latrines," Robert said. It was obvious to Wainwright that the orderly had either never seen the humor to be found in their little bouts of verbal jousting, or else had grown tired of the exchanges. Wainwright realized he should not be hassling the man in this way, as Robert was just trying to do his job, but he found that minor rebellions of this sort were one of the few defense mechanisms at his disposal for dealing with his present situation.

Wainwright and Robert went through this routine, or some variation of it, every Wednesday morning. It had become something of a game, at least for Wainwright, beginning several months earlier, after deciding he had been subjected to more than enough of the air force's misguided ministrations over his so-called well-being. He had been a guest here for nearly two years, following a diagnosis of what one military physician had termed *post-traumatic stress*, which to Wainwright had sounded like a fancy name for a nervous breakdown. That the apparent condition had manifested itself after more than two decades spent in service to a top-secret military program and the fatigue, anxiety, and sheer terror that had come with that assignment, seemed not to matter to those who had put him here.

He had spent his fifty-third and fifty-fourth birthdays here, treated to a slice of chocolate cake provided by the hospital's cafeteria. All of the other days had been spent either being subjected to tests, participating in one-on-one or group therapy sessions with a rotating roster of psychiatrists and other mental health professionals, or desperately seeking anything to help fill the hours. He felt no ill effects, but was told that was a symptom of someone suffering from deep emotional or other psychological issues. The boredom was alleviated by visits from friends and family, most notably his son, Michael, and of course Allison Marshall, his longtime friend, partner, and lover. Having recently retired from the air force, Allison had moved to the San Antonio area to be close to him, and her visits were frequent and anticipated. She was the one bright spot in all of this, giving Wainwright something on which to focus in the hopes that the military in its infinite wisdom would one day see fit to discharge him from his veritable prison.

As for the condition from which he supposedly suffered, Wainwright in a way felt as though he was undeserving of such a judgment. Instead, he, like many others, felt the diagnosis more aptly described the shock, pain, and suffering endured by soldiers who had faced combat or other disturbing experiences. Being handed such a determination, at least to him, seemed to dilute the real problems with which those scarred by battle were coping. Wainwright had not seen war, at least not for more than twenty-five years. Were some of his own experiences during the past two decades on par with the brutalities of actual war? There might be those who agreed with that notion, but he was not one of them.

"I'll be back in an hour, sir," said Robert stepping backward through the open door. "I recommend shaving, combing that mop you call hair, and I definitely suggest brushing your teeth. You know the doc's got a thing about people and their breath."

"Is he expecting me to kiss him or something?" Wainwright offered a small smile to show that this was still part of their banter. In truth, he held no bad feelings for Doctor Silverman, who had only been working at the hospital for the past three months. Unlike his predecessors, Silverman seemed content to let his patients talk at whatever length suited them, only asking questions to guide discussion when the other party seemed unsure as to how to proceed. One thing that definitely worked in the doctor's favor was his reluctance to use medication in place of actual sessions with his patients. For that reason among several others, Wainwright had come to respect the man, and if anyone was going to see to it that he was freed from this place, it was Silverman.

Seeing that Robert was getting antsy, Wainwright offered a mock salute. "I'll be here," he said. The orderly said nothing else, but instead just shook his head before exiting the room and leaving Wainwright to his book.

He managed to read two pages before he was interrupted again.

"Mister Wainwright?"

Startled by the voice behind him, Wainwright bolted from his chair, turning to see a man standing just outside the doorway leading to the bathroom. The new arrival was dressed in a dark gray suit with matching tie over a plain white shirt. A gray fedora rested atop his head with the brim pulled low, and Wainwright noted the man's pale, almost yellow skin. The eyes were dark, and there was no mistaking the intelligence behind them.

Even with the hat in place to cover what he knew were pointed ears, Wainwright recognized him at once. "Mestral?"

The man—no, *Vulcan*—nodded. "It is agreeable to see you, again, sir, though I am distressed about your present living arrangements."

How long's it been since I last saw him? At least three years, if Wainwright's recollection was correct. "What happened to you? The last I remember, you were on your way to New York City. We were investigating those . . ."

He stopped short of saying the word *aliens* aloud. For more than two decades, he had worked and lived under a strict veil of secrecy, tasked with investigating things the government wanted kept from the public while at the same time helping his superiors to devise ways to defend those same people from things about which they remained blissfully ignorant. It had been tireless, thankless work, at least to those who might most benefit from such effort, but Wainwright and others forever connected to the covert organization known as Majestic 12 knew that they had been a part of something important to the safety of every living thing on this planet.

Until they decided they didn't need me anymore, that is.

As though sensing his desire for vigilance in the event unwanted ears might overhear their conversation,

Mestral nodded. "You are correct. I ran into some . . .
difficulty . . . while in New York, which resulted in a
rather remarkable detour. I'm afraid I cannot share the
details of that incident with you."

"Can't share?" Wainwright made no effort to dis-
guise his surprise. "With me? You were working with
us, remember?" He still recalled that day in the summer of 1958 when the Vulcan walked into the office
he had shared with his assistant, Allison Marshall, at
Wright-Patterson Air Force Base in Ohio. The two of
them were in the midst of their nearly twenty-year association with MJ-12 and Project Blue Book, which to
that point had consisted in large part of unconfirmed
sightings and unverified reports of contact by various
people with extraterrestrial beings. Though Wainwright and Marshall had seen with their own eyes that
such things were real, attempting to monitor the movements and activities of alleged aliens from other worlds
had proven a daunting task.

"The Certoss," Wainwright said, keeping his voice
low. "You were helping us hunt the Certoss."

Mestral nodded. "And it was while assisting you
with that effort that I became aware of another effort
to monitor and even influence events here on Earth,
though in this case it was for benevolent purposes."

"Well, that's a nice change of pace." The Certoss had
been a problem for Wainwright and Marshall for several
years, even before the Blue Book agents had even known
who or what they were hunting. It was Mestral who had
arrived on their doorstep, bringing with him information

he had acquired about the aliens after his own firsthand experiences with them. The Vulcan had told Wainwright and Marshall how a small group of these aliens had traveled through both time and space to Earth at the height of World War II. Even as the United States was battling German forces in Europe while at the same time waging a campaign in the Pacific against Japan, these Certoss agents had come to destroy all of humanity. It had been a lot for Wainwright to accept, but Mestral had convinced him through an extraordinary technique that had allowed the Vulcan to join their minds. Through this process, Wainwright had become convinced of Mestral's sincerity and desire to assist them. That was what he was doing when he traveled to New York City, ostensibly to investigate a lead on a possible location for the Certoss, who to that point had done a remarkable job of concealing their whereabouts and activities.

"So, who are these other people you're talking about?" asked Wainwright, his attention shifting between Mestral and the door. He half expected Robert to come barreling into the room again. A look at the clock on his nightstand told him it had only been a few minutes since the orderly's last visit, but that did not discount the possibility of him or another member of the hospital's staff wandering in to bother him for any of a dozen reasons.

"They are friends." Mestral stepped closer. "They're humans, working for an agency that is not affiliated with your government or any other organization born of this planet."

Wainwright frowned. "How is that even possible? Who funds them? How do they operate? Where are they?"

"They wish their location kept secret," said Mestral, "and I have promised to honor that request, but they have sent me to talk with you because they believe you possess information about certain alien activity on Earth."

Moving to his bed, Wainwright placed a slip of paper into the book to mark his place, then laid the novel on his nightstand. "What sort of alien activity?"

"My friends are searching for beings who call themselves Iramahl. What we don't know is whether you or any of your fellow agents may have encountered members of this race during your investigations of extraterrestrial activity."

"I don't recall ever hearing that name," Wainwright said, shaking his head. Ferengi, Certoss, and Vulcan were the ones he himself had encountered and for which he had a species name. Mestral himself had offered hints about dozens—no, hundreds—of other races inhabiting planets throughout this "quadrant" of the galaxy.

Mestral replied, "It is entirely possible that you met such beings and either did not realize it, or else any memories of a particular incident may have been suppressed."

"Suppressed?" Wainwright did not like the way that sounded. "You mean like brainwashing?"

It seemed to take the Vulcan a moment to ponder what Wainwright had said, before his right eyebrow rose. "An interesting choice of phrase. Informally expressed, but essentially correct. Do you recall how I joined my mind to yours?"

"Of course." It had been a bizarre experience, to say the least, but it had not been painful, and Mestral had even expressed concern about having performed the task, or that he may have crossed some sort of ethical line.

"I would like to repeat that act, if you will permit it."

Wainwright nodded. "Sure. I don't suppose you can take me somewhere else to do that?" He gestured around the room. "I'm getting pretty tired of staring at these same walls all the time."

Instead of replying, Mestral approached him. As he had done all those years ago, the Vulcan pressed the fingers of his right hand to key points along Wainwright's face. Wainwright immediately felt the odd tingling sensation beginning to well up from his subconscious.

"Our minds are merging, James," Mestral said, his voice almost a whisper. "Our minds are one."

Wainwright was staring out the window when he heard the door open behind him, followed by the voice of his favorite orderly.

"You're kidding me, right?"

Shifting in his chair, Wainwright turned from the window to see Robert standing in the open doorway, staring at him with a disapproving expression.

"What?"

"Doctor Silverman, remember?" asked the other man. "You're supposed to be meeting with him in ten minutes."

What the hell?

Looking down, Wainwright saw the paperback novel resting in his lap. Had he fallen asleep? The piece of paper he had been using as a bookmark was stuck inside the book's back cover, meaning he must have dozed off and let the book fall from his hand, losing his place.

"I must've . . . wasn't I just talking to . . . ?" There was a fleeting image of another figure standing before him, but Wainwright couldn't bring the odd thought or memory into focus. He looked to the clock on his nightstand and saw that it had been nearly forty-five minutes since his last conversation with Robert. Had he really fallen asleep, that quickly?

Stepping into the room, Robert offered an expression of restrained irritation. "Yeah, whatever. Come on, sir. We need to get you ready. You know the doc hates to be kept waiting."

"Mestral."

That was a name he had not heard or said aloud in a while, and yet there it was, bubbling up from the depths of his memory. Why would he give thought to the Vulcan now, after all this time? How long had it been since he had last seen him? Two or three years.

"I'm sorry?" asked Robert, and when Wainwright looked at him the orderly was staring back in confusion. "Who or what is Mestral?" Of course Robert would have no idea to what Wainwright was referring.

Other than himself, there were only two other people on the planet who even knew of Mestral's existence. Wainwright had not even told Doctor Silverman, who had been briefed into many of the aspects of Project Blue Book—but not Majestic 12—so as to have a clearer picture of what he was dealing with while treating his patient.

Shaking off the odd sensation, Wainwright made a dismissive gesture. "Sorry. I was just lost in thought."

Maybe I am crazy.

Fourteen

"It is unfortunate that he has to remain in that facility."

Sitting at the oversized desk in Gary Seven's office, Roberta Lincoln nodded as she swiveled the desk's high-backed chair to face Mestral. The Vulcan stood at the windows, hands clasped behind his back. He had removed his fedora, exposing his pointed ears, and he presented quite the image, dressed as he was in the charcoal-gray suit that was similar to so many others Roberta might encounter on the streets of her home city.

"I agree with you," she said, "but pulling him out of there would just raise questions and alarms. Considering everything he knows, the military would waste no effort trying to find Wainwright and make sure he wasn't blabbing government secrets to the newspapers or the evening news." Though Roberta did not think that a likely scenario, it was easy to imagine the top-secret Majestic 12 organization sending agents on a hunt to find one of their own who they believed may have "wandered off the reservation," as the saying went.

For better or worse, she knew that James Wainwright was safer in the care of the air force, at least for the time being. In that way of his that was both vague and infuriating, Gary Seven had told her that his stay at the hospital in Texas would be a temporary one.

"Did you not have similar concerns when you liberated me?" asked Mestral, turning from the window.

Roberta shrugged. "For a minute, but your case is a bit different." She smiled. "You're an alien, after all."

"I am aware of that, Miss Lincoln." Mestral punctuated his reply with an arching of his eyebrow.

"So, Majestic can't just throw out an all-points bulletin to local police departments and news outlets, warning everybody to be on the lookout for the man in the sharp suit and pointed ears." Roberta had instructed the Beta 5 to monitor government and military communications for any mention of Mestral or anything that might relate to an escaped prisoner or a simple hunt for a person of interest, but the supercomputer had so far found nothing of note. This actually surprised Roberta, in that she would have expected chatter within the first hours of the Vulcan's mysterious disappearance from the classified facility in California. Was it embarrassment on the part of Majestic, or was the secretive group proceeding with even greater stealth and deliberation as they tried to figure out what happened? If there was one thing MJ-12 knew how to do with great effectiveness, it was to remain cloaked in shadow. Very little of what they did was recorded anywhere on paper or in a computer file, at least not anywhere accessible to anyone outside their compartmented, protective veil of security.

This was what had made tracking Mestral's whereabouts so difficult when Roberta and the Beta 5 had attempted to find him. After tracking down a report from the fall of 1970 in San Diego, Mestral's last reported location, she and the computer surmised that the Vulcan had been taken into custody. Eliminating regular law-enforcement agencies was simple, as was ruling out conventional military forces, such as the navy or Marine Corps installations in San Diego or Camp Pendleton, the Marine base farther north. That was when Roberta had set the Beta 5 to scour through whatever classified communications and other reports it could find. A single report of a prisoner transfer from a secure facility tucked inside the El Palomar Marine Corps Air Station in California had been the first tangible clue, noteworthy because of its distinct lack of a name for the person being transferred. That was a tactic the military liked to employ when moving high-value prisoners around. The Beta 5 had also recognized one of the names on the order: Jeffrey Carlson from Majestic 12 and who currently was working on some rather interesting projects at a secret base in the Nevada desert. Not entirely sure whom she might find, Roberta had followed the computer's lead to California and found Mestral.

"They will exhaust every effort to find me," said the Vulcan.

Roberta shrugged. "Sure, but it'll be an uphill climb

for them." While she had no doubt that MJ-12 was searching for him, she also knew that they would have to conduct their little hunt on their own. With her helping him, she was sure she could keep the Vulcan a few steps ahead of them, at least until something of greater import seized their attention.

"Were you able to learn anything from Wainwright?" she asked.

"His knowledge of the Iramahl is very limited," replied Mestral. "So far as I was able to determine, Mister Wainwright had only the one encounter with them. Interestingly, I believe it was his first meeting with any extraterrestrial following the events in Roswell. Of course, his memory of this incident was suppressed."

"It wouldn't be the first time," replied Roberta. A review of the Beta 5's information on James Wainwright revealed that he had been visited by other members of the Aegis before that mysterious organization had sent Gary Seven to Earth. Even now, three years after learning the truth behind Seven and the Aegis, Roberta found it hard to imagine that humans had been taken from Earth thousands of years ago, and that they and their descendants had been trained and genetically enhanced over uncounted generations. It still amazed her that the aliens behind this effort had invested such a staggering amount of time and resources before deciding when the time was right to deploy their prodigies to Earth. The proof of that was Gary Seven, as well as those agents who had preceded him, each bearing the burden of their broad, all-encompassing mission that was—as Seven had described—to "prevent Earth from destroying itself before it can mature into a peaceful society."

Two such predecessors had tracked one of Wainwright's investigations to Carbon Creek, a small mining town in Pennsylvania, in late 1957 where a mysterious object was seen to have crashed. As it happened, it was a Vulcan ship that had come down, and a member of its crew now stood in Gary Seven's office.

Pretty weird, the way we're all connected like that.

"We've had to step in more than once to keep someone like Wainwright from learning too much about the wrong thing at the wrong time." There were times when Roberta had hated being forced to take such action, especially when they were people who might well be able to serve as allies in the mission she and Seven faced. However, her inscrutable employer was far more reluctant to bring "civilians" into the fold, preferring instead to maintain his and Roberta's relative anonymity as they watched over Earth and its people.

"It would appear the Iramahl or some other party shared your concerns," Mestral said, moving around Seven's desk and beginning to pace the length of the room. When he came to where the Beta 5 had swung out from its hidden wall alcove, he spent a moment studying its control panel and display screens. "The technique used to suppress his memories was crude, but effective. Rather than isolating and eliminating recollections of specific individuals or events, an entire period of time was compartmentalized and rendered inaccessible. It required great effort on my part even to locate those memories, let alone read them."

"Can they be restored?"

Mestral shook his head. "Not through a mind-meld. To be more precise, doing so is beyond my capabilities. A Vulcan High Master might be able to do it, though such individuals are in rather short supply here."

"Seven might have access to technology that can do it," Roberta said. She added it to the growing list of things she wanted to discuss with her employer upon his return from wherever the Aegis had seen fit to send him this time. With the amount of time the veteran agent was spending away from Earth, it was hard for her not to wonder if they could be preparing for some kind of global or even interstellar catastrophe that might be coming down the line.

You're just being paranoid.

"What about these other aliens that are supposed to be hunting the Iramahl?" she asked. "The Ptaen?"

"Mister Wainwright's knowledge of them is even more limited," Mestral replied, turning away from the Beta 5 and continuing his pacing. "His memories are very short and chaotic. There are only fleeting glimpses of them, but the images I was able to see match the descriptions you provided."

Roberta sighed. "We need more information."

"That is always helpful." Having crossed the length of the office, Mestral stopped before the shelves that had split and slid apart, revealing the vault concealed behind them. Roberta watched him study the compartment's interior, which of course only appeared to the casual observer as a simple vault. When he turned back to face her, his right eyebrow had risen.

"There is one way we might be able to obtain that information."

It took Roberta a moment to comprehend what the Vulcan was suggesting, and she began waving her hands as though to scare the very idea from the room. "Oh, no. I know what you're thinking, and there's no way that's going to happen. After that business with the Certoss, Seven read me the riot act."

Her employer had been livid upon learning of her use of the Aegis technology at her disposal to deal with the renegade Certoss agents. Having managed to insinuate themselves into the fledgling American space program, including a top-secret initiative to launch a nuclear weapons platform into orbit, the Certoss had moved to within a hairbreadth of succeeding in their plan. Roberta thwarted them, with an assist from Kirk and Spock.

Though she had understood the risks posed by any sort of time travel, Seven had expressed supreme reluctance to use such tactics here on Earth, where the primary mission was protecting humanity from destroying itself. Inserting themselves into past events was a risk Seven was unwilling to take in all but the direst of circumstances.

"I'm not allowed to time travel here on Earth unless it's a super emergency. You know, like the world's on fire and the flames are visible from Mars kind of emergency."

Mestral seemed to consider this response, before offering her an odd look. "It is interesting that before I met you and Mister Seven, I believed time travel to be impossible, in keeping with the findings of the Vulcan Science Directorate."

"Yeah, well, their opinion will be changing one of these days." Rising from the chair, she crossed the office to the Beta 5. "In the meantime, we're going to have to do this the hard way, with good old-fashioned detective work." She laid a hand on the computer's console. "Thankfully, we've got an ace."

Based on the information Mestral had been able to glean from his mind-meld with Wainwright, the one true lead they had for the continued presence of the Iramahl on Earth was still twenty years old. She had tasked the computer with cross-referencing maps and information on the area against its storehouse of U.S. government and military records obtained over the course of many years by the Aegis agents who had preceded Gary Seven's assignment to Earth. Among that vast collection of data were digital copies of reports submitted by case officers from Project Blue Book and its predecessors after investigating sightings and other eyewitness accounts pertaining to unidentified craft as well as extraterrestrial beings. It had taken the Beta 5 little time to find the rather unremarkable, even boring report James Wainwright had submitted in September 1951 detailing his interview with the Clarkes.

"Besides," Roberta continued, "it's not really the Iramahl who are the concern. If what Kirk told me is true, then they're simply trying to hide until their own people find them. It's these other aliens, the Ptaen, who are the bigger problem."

"Yes," Mestral replied, moving away from the vault. "If they have also been on Earth for an extended period, then like the Iramahl, they have done remarkably well concealing their presence."

Roberta crossed her arms. "They probably have more technology at their disposal too. If the Iramahl ship crashed here, then it was destroyed, or else so damaged that repairs were impossible. They would've salvaged whatever they could carry, but how much would that end up being, especially if their main concern at the time was simple survival?" She reached up to rub the bridge of her nose. "Seven's so much better at this than I am."

Uncounted hours of study over the past three years and working under the guidance of both Seven and the Beta 5 had seen to it that Roberta received a crash course in all manner of topics with the potential to influence the mission she had so unwittingly joined on that fateful day in 1968. While that overdose of education had served to broaden her thinking so far as examining problems from a global and—occasionally—interstellar perspective, she was still learning the ropes here. Was there some key component to the present issue she was missing? Something she had overlooked? When she had briefed Seven on the odd message sent to her by Admiral Kirk and the preliminary steps she had taken to investigate the potential of finding the

Iramahl refugees, her unlikely mentor had expressed his satisfaction with her work, encouraging her to follow the information wherever it led, and her gut wherever it took her. Despite his reserved, even aloof demeanor, Gary Seven had a way of quietly motivating her that did not seem condescending or overbearing, and he more than once had expressed his admiration at how she had thrown herself into her work. It was an issue of pride with her, wanting to show Seven and his masters that Earth was worth saving. To that end, Roberta often wondered if he muttered the occasional judgmental remark about the human race for her benefit, particularly when he made some observation about Earth "at this point in its development," or expressing his frequent surprise that "her people" had managed to persevere through their own shortsightedness and even stupidity. Likewise, she found it interesting that Seven never seemed to include her in these observations and commentaries.

He's the worst teacher ever, except when he's being the best teacher ever.

Mestral, now standing next to her at the Beta 5, said, "I would suggest instructing your computer to begin searching government and military records for anything pertaining to unidentified craft that have been investigated and which cannot be ruled out as being either Iramahl or Ptaen in origin, with an emphasis on the latter. It is probable that examples of their technology are more prevalent, despite their efforts to conceal it."

"Way ahead of you, Mister Vulcan," Roberta replied,

tapping the computer console. "She's already dug out the Project Sign case file for the sighting Wainwright was investigating in 1951. Remember, this was back when the air force was actively hunting for potential threats, along with technology they might be able to tear apart, re-create, and all that other stuff. There were other investigators working the case, and the main file contains interviews with descriptions of the craft that was seen, along with the usual assortment of blurry, useless photos and even a couple of sketches. It's not the greatest source of information, but it's a starting point." There had to be other files somewhere, buried deep within the convoluted network of secret bases, warehouses, and whatever holes in the ground Majestic 12 had utilized for more than twenty years to safeguard its secrets. It was just a process of finding first which haystack in which to look, then extracting the needle that MJ-12 had put there as a feint to distract unwanted attention, and then figuring out which way the clandestine agency did not want curiosity seekers to look.

"The thing is," she said after a moment, "this could all just be a wild-goose chase. For all we know, the Ptaen found the Iramahl years ago."

Moving once more to the window, the Vulcan had resumed looking out at the surrounding city, hands behind his back. "For the moment, it's logical to assume that the Iramahl are here. Even if they have died, they would seem to have eluded their Ptaen pursuers. The truth is simply waiting for us to find it."

"Yeah, well, the truth might be waiting awhile." Roberta sighed. "This is probably going to take a pretty long time."

Mestral nodded. "As you've noted, Miss Lincoln, time seems to be an ally."

"For now, anyway."

Turning from the window, the Vulcan regarded her with that eyebrow of his, and Roberta mimicked his expression.

"Yeah, I know. I'm hilarious."

Fifteen

No sooner did Kirk lower his tired body into the recliner in front of his fireplace than his desk communicator sounded.

"Damn."

With a heavy sigh, Kirk pushed himself from the chair. For a moment, he considered leaving his glass of brandy behind, but then decided against it. Whoever was calling him at this hour would just have to bear the reality of having intruded on his solitude. Stepping away from the pair of recliners that represented his favorite place to relax after a long day, he crossed his living room to the desk terminal. He smacked the activation switch on the Starfleet-issued communications panel with more force than was necessary, wondering if he might break the thing.

"Kirk here."

Much to his dismay, the terminal activated, its compact screen flaring to life and coalescing into the image of Admiral Nogura. The older man was staring out at Kirk with a knowing gleam in his eyes.

"There you are. I thought you may have made your escape."

"I obviously didn't kill enough guards." To punctuate his reply, Kirk took a deliberate sip of his drink.

Nogura seemed not to notice the jab. *"My spies tell me you weren't enjoying yourself at the reception."*

"It was a bunch of diplomats and other stuffed shirts. I've never enjoyed those sorts of glad-handing affairs." Kirk shrugged. "On the other hand, they're far better suited than I am for taking care of our new friends."

"I won't argue with you on that."

Kirk had been more than happy to follow Nogura's suggestion and bring the Iramahl delegation back to Earth, where the full resources of the Diplomatic Corps and other Federation departments could be brought to bear. He knew from experience that making first contact with a new civilization was always tricky and that the situation became even more complicated when it was the other party prompting the initial meeting. Kirk considered himself a competent representative of Federation interests in his capacity as a Starfleet officer, but he much preferred to leave the intricacies of diplomacy to those individuals who possessed far greater expertise and talent for such things. Kirk did not like it when outsiders attempted to tell him how best to do his job, and he was reluctant to do the same to anyone else.

"What happens now?" he asked.

Leaning back in his black leather office chair, Nogura replied, *"For the time being, we leave it to the* diplomats. There's a lot of ground to cover now that official first contact has been made. We're preparing our own delegation to travel to the Iramahl homeworld to continue these initial conversations on their turf. They may have come to us, but there are still Prime Directive considerations we need to address, particularly given the Iramahl's still contentious relationship with the Ptaen. Even though they've declared their independence from this Consortium, that doesn't mean the Ptaen are necessarily planning to go quietly into that good night. After all, they're supposedly on something resembling decent terms with the Klingons."

"But we're not just going to stand by and let the Klingons help the Ptaen subjugate the Iramahl all over again, are we?" Kirk knew the Federation would not be eager to wade into such a dispute. But would there really be a choice, if the Ptaen opted to force the issue? He did not see how any sort of diplomatic initiative between the Federation, the Iramahl, and the Consortium—and even the Klingons, if it came to that—could be avoided at that point.

"We're not there yet, Jim," replied Nogura. "The Federation Council and the Diplomatic Corps are confident an understanding can be reached and foster discussions for a formalized agreement down the road. A large part of that will of course depend on how willing the Ptaen are to just call it a day."

"How likely is that?"

Nogura shrugged. "Nobody knows at this point. A message has been sent to the Consortium, but it'll be

*some time before we can expect a reply. Let's all keep our
fingers crossed. Enjoy your evening, Jim. You've earned it.
Nogura out."*

The screen faded, taking with it the admiral's visage
and leaving Kirk to stare at the blank monitor for a moment. Whatever was to happen next, it would involve
politicians, but that did not mean he should not be
thinking ahead. There was still much he could do to
prepare Starfleet for the movement of resources needed
to support the Iramahl if the diplomats from all sides
were unable to craft an accord—or somehow managed
to make things worse.

Because as we all know, he mused as he sipped his
brandy, *that sort of thing* never *happens.*

Kirk had made his way back to his recliner and the
inviting fireplace when he realized that some deity with
nothing better to do had to be deriving entertainment
at his expense, for it was at that moment that his door
chime sounded.

Someone has a death wish.

Choosing this time to place his drink aside, Kirk
left the glass on the recliner's arm and stepped toward
the door, which opened at his approach. He stopped,
frowning at the blond woman darkening his doorstep.
It took an extra moment for him to recognize his unexpected visitor, Roberta Lincoln.

"Hello, Admiral. It's nice to see you again." Though
she appeared several years older than the last time he'd
seen her, there was no mistaking her wide smile or her
bright blue eyes. She was dressed in a simple dark blue

pantsuit with a pearl-white blouse, which Kirk took to be normal fashion for the late twentieth century.

"Miss Lincoln. This is a surprise." Remembering his manners, he stepped aside and gestured for her to enter his apartment. "I guess it's been a while."

"In a lot of ways." Walking into the living room, she took a moment to study the decor, including his collection of antique weapons and other mementos he had acquired during his career. She turned to the window and its vantage point overlooking San Francisco Bay. "Nice view." After another lingering gaze at the bay and the cityscape beyond it, she turned to him. "Congratulations on your promotion, by the way."

Kirk smiled. "It was a while ago, but thank you. Obviously, you're still working with Mister Seven. How long has it . . . ?"

"Seventeen years, give or take the odd trip back and forth through time. Speaking of which? I got your message, but you probably already knew that." She made a show of looking around the apartment. "Got anything to drink around here?"

Once both of them had situated themselves in the recliners before Kirk's fireplace, each with a brandy in hand, he said, "All right, so you got our message, but I don't understand. Spock programmed the probe to travel back to a point closer to the time of our first meetings with you, and after that business with the Certoss. Did he miscalculate?"

Roberta shook her head. "Not at all. Mister Spock was on the money with his computations. The probe arrived in late 1970, more or less right where he was aiming." Shrugging, she held her hands away from her body in a gesture of regret. "We still haven't found them, but the data you sent was very informative and helpful. It just took us a while to dig up anything worth reporting back to you."

"How long?"

Sipping her brandy, Roberta blew out her breath. "It's nineteen eighty-five back home." No sooner did she say the words than she chuckled. "That sounds so weird when I say it that way."

"Fifteen years." Kirk shook his head. It had been less than a day since Spock had deployed the probe and sent it on its warp-speed voyage around the sun.

"Yeah. Seven and I have been kind of busy since the last time you saw us." Roberta frowned, casting her gaze toward the fireplace. "I mean, since the last time we saw you. Whatever." She waved a hand as though trying to shoo away a bothersome insect. "As rough as the sixties were? The seventies weren't that much of a picnic, and the eighties are shaping up to be all kinds of crazy."

Kirk said nothing, content instead to listen to this woman who had led such a remarkable life. Gone but not completely forgotten was the young, naive secretary Roberta Lincoln once had been. Now she was a mature, wise woman who had seen and done things beyond the comprehension of almost anyone with whom she had not shared that experience. Even Kirk's own shared adventures with her and the mysterious Gary Seven had given him only a fleeting glimpse into the demanding reality that was the lives of these two remarkable individuals.

The 1980s, Kirk thought. Even with the incomplete records of that era that were available to modern historians, students, and other curious parties, he knew that the late twentieth century was something of a precipice for human civilization. This would be only partially understood at the time, and even in the decades immediately following that tumultuous period. The dawn of the twenty-first century would bring its own problems, of course, along with all manner of triumphs as humanity fought to stretch its wings beyond the confines of its own planet while at the same time struggling to keep that world from descending into everlasting chaos. Even as the first footprints disturbed the parched soil of Mars and humans stared with unaided eyes at the breathtaking beauty of Saturn's rings and the storms of Jupiter, Earth was marching toward oblivion. And yet, somehow, the people of this world found a way to survive the destruction and despair that would all but consume it. How much of what humans finally became after scratching, scraping, and pulling themselves from the ruins of famine, environmental calamity, and nuclear war was due to the unheralded efforts of Gary Seven and Roberta Lincoln?

Kirk suspected he would never know the depth and scope of the answer to that question, although Seven had provided a few insights. It had been during a meeting with the furtive human agent some years ago, aboard the *Enterprise* near the end of Kirk's five-year command. Seven had arrived much older than he had been during any of their previous meetings, and to this day Kirk was unsure whether the man had used time travel to visit him, or if he simply had enjoyed a prolonged lifespan thanks to the genetic enhancements imbued into him and his ancestors. The Eugenics Wars had been the crux of that conversation, but it had given Kirk reason to consider the impacts of other conflicts that had so burdened those times, such as the various Middle East clashes of the early twenty-first century and—eventually—World War III.

Even if we had some extra help, we made it through all of that. I'll take it. Thank you, Mister Seven.

"Thank you, Miss Lincoln."

Shifting in her seat, Roberta eyed him with confusion. "Thank me for what?"

Only then realizing he had said the words aloud, Kirk sipped his brandy and smiled. "You and Seven, and everything you've done, or will do. It'd be nice to hear about it all someday."

"Well, it's funny you should say that. We had our share of help over the years. You know that, seeing as you've helped us a couple of times, yourself." Roberta paused, finishing her drink. She drew a deep breath, savoring the last of her brandy, before returning her gaze to Kirk. "I could use your help again. Yours and Captain Spock's."

"Our help?"

"Like I said, it took us fifteen years to get any kind of a decent lead on these guys. They'd been hiding on

Earth for more than a hundred years before you contacted me, and it looks like they'd gotten pretty good
at it. Other than one verified encounter in the nineteen
fifties, there was nothing concrete, but now we've got
something solid: their ship."

Kirk said, "Really?"

Nodding, Roberta replied, "Beta 5 thinks we might
be able to use it to attract the Iramahl's attention, but
there's also the Ptaen to deal with. They've managed
to stay off our radar for years, as well, but now that
we've got a pretty good idea how to find the Iramahl,
we think the Ptaen will be coming hard." Roberta
shrugged. "So, I'm stacking the deck a bit."

Kirk considered this. "What does Seven say?"

"I'm sure he'll be annoyed when I tell him." When
Kirk laughed at that, it evoked another smile from Roberta, but it was short-lived. "Just you and Spock, like
last time. We get in and get the job done, and I get you
back here, hopefully with the Iramahl."

Sighing, Kirk shook his head. "My file with the Department of Temporal Investigations is about to get
bigger, isn't it?"

"Probably."

A rather insulated branch of the Federation Science
Council, the DTI was tasked with the unique challenge of studying and reporting on any instances of
time travel or encounters with temporal phenomena.
Stories had circulated for years that the group had a
special file just for Kirk, though no one at that agency
had confirmed such rumors. Kirk himself preferred to

think that such a dossier did exist. After the numerous bizarre run-ins he and the *Enterprise* had experienced with time-related oddities, he would be disappointed to find out no one had been recording such incidents for posterity.

Maybe it'll all make for a good book or two someday.

"I'll contact Spock," he said, using the opportunity to drain the rest of his brandy. "He's going to love this."

Roberta regarded him with a sidelong glance. "What about your superiors? What will Admiral Nogura say?"

Echoing her earlier remark, Kirk replied, "I'm sure he'll be annoyed when I tell him." In truth, Nogura and Admiral Morrow would likely fly into a monumental rage when they learned what Kirk proposed to do. "So, I'll tell him when we get back." He studied his now empty glass. "Time travel. You know, I'm never going to get used to this sort of thing. Given everything that's at stake, how do you stay so calm?"

Roberta said, "There's really no need to rush when we're talking about time travel." Pushing herself from the recliner, Kirk noted her sudden wide, enthusiastic smile. "Oh, wow, speaking of time travel, that reminds me: There's this great movie that's playing. Maybe there'll be a chance after all of this for you to see it. There's this kid, and he's got a friend who turns a car into a time machine. It's insanely funny."

Kirk eyed her with amusement, only partly understanding her meaning. "What year are you taking us to, again?"

Sixteen

United States Coast Guard Cutter
Polar Sea—The Northwest Passage
August 8, 1985

Never in his young life had Charlie Atwell seen anything so beautiful.

Leaning against the rail, cigarette in his hand and enjoying the crisp Arctic air, he smiled at the wonder that was the ice field surrounding the ship as well as the coastline to starboard. He listened to the sound of the hull breaking the ice ahead, and felt the vibrations in the railing and the deck beneath his boots, as the *Polar Sea* made its way ever forward with slow, steady determination.

"Something else, isn't it?"

Atwell turned to see his friend Susan London making her way along the deck toward him.

"Yeah, it's something," he replied, taking a drag on his cigarette.

Gesturing toward the water, which now was home to thick sheets of ice as well as larger chunks that had broken away from the glaciers lining both sides of the channel, London said, "Kind of like poking Mother

Nature in the eye with a sharp stick, right? She says you can't come up here, and we say, 'Screw that.' Kind of like climbing a mountain or going to the moon, right? We just decide to do something, and it gets done." She pointed toward another massive glacier looming ahead, some distance off the ship's starboard bow. "You don't see this kind of thing in Florida, that's for damned sure."

"Do you even have ice in Florida?" asked Atwell.

London shrugged. "In freezers, and in drinks, but that's about it."

"I've seen crazy ice storms every once in a while," replied Atwell, "but nothing like this." As a native of Independence, a small Missouri city just to the east of Kansas City, he had seen his share of what he thought were harsh winters, but all of that went away upon his posting to the *Polar Sea*. Even the pictures his grand-parents had brought back from their two-week Alaskan cruise, which had included a transit through the Inside Passage and the Gulf of Alaska, had not prepared him for the pure grandeur that was the Arctic Circle.

"This ain't nothing." London grinned. "Wait until they send us down under."

Atwell had read about the ship's previous mis-sions to Antarctica, which included breaking channels through the ice floes of the Ross Sea so that a string of supply ships could bring food, fuel, and all manner of other cargo to McMurdo Station, the permanent inter-national research center that was home to several hun-dred scientists, engineers, and other support personnel.

London had already made one such journey to that inhospitable region, and Atwell could not wait for his turn. The trip would take nearly six months to complete, but it would be worth it for him to go to a part of the world visited by none but a privileged few.

Life in the coast guard had delivered several of the so-called promises offered on that fateful day the previous summer when Atwell decided to visit a recruiting office, travel being chief among them. Until his enlistment, and not counting routine hops across the state line into Kansas, he had never ventured out of Missouri. The farthest he had been away from Independence was St. Louis, and then only to see his hometown Chiefs take on the Cardinals. A brief stint in the coast guard offered more opportunity than he would ever have if had stayed home and gone to work in the family furniture store, and once his tour was done he would go to college. Maybe he would decide on the University of Kansas or perhaps one of the schools in or around the Seattle area that was the *Polar Sea*'s home port.

For now, though, this life would do quite nicely.

"Any word from topside?" he asked, taking the last pull from his cigarette before snuffing it out and beginning the process of "field stripping" the butt by removing the unused tobacco and balling up the filter and leftover paper. Though smoking was allowed on deck, it was considered a mortal sin in the military to flick a spent cigarette overboard, or to the ground if they were ashore. The nearest butt can was hanging on the bulkhead next to the hatch where Atwell had come outside from the galley. He would toss his remnants there on his way back inside.

Watching this process with no small amount of amusement, London replied, "There was some squawk this morning, but nothing since then." Unlike Atwell, who worked in the ship's engineering spaces, his friend worked in the communications shack close to the bridge. Because of her job, including the incoming and outgoing message traffic she saw every day, London was privy to news, rumors, and gossip well ahead of most of the *Polar Sea*'s crew.

The situation had been tense for more than a week, ever since the ship began its transit of the Northwest Passage on its way from Greenland to Alaska. What had begun as a simple supply mission had become an international incident between the governments of the United States and Canada.

Canada? Who the hell provokes Canada? Is that even possible?

The idea behind the transit had been easy enough, in that the coast guard higher-ups had figured out that the passage represented a shorter, less costly route than sending the *Polar Sea* south and through the Panama Canal. While this was obvious to almost anyone who could read a map, the problem with the idea was that ownership of the passage was in dispute. Canada had declared the route to be within their borders, whereas the United States held the position that the passage was within international waters and therefore open to shipping traffic. Granted, navigating the region was all but impossible most of the year, save for vessels like the *Polar Sea*, with hulls and the engine power to drive the ship through the otherwise unyielding ice, but the politics of the matter were of greater concern.

Despite a lack of official authorization from the Canadian government, the coast guard ordered the *Polar Sea* into the passage, and the ship had begun its transit just over a week earlier, on the first day of August. From what he had heard from brief snippets of radio news broadcasts, the trip was making headlines across the United States and Canada as well as countries abroad. Even the Russians were taking an interest in the affair, with their government even going so far as to support Canada's claim of sovereignty over the passage.

We got the Commies siding with Canada. How does that even happen?

In sharp contrast to the public perception of deep political tension between Canada and the United States—at least some of which was well earned, the way Atwell understood things—and regardless of how diplomacy played out over the next days and weeks, things at the moment were far more pleasant on the *Polar Sea*. A team of Canadian observers was traveling aboard ship, and for the most part, they had been polite, at least during the few instances where their paths had crossed with Atwell's. One advantage of being a machinist's mate was that you could duck and avoid "dog and pony shows" and guided tours for guests who were not very interested in seeing the guts of a naval vessel. Better to keep those people topside, with the portholes and the hot coffee.

Speaking of coffee, Atwell mused, *that sounds like a damned fine idea.*

"I'm heading back inside," he announced, closing his fist around his spent and stripped cigarette butt and crushing it into an even tighter ball. "Going to grab a cup of coffee before I head back below. Interested?"

London nodded. "Sounds like a plan." Her expression shifted, and Atwell saw her eyes widen as she pointed to something away from the ship. "Holy crap! What is that?"

Turning to look in the indicated direction, Atwell saw that the *Polar Sea* was coming abreast of yet another mammoth glacier, and he watched an enormous hunk of polar ice in the final seconds of calving away and falling into the sea. The plunge forced plumes of water into the air that showered down upon the newly formed iceberg as it bobbed and listed to one side before righting itself. Ice already in the vicinity of the point of entry was pushed away, crashing into still more unbroken ice as everything seemed to shift and make room for the new arrival. Seconds later, Atwell was sure he felt the ship itself heave as ripples carried along the water beneath the ice pushed outward across the channel.

"That's incredible!" Atwell said, making no effort to hide his astonishment at what he had just witnessed. He had seen this sort of thing only on television. Observing it in person was even more awe-inspiring.

London chuckled, no doubt amused by his reaction. "I know, right?"

So intent was his focus on the iceberg, or *ice island* as he was already calling it, imagining it as the secret lair of some kind of comic book super villain, that it took Atwell an extra moment to notice the dark spot on the side of the glacier that was now exposed thanks to the calving.

"Do you see that?" he asked, pointing to the odd dark shape sticking out of the ice. Even from well over a mile away, the discoloration was obvious.

"Yeah, I see it," replied London. "What is it?"

It took them almost two full minutes to scale ladders and run the length of the deck to where a set of field glasses was mounted. Several other members of the ship's crew had already gathered around the oversized naval binoculars, which were aimed at the glacier.

"Looks like a plane or something," said the man looking through the glasses.

"How long you figure it's been there?" asked another crewmember.

"Maybe it's Amelia Earhart."

"You bonehead. She crashed in the Pacific."

After several minutes of waiting, Atwell was able to get a turn with the glasses. As he peered through the eyepiece, the dark object sticking out of the glacier leapt into sharp relief.

"So what the hell is it?" he asked, to anyone who might answer.

Seventeen

Raven Rock Mountain Complex—
Blue Ridge Summit, Pennsylvania
August 9, 1985

It was a ship.

"What else could it be?" asked Major Daniel Wheeler as he studied the set of glossy photographs. Each picture bore the ever familiar "TOP SECRET/ MAJIC—EYES ONLY" warning stamped in one corner, and each possessed its own coded file number. The one he now held carried the designation MJ12-29I4495-850808D, identifying it as the fourth in this series of twelve photographs hand delivered to him by a courier. The folder in which the pictures had arrived also featured the stern MAJIC stamp. Wheeler knew that each of the photos had been taken by reconnaissance aircraft at an extreme altitude and using state-of-the-art high-speed cameras.

"If it is a ship, then it's not like anything we've seen before, sir," said Lieutenant Joseph Moreno, the Marine officer assigned to Wheeler as his aide, from where he stood before the major's desk. The lieutenant was dressed in green uniform trousers and a tailored

short-sleeved khaki shirt with his silver rank insignia
displayed on his collar tips, but his chest was notably
barren of decoration save for a single multicolored rib-
bon that told the knowing that Moreno had served a
tour at an overseas installation or perhaps aboard a U.S.
Navy ship. How long had the man been in the service?
Just a few years, if Wheeler's memory served him, and
he was not certain that it did.

"I've already sent people down to the vault to
double-check everything just to make sure," Moreno
continued, "but based on what our research team has
been able to suss out, the configuration doesn't match
anything in our files." Stepping closer to the desk, he
pointed to one of the papers that had accompanied the
photographs inside the file. "Did you see this?"

Setting aside the photograph, Wheeler reached for
the schematic that he recognized as coming from one
of the group's engineers. It was labeled as a conjectural
depiction of the object in the pictures, but even with
the limited amount of time the research team had been
given to study the photos and render opinions and
recommendations, it was still a detailed piece of work.
The drawings offered several orthographic depictions
of the engineer's best guess as to the craft's basic form.
To Wheeler, the thing looked like a wedge, thin and
lean. Comparing the drawings with the photographs,
he could see where the artist had been forced to theorize about the ship's overall shape, given the amount of
damage that was apparent on the actual object's hull
and what likely was still buried within the ice. There

also was a handwritten note, with an arrow pointing to one end of the vessel, which read, "Bow or Stern? Section Missing?"

"If the guys downstairs are right about this," Wheeler said, returning the drawing to the file, "then you're right. It's not like anything we've come across before." He tapped his fingers on the photos. "I wonder how long it's been there."

Moreno replied, "There's no way to be sure, sir. Our first response team has already quarantined the area and started taking ice and soil samples, but it'll be a while before they figure out anything conclusive." He checked his watch. "At last report, excavation equipment hadn't arrived yet, so they won't be able to get into the thing for a while."

Swiveling his chair, Wheeler cast his gaze toward the ceiling tiles, which along with the wall paneling and carpeting did its level best to fool him into thinking he was not sitting inside a mountain. The entire Raven Rock complex was a multilevel maze of tunnels and chambers cut into the subterranean rock. Originally constructed in the 1950s by order of then President Harry Truman, the hardened installation had continued to be expanded and fortified during the ensuing three decades. It was envisioned as both a protective bunker and an emergency operations center for the government as well as the armed forces, predating even the massive Cheyenne Mountain Complex in Colorado.

Wheeler hated this place. Despite working here for nearly a year since the relocation of this top-secret unit from Wright-Patterson Air Force Base, he had never been able to shake what he knew was the ridiculous fear that the entire mountain was going to come crashing down on his head. Though he did not devote much time or energy to such thoughts, one emerged every so often from the recesses of his subconscious, taunting him as he went about his duties. He kept such things to himself, or attempted to push them away with humor, such as thinking the calamitous event would take place while he was in the bathroom.

"Here's another question," Wheeler said, once more setting aside the errant thoughts. "Is it there deliberately, or was it an accident?" He retrieved one of the photographs. "It looks to me like this thing is damaged. If it crashed, then maybe there's a crew inside, and if it's been stuck in the ice since it got here, then any bodies we find might be well preserved."

Another thought struck him, and he reached again for the engineer's drawing. "He says here he thinks there's a piece missing. If I'm looking at this thing the right way, it could be a pretty major hunk of the ship. Some kind of detachable module? Maybe even a lifeboat?"

"It's as good a guess as any, sir," replied Moreno. "Have you run into anything like that before?"

Wheeler shrugged. "We've run into a lot of things where we end up making a best guess. Then we move on to the next thing and end up forgetting about whatever it was that seemed so important at the time. That was just one of the problems with having one group operating under so many different mandates, which is why we came up with this new approach."

After more than two decades spent grappling with the numerous issues that came with attempting to understand the realities of extraterrestrial activity on Earth, the clandestine organization known in very limited circles as Majestic 12 had closed in on itself. Shutting out anyone and anything that did not fall within their protected realm, the group's leadership, who, like the cabal they represented, existed more as whispered theory or unsubstantiated rumor, redirected their attention and their energies away from often competing goals in order to focus on a single, straightforward mission. Rather than simply investigating or *truth finding*, as some liked to call it, this new initiative's prime thrust was to locate and retrieve any and all evidence of extraterrestrial activity or technology on Earth, and to exploit those discoveries in order to defend the planet, period. So compartmentalized was this new effort— code named "Project Cygnus"—that Wheeler, himself an MJ-12 veteran, had not known of its existence until he was assigned as its commanding officer thirteen months ago.

In truth, this effort was a renewal of MJ-12's original mission, as outlined by President Truman in 1947 following the incident in Roswell. Additional efforts, beginning with Project Sign and Project Grudge and their better-known descendant, Project Blue Book, had concentrated on verification of sightings and encounters by members of the public. After Blue Book's deactivation in 1970, MJ-12 continued its own research behind a thick veil of secrecy. Most of the people involved with the public face of the air force's efforts to understand UFOs were reassigned, retired, or simply removed. Assets and information amassed over a twenty-year period were stored at facilities around the country, and much of that treasure trove remained hidden away. Wheeler was certain much of it would never again see the light of day, at least until a genuine alien crisis presented itself.

Indeed, this pronounced lack of an imminent threat had challenged Project Cygnus during its early years. Activated in 1975 as the United States' involvement in the Vietnam War was coming to a close, the effort had progressed in near total obscurity, its members unhindered by the usual machinations of government and military affairs. However, the lack of verifiable sightings of alien craft or other evidence of extraterrestrial activity had led those few government leaders with knowledge of Cygnus to question its viability. On the other hand, the project retained a handful of faithful champions who knew from experience that the threat from beyond the stars was very real. Project Blue Book had proven that much, regardless of the ignoble ending it had suffered.

What had prompted the creation of Cygnus in the first place? Wheeler credited that to a rare moment of clarity by the highest levels of leadership, who for the first time seemed to realize that the United States was not the only country on the planet dealing with these sorts of issues. Other governments—whether ally or adversary—had created organizations similar to Majestic 12 and charged them with similar missions, and some of those groups were dealing with the same things faced by MJ-12 and Blue Book. Russia, Japan, and Australia had shared their findings during secret summits held at different locations around the world, and England's effort was ongoing. Wheeler had read numerous reports submitted by the British military task force that had been dealing with its own extraterrestrial threats for years. Despite the political games being played by the world's governments, people who toiled within these covert organizations knew that the potential for alien invasion was a global problem, with no regard for the trivial squabbles in which humans chose to embroil themselves.

Even before his assignment to Cygnus, Wheeler had immersed himself in the legacy of the mission he had undertaken. This meant studying as much of MJ-12's archives as he could access, along with the repositories of information collected since the 1940s by Blue Book and its predecessors as well as similar organizations and units from around the world. It was equivalent to cramming for a dozen college final exams at once, but the effort had paid off. In less than six months, he had become a leading authority on everything accomplished by Majestic and its satellite organizations and projects, second only to those few men from the original MJ-12 roster who remained alive.

"Has the scout team come up with an estimate on what it'll take to get this thing out of the ice?" asked Wheeler, gathering the photographs and returning them to the file.

Moreno replied, "Not yet, sir. They haven't even had a chance to retask a satellite to make a pass over the area. All we've managed so far is the recon flight that gave us those pictures, from an SR-71 out of Kadena." The top-secret reconnaissance plane, one of a squadron of such craft assigned to Kadena Air Force Base on the Japanese island of Okinawa, normally was charged with flights over the Soviet Union at extreme altitudes while traveling at more than three times the speed of sound. Redirecting one of the planes back to North America for the flyover had been far simpler and faster than altering the flight path of an orbiting satellite, but Wheeler had already set that action in motion as well. One of the perks of being the Cygnus commanding officer was an almost unlimited ability to call on any resource in the United States' arsenal of weapons or technology, and he had no problem exercising that authority for something like this.

"At least we can dig it out, rather than have the damned thing sticking out of the side of the glacier." Excavating the mysterious object while standing on a ship next to a wall of ice that had already demonstrated a propensity for chunks of it to fall into the sea was not something he wanted to try. It would be far easier to dig the thing out of the ice from the top. "Where are we with the icebreaker crew?"

"The *Polar Sea* reached Tuktoyaktuk this morning, sir. It was late thanks to all of this, but our cover story is that ice conditions in the Amundsen Gulf slowed the ship's arrival." Moreno shrugged. "The Canadian government wasn't very happy, particularly because of the observer team traveling with the ship, but our liaison in the RCAF is helping to smooth things over."

Wheeler nodded. Though the Royal Canadian Air Force had no specific counterpart organization to Majestic 12—at least, none he was aware of—they had been working with the United States for years thanks to efforts like the Distant Early Warning Line radar tracking stations stretching across Alaska and Canada.

"So the observers are cooperating?"

Moreno chuckled. "That's one way to describe it, sir. They're not happy, but they're not raising too much of a fuss. I think they're tired of shipboard coffee. They did last a whole week, though."

"In the crew's defense, their coffee is better than ours." Pushing away from his desk, Wheeler stood and straightened his uniform jacket. "What about the debriefings?"

"The first interviews are already under way, starting with the captain and officers, with the rest of the crew to be completed in the next couple of days. By all accounts, only a small percentage of the crew even really saw anything, but our team's talking to everyone."

Wheeler stepped around his desk on his way to his

office door. "Good. Let's get those done as fast as possible, and let the *Polar Sea* get on her way. That ship's already caused enough trouble, but at least it gives us some cover." Reaching the door, he stopped and turned back to Moreno. "Ever been to Canada?"

The lieutenant shook his head. "No, sir."

"Dress warm. We leave in an hour."

Eighteen

Wheeler had seen something like this in a movie once.

"That is incredible," he said to no one in particular as he studied the object extending from the ice. Even the stark clarity of the SR-71 recon photos had not done proper justice to this thing's size. The exposed portion rose nearly ten feet into the air, and its circumference was at least twice that. Dark metal reflected the afternoon sun, appearing to have been cast in a single piece rather than assembled from individual plates or other components. Wheeler ran a hand along its smooth length, crouching down to where metal met ice. There were several dents and scars marring its surface. The protrusion's ghostly outline descended into the ice, and thanks to the sunlight, he was just able to make out the silhouette of something larger, several feet below the surface. He tried to picture what the rest of this thing must look like. How close had the computer imagery created from the photographs come to portraying reality?

We'll find out soon enough, I suppose.

"You're sure about the radiation readings?"

Standing next to Lieutenant Moreno and, like everyone else, dressed in a bright orange parka, Doctor Kayla Iacovino replied, "Nothing on the Geiger counter, Major. A thermal scan shows some very, *very* minor activity inside, but our best guess right now is a battery of some kind." She reached up to push aside her parka's thick collar and scratch the tip of her nose, which was all that was exposed beneath her oversized goggles.

"Tell me this doesn't beat stomping around some volcano," said Wheeler, unable to suppress a grin.

Iacovino smiled. "Depends, sir. If it's Mauna Loa, I'd be all right with it."

"I'll see if I can't find a reason to send you to Hawaii once this is all over." Wheeler had read about the volcano's eruption the previous year after being quiet for nearly a decade. Though Iacovino had not been the one to suggest the eruption might be the result of extraterrestrial activity, she had been the first to volunteer to fly to Hawaii and investigate. Wheeler gave her credit for lodging her request while maintaining a straight face.

A geologist by profession, Iacovino and a number of civilian scientists representing several fields and disciplines had been recruited by the air force to assist in sensitive matters such as the one buried in the ice before them. Though examination and interaction with alien technology had not been her original course of study, Iacovino and other specialists like her had more than proved themselves as invaluable assets to Majestic's mission dating back to the 1940s. There were those in the higher levels of military leadership who questioned the use of civilians, often expressing worry that they might share secrets with friends or family, but Wheeler had never given much thought to such concerns. Treason and federal prison were frightening prospects to anyone regardless of whether they wore a uniform. In his experience, people like Iacovino were quite happy to sign the same nondisclosure agreements he had in exchange for the unique opportunities provided by working for a top-secret government program that investigated aliens.

"A power source?"

Iacovino shrugged. "Could be. No idea what it is or how it works though." She gestured toward the object. "We need to get inside to find out."

"That's going to be some trick," said Lieutenant Moreno. "I just checked, and the heavy equipment we need won't be here for at least another eighteen hours."

This was disappointing though not unexpected, conceded Wheeler. He and his small group were standing in one of the most uninviting regions on the planet. Access was limited to special ships and aircraft, of which few were available to him at a moment's notice. Still, he had pulled as many strings as he was able to see to it that excavation equipment was on its way here. Whatever awaited them in the ice, he wanted it treated like the priceless artifact it was, even though any potential monetary value it might hold was nowhere in his thoughts. Along with Moreno and other Cygnus personnel, Wheeler had been airlifted by helicopter from Tuktoyaktuk, the small hamlet on Kugmallit Bay that also served as one of the Distant Early Warning radar stations. The trip here from "the Real World" had been circuitous, at best, requiring flights between the air force bases at Andrews near Washington, DC, and Elmendorf in Anchorage, Alaska. This had come after a lengthy briefing with the chairman of the Joint Chiefs of Staff to update him on the current situation. Another flight to the remote town of Inuvik had preceded an even shorter yet far more harrowing jump to the small airport in Tuktoyaktuk, where an MH-53J Pave Low III helicopter was waiting to bring them out to the site. Wheeler, a former helicopter pilot himself, whose last flights had been as training exercises in the waning months of the Vietnam War, had enjoyed this last leg of the trip most of all, and for a moment he had grown nostalgic for those distant, simpler days.

Nah. This is way more interesting.

"I've got a crew rigging up screens and netting to shield the site," said Moreno, gesturing skyward. "Just in case anybody else gets curious."

Wheeler turned to where a crew of enlisted personnel, overseen by an air force lieutenant whose name escaped him, was unpacking rolls of white and light gray netting and canvas. In short order, the materials would be erected on metal poles with stakes driven into the ice, forming a web of camouflage tarpaulins that would render the site all but invisible to high altitude reconnaissance aircraft and satellite surveillance. That would leave Wheeler's team free to operate without worrying about unwanted eyes, though the likelihood of any sort of visit by the Russians or another potentially troublesome party was slim. Still, in this line of work, it had long ago become prudent not to take anything for granted.

"What are you planning to do with it once you've dug it out of there?" asked Doctor Iacovino. "It's not like it's going to fit in the back of that helicopter."

It was a reasonable question, one to which Wheeler had given considerable thought during the journey from Raven Rock. The truth was that he did not have the first clue how they would proceed, assuming they were successful in excavating the object from its icy grave. He hated the idea of cutting up the ship—or whatever it was—just to get it shipped out of here. Perhaps an aerial crane helicopter, provided one was available, could be used to get the artifact to an airport large enough to accommodate an air force heavy-lift cargo plane.

Getting ahead of yourself, there, Dan. One thing at a time.

The sound of running footsteps across the ice made Wheeler and the others turn to see Lieutenant Anthony Lucas, another air force officer under his command, coming toward him. The younger man was in charge of the communications center that was being established in a tent pitched beneath the snow camouflage cover, but his orange parka made him stick out against the surrounding white-blue terrain.

"Major!" The lieutenant was waving something in the air, and it took Wheeler a second to realize it was a clipboard. Whatever had driven Lucas from his tent and its space heater, it must be important.

"Slow down, Lieutenant," Wheeler said, holding up a gloved hand. "You're liable to go sliding over the edge or something." Lucas slowed his sprint to a walk and began catching his breath, offering the clipboard to Wheeler before pointing to the mysterious metal protrusion.

"That thing is transmitting."

Wheeler frowned, taking the clipboard. "What? You're sure?" As he asked the question, he noted Doctor Iacovino trying to peer around his arm at the paper secured to the clipboard.

"Yes, sir," replied Lucas between breaths. He gestured to the clipboard, which held several pieces of green-and-white computer paper. "It's all right there."

The paper was a printout of a graph chart, which was marked with time stamps at fifteen-minute intervals, with the earliest time indication being less than two hours ago. Wheeler figured that had to be about the time Lucas and his people had set up their communications equipment and began transmitting status reports back to the DEW station at Tuktoyaktuk, which in turn would send the information on through an encrypted air force radio network back to Raven Rock. Though they had the ability to send and receive communications via satellite equipment, Wheeler had decided not to trust the connection with sensitive information, as rumors abounded that the Russians had cracked some of the encryption ciphers used for secure military message traffic.

His breathing having returned to normal, Lucas said, "It's a constant, steady signal, sir, on a very low frequency. Still, it's got enough power so that anyone who knows what to listen or look for can pick it up."

"And who would be listening or looking for this?" asked Lieutenant Moreno.

Lucas shrugged. "I don't know, Joe. I just deal with the comm, remember?" He nodded to Moreno. "The who and what is your thing."

"What kind of signal is it?" asked Iacovino.

"It's some type of acoustical beacon, cycling through at intervals of twelve seconds." Lucas reached up to warm his face with his glove. "I've got no idea what it might be trying to say. Could be a distress call, or somebody trying to order a pizza, for all the hell I know. I'll have to double-check, but I don't think it's like anything we have on file."

"Perhaps we can help with that."

The female voice was not Iacovino's, which was a problem, as she was the only woman on Wheeler's team. Looking up from the clipboard, he saw three people standing twenty feet from him, dressed in thick white parkas, trousers, and gloves that reminded him of a sniper's ghillie suit. Hoods and goggles disguised their faces, but Wheeler figured the smaller of the trio was the one who had spoken. The new arrivals had apparently come from the direction of the camp his team had established, making him wonder how they had gotten this far without being detected or challenged.

"Who the hell are you?" he asked.

The smaller figure held something thin and silver in her right hand, which was pointed in his general direction. "You probably won't believe me, Major, but we're friends and we're here to help."

Then all the white in Wheeler's field of vision went black.

Kirk watched as the servo acted with its customary efficiency, stunning the three men and their female companion. Their bodies stiffened and their expressions went flat, and the clipboard carried by the one male officer clattered to the ice.

"Okay, people," said Roberta Lincoln. "Everybody lie down right where you are and have yourselves a nice little nap."

Unable to suppress a smile as the four officers dutifully complied with her request, Kirk shook his head. "I really need one of those things. There's a long list of admirals and diplomats back home who are perfect for it."

"I'll see what I can do," replied Lincoln as she returned the servo to a pocket on her parka's left sleeve.

Standing next to Kirk, Spock reached into an oversized pocket of his parka and removed a tricorder. The Vulcan stepped closer to the alien object and activated the unit, which began emitting its familiar high-pitched warbling whistle.

"Definitely Iramahl in design, Admiral," Spock reported after a moment. "According to my scans, this craft has been here for more than a century. Stresses and gaps in the ice beneath it suggest upheaval, possibly due to seismic activity or other environmental factors, which could explain why it's not buried deeper within the glacier."

Lincoln said, "There won't be any records to verify that sort of thing. Not for this part of the world, anyway. The only things living around here are polar bears."

"No, but the timing works out pretty closely," said Kirk.

After pausing to further study his tricorder readings, Spock added, "I am picking up residual traces of Iramahl bio-matter. Two adults; a male and a female. Readings suggest they have been here for the same length of time as the vessel itself."

"Died in the crash?" asked Lincoln.

"A logical assumption. The section of the ship containing the readings suffered tremendous dam-age, including buckling of the outer and inner hulls, suggesting it was this portion of the vessel that bore the brunt of the crash landing. Anyone in that section likely was fatally injured on impact."

"So we know at least three survived," said Kirk. "That's more to go on than we had five minutes ago." Studying the protrusion, he frowned. "How big is this thing, anyway?"

Spock replied, "Approximately twenty meters in length, thirteen meters across at its widest point. It consists of three sections: a cockpit, a storage or berth-ing compartment, and an engineering space. Based on the schematics we were given, this is the control pod section of the larger craft."

"And with the rest of the ship in the Mariana Trench," Kirk said, "this is the only piece that presents an immediate problem." Soon after Lincoln's arrival in the twenty-third century, Admiral Nogura had relayed the news that deep ocean sensor sweeps had found the wreckage of the Iramahl vessel almost eight kilometers below the surface of the Pacific Ocean near Guam. It was not quite the deepest place that could have been selected, but it was more than sufficient, as it had taken several attempts to pinpoint the vessel's location. By present-day standards, the wreck was all but unreachable. According to the historical records Spock had been able to search, there was no record of the ship ever being discovered.

Small favors, I suppose.

Turning away from the protrusion and looking to the camp they had infiltrated, Kirk regarded the unconscious officers Lincoln had disabled, and the others underneath the tarps and inside the tents. After using the transporter device in Gary Seven's New York office to travel here, Spock had used his tricorder to pinpoint the location of everyone in the encampment. Then he and Kirk had remained at a safe distance as Lincoln moved through the camp with ease, disabling each of the military and civilian personnel with the same effectiveness she had used here.

"What about all of these people?" he asked. "How are they going to explain what happened?"

Shrugging as she studied the Iramahl ship, Lincoln replied, "Most of them won't even know what hit them."

She gestured to the last four people she had immobilized with her servo. "I can wipe away the short-term memory of them seeing us, but it's not as if they don't know aliens are hanging out on Earth." She placed a hand on the craft's exposed hull section. "Besides, when they wake up, we'll have given them something else to freak out about."

It took Kirk an extra moment to understand her choice of terms, which was somewhat embarrassing once he realized her meaning. "We're taking this thing with us?"

Lincoln nodded. "That's the plan."

Before Kirk could ask how she intended to accomplish such a feat, Spock said, "I am detecting energy readings." The Vulcan had moved closer to the ship and was still conducting scans with his tricorder. "They're very limited. I suspect some form of reserve battery power source."

"After more than a century buried in ice and subfreezing temperatures?" Kirk asked. "That's some power source. Is it dangerous?"

Spock replied, "I am unable to make that determination based on these readings, Admiral. However, scans are also detecting a low-frequency communications signal." He adjusted one of the tricorder's controls. "From the Iramahl language database Jepolin provided us, this appears to be a form of homing beacon, transmitting location coordinates based on the mapping systems employed by the onboard computer. It's not powerful enough to escape the atmosphere, but someone with the proper monitoring equipment would be able to detect the signal and use it to track the ship's location."

"Meaning the Iramahl survivors," said Lincoln, "or the Ptaen hunting them."

"Precisely."

Kirk eyed the alien ship. "Can we stop or mask the signal somehow?"

"Not without gaining entry or destroying the vessel," replied Spock.

"I have a better idea." Reaching for her parka sleeve, Lincoln retrieved her servo. "You fellas might want to stand back. I don't know how or even if this is going to work."

She twisted the silver fountain pen that was so much more than its outward appearance suggested. Kirk heard an almost musical succession of electronic tones, and a moment later the very air seemed to tingle as a now quite familiar blue mist appeared as if from nowhere. Unlike the fog-like environs of the vault housing Gary Seven's mysterious transporter device, the mist was free-form as it fell across the alien ship. Then Kirk was sure he heard the sounds of ice cracking and water falling, and he took an involuntary step away from the craft.

A moment later the blue fog and the ship it embraced was gone.

"Fascinating," said Spock.

Lincoln smiled. "Neat trick, huh? I just hope I set this thing correctly and didn't send that ship to Times Square or something."

Nineteen

From the outside, the three-story warehouse looked no different from the dozens like it scattered across the former shipbuilding facility. Facing northwest with Manhattan in the distance, he took in the abandoned dry docks and piers forming a perimeter around the yard's basin. It had been several years since any ship construction had taken place here, and the area was falling into neglect. This worked to their advantage, Kirk decided as he inspected the buildings and dry docks to either side of the warehouse where he now stood.

It was only a short walk to the nearest ship berth, which was tucked into the yard's southeastern corner. Kirk had inspected the building itself along with its immediate surroundings upon their arrival, as much out of curiosity as to ascertain its location, avenues of approach, security, and any points of vulnerability. The warehouse's exterior was a combination of brick and concrete, and he had found a cornerstone noting the building's construction as having taken place in the year 1912. Observing outside activity for more than thirty minutes after arriving, Kirk had concluded that there was no vehicular or pedestrian traffic anywhere in the immediate vicinity.

"I told you, Admiral," said Lincoln as he stepped back into the building, the reinforced door closing and locking behind him. She was leaning against a waist-high counter separating the passageway from a cubicle that would serve as a receptionist's workspace, if this building were playing host to a real company. As it happened, Aegis Information Technology, Inc., was little more than an elaborate front, unremarkable to anyone who might happen past it, let alone make it through the security door and into the building itself. Of course, the likelihood of that happening was rather remote.

"This place is like a vault," she said. "The surrounding area is a ghost town. There are a few businesses and tenants scattered here and there, but that's farther down, closer to the piers. Around here, it's just us and the rats." She made a show of looking around the reception area. "But they're pretty big rats, I have to tell you. Keep your phaser handy."

"I'll keep that in mind," Kirk said. Glancing around the room, he added, "It never occurred to me before today that you and Mister Seven might have another base of operations, but it makes perfect sense, the more I think about it."

Lincoln replied, "It's not something we use very often, but there are times when we need more space for our work than the office provides. Plus, this has the added benefit of not being in the middle of Manhattan."

"Where is Seven, anyway?" asked Kirk.

"Off-planet, again." Lincoln sighed. "That's been happening a great deal lately. It's been pretty hectic these past several years. There's a lot going on in the world, Admiral."

Kirk nodded. "I can imagine." The late twentieth century had been a tumultuous period of Earth's history, as he recalled. The Eugenics Wars were but a few years in the future, and Kirk already knew that Seven and Lincoln would play a role in that clandestine conflict that had raged around the planet, all while lurking in the shadows of civilization. He had to remind himself that for this Roberta Lincoln, those events had not yet happened. Even if she possessed specific foreknowledge of the future, discussing such matters carried with it the danger of altering the history that was yet to be written.

"I expect he'll be back soon," said Lincoln. Pushing away from the counter, she headed for one of the room's two other doors. To Kirk, both interior portals looked every bit as robust as the one leading outside. A numerical keypad was set into the wall next to the door, and she entered a ten-digit code before pressing a key marked Enter. Kirk heard a solid metallic clicking sound before the door swung inward.

"The inner sanctum," she said, leading the way through the door.

As much as the area behind him looked every bit

a twentieth-century working environment, this much larger chamber also supported that illusion, but only to a point. Fashioned from cinderblock and featuring no windows that might allow curious eyes to see inside, there were metal tables and workbenches lining the walls and an enclosed office area at one end, complete with a vault not unlike the one in Gary Seven's New York City office. Set into the room's opposite wall were two more doors, seemingly identical to the one through which Kirk and Roberta had just passed. Resting in the center of the room's concrete floor was the Iramahl ship, and standing in front of it was what Kirk hoped to be one of only two Vulcans on the planet.

"Mister Mestral," said Kirk as he and Lincoln drew closer. "It's nice to see you again."

The Vulcan, dressed in twentieth-century business attire, offered a formal nod. "It is agreeable to see you again, as well, Admiral. Miss Lincoln has explained to me the circumstances under which you have been brought from your own time to work with us. I must admit that I still find the concept of time travel to be most . . . intriguing."

"It's okay to say it's weird, Mestral," said Lincoln, smiling.

Kirk turned his attention to the Iramahl ship. With it now excavated from the ice that had been its home for more than a century, he was able to admire the simple beauty of its design. It resembled a massive arrowhead, towering above him as it seemed to reach for the room's arched ceiling. The scars of its journey marred the ship's hull from end to end, in the form of dents and gashes and even pieces of the outer skin that were missing.

Chief among the damage was the buckled area of the hull near the bottom and rear of the craft. It was easy for Kirk to envision what that section of the vessel must have looked like before its crash, which made its current appearance even more alarming. Severe inward buckling of the hull, as though a giant fist had simply collapsed that portion through brute force, told the tale. According to Spock's readings upon their arrival in New York, that area of the ship had been a berthing compartment, where at least two members of the crew had been during the crash. They had stood no chance.

Despite the ghastly wounds inflicted upon the ship, Kirk could see no lines where hull plates or armor components had been joined, aside from the obvious circular section that Spock had already confirmed was an access hatch. There was an aesthetic beauty to the craft, as though its creator had been an artist as well as an engineer.

"This entire room is shielded," said Lincoln as she moved to stand next to him. "It acts as a dampening field that lets us control any signals coming in or going out. So far as anyone who might be trying to track it is concerned, this ship just fell off the face of the planet."

Kirk nodded in approval. "Is there any way to know if anyone attempted to respond to the signal? To communicate with the ship or access its onboard computer?"

"Not so far as we have been able to determine," replied Mestral.

Lincoln added, "The Beta 5 hasn't been able to interface with the ship's computer." She pointed to a table standing next to the ship, atop which sat a computer that appeared to be commensurate with present-day technology standards, though Kirk suspected the machine's innards were far more advanced than anything 1985 Earth had to offer. Positioned atop the computer's oversized, bulky display monitor was a green cube like one he had seen on the desk in Gary Seven's office. Whatever powered it was giving the alien device a steady, pulsing glow, as though it might be communing with the comparatively primitive-looking twentieth-century computer.

The low whine of a tricorder heralded Spock's appearance from around the rear of the vessel. Like Kirk, the Vulcan was dressed in contemporary civilian clothes, in his case tan trousers and a blue button-down shirt with black shoes. A windbreaker would complete his ensemble should he and Kirk need to leave the building, along with a wide-brimmed bucket hat that would do a serviceable job of concealing his pointed ears.

"What is it, Spock?" asked Kirk, noting his friend's intense scrutiny of his tricorder readings. "You look troubled."

Continuing his slow circuit of the craft, the Vulcan replied, "I am detecting a new energy reading emanating from the vessel, Admiral. According to my scans, it began shortly after Miss Lincoln modulated this building's dampening field to block the ship's transmission. The ship's internal power systems have increased and energy is being directed to the propulsion system, though I find no evidence of the craft attempting to engage that system."

Frowning, Kirk said, "But it's obviously a reaction of some sort."

"That seems a logical assumption."

Mestral added, "It is also possible that the mere act of moving it from its previous location was enough to prompt a response."

"To verify that," said Spock, "we would need direct access to the vessel's power and computer systems." He stopped before the circular hatch set into the side of the ship's hull near its midpoint. "We are still endeavoring to gain entry."

"The Beta 5's been chewing on it," said Lincoln, gesturing to the green cube sitting atop the contemporary computer. "It's been scanning the ship inside and out since we brought it here."

Mestral said, "That may also have been the cause of this new energy reading."

Behind them, Roberta Lincoln's little green cube chose that moment to emit a series of pinging tones as though demanding attention, and Kirk saw on the computer's monitor columns of green text scrolling past, almost too quickly for him to follow. Lincoln moved to the computer and tapped its keyboard, and in response to that simple command, the text froze on the display.

"Mister Spock, stop scanning," she said. "Stop scanning *right now*."

"What is it?" Kirk asked, hearing the alarm in her voice.

Turning from the computer, Lincoln stared at the ship. "It's a self-destruct protocol. We had to have triggered it by moving the thing, and the dampening field is only pissing it off that much more." She looked to the green cube. "Computer, how do we stop this?"

"Insufficient data to recommend course of action," replied the stilted yet feminine voice of the Beta 5, its response coming from the desktop computer.

"What can you tell us about the self-destruct protocol that has been activated?" asked Mestral. "What would be the result of the procedure being executed?"

"Resulting explosion sufficient to destroy significant portion of this building and surrounding area. High risk of casualties, as well as infrastructural and ecological damage. Area rendered uninhabitable due to radiological contamination."

Kirk sighed. "We should probably try to avoid that."

"Computer," Lincoln said. "Deactivate the dampening field."

"Warning. Eliminating dampening field increases risk of signal detection."

"All right, then lower the field's intensity until you detect a change in the ship's energy readings."

Spock renewed his study of the alien ship with his tricorder, and after a moment said, "Readings are stabilizing. Though the protocol does not appear to have been rescinded, there is a noticeable reduction in the power being routed to the propulsion system."

"Like a holding pattern?" asked Lincoln.

The Vulcan nodded. "That is an apt analogy."

She eyed the computer monitor. "The dampening field's still active, but only at thirty-six percent."

"That should be sufficient to thwart most current monitoring or tracing equipment," said Mestral, "but the Iramahl or Ptaen should still be able to detect it."

"Good," said Lincoln. "If it's transmitting to the Iramahl, they're going to want to know why their ship was moved. It's obvious they kept it around in case they needed it for something, otherwise they would've destroyed it a century ago."

"Perhaps," replied Spock, "though the ship's usefulness is limited. Its propulsion system is insufficient to escape Earth's gravity."

Lincoln said, "But that doesn't mean it can't be used to get around the planet. At the very least, it makes for a decent enough emergency shelter." She shrugged. "Of course, all of that's dependent on any of the Iramahl still being alive."

"So," Kirk said, "I guess our best play for the moment is to wait."

"And if they are still alive," replied Lincon, "that means the Ptaen are still looking for them, so we wait for them too."

It was as good a plan as any he might devise, Kirk decided. If they were going to shift this protracted game of hide-and-seek to their favor, they would need to take actions such as what Lincoln had put into motion.

"You do realize, Admiral," said Spock, "that in addition to increasing the risk to our personal safety and that of Mestral and Miss Lincoln, our presence here also carries the potential to be a hazard to time itself."

"Of course I realize that," Kirk said. He released a sigh and forced a smile. "Look on the bright side. We'll be talking to our friends at Temporal Investigations again when this is all over."

Assuming we don't end up destroying the space-time continuum or something. This should be fun.

Twenty

Grover's Mill, New Jersey
August 12, 1985

The alert tone roused Drevina from slumber, and for a moment she was uncertain she had heard anything. She stared up at the cabin's wooden ceiling, listening to the breathing of her companions, before the alarm sounded again.

"What is that?" asked Canderon as he awakened and sat up, the blanket he used to cover himself falling to his waist.

Drevina rose from her own sleeping area on the cabin's floor. "It appears to be an intercepted transmission." Crossing the room, she moved to the table where Glorick had positioned their lone remaining communications scanner. Its flat display had begun a continuous scroll of text along with a rapid succession of computer-generated imagery.

"It is from the ship."

"Are you certain?" asked Glorick, who also had shaken off sleep and now moved to stand beside Drevina at the table. "After all this time?"

Drevina replied, "It would seem so." As humans

measured time on Earth, it had been more than one hundred forty years since she and her companions crash-landed in the planet's inhospitable Arctic region. They had salvaged as much as they could carry from the wrecked vessel, but Drevina had elected not to destroy it. There still were items that could one day be of use, and components from the ship itself might also be recovered if needed. Canderon had put the craft's onboard systems into a hibernating state, reducing its energy output to the absolute minimum needed to power the distress beacon they would use to keep track of the ship's position. If his calculations were correct, this configuration would allow the craft to transmit via the beacon for at least another century. With the vessel as secure as they could make it, and already half buried in the ice thanks to the violence of its crash landing, Canderon took the additional step of using the pulse weapon from one of their survival kits to melt the ice around the craft so that the ship settled even deeper into its resting place. The process had taken hours, after which the craft rested within its icy tomb. Occasional checks over the decades were enough to tell Drevina and the others that the vessel remained—more or less, due to shifting ice in that glacial region—where it had landed.

Using the scanner's touch-sensitive interface, Drevina instructed the device to answer the signal and request a report on the vessel's current status. It was the first time she had done so since their arrival, due to the additional drain on the ship's limited power systems. When the scanner returned its results, Drevina stared at the data for a moment, not believing what she was reading.

"The ship has moved."

Moving to stand on her other side and better see the scanner, Canderon said, "Moved? Has someone found it?"

"Or perhaps the glacier on which it resides has melted or broken apart, and the ship has fallen into the sea?"

It may have sounded like an odd scenario, but the glacier that was the ship's resting place had moved thanks to melting, new ice accumulation, and refreezing over the decades. Whereas the ship had been several kilometers from the nearest water at the time of the crash, the glacier had flowed south toward the sea during the ensuing decades. That much had been evident from Drevina's periodic checks of the ship's beacon.

None of this explained the vessel's current location.

"It has moved more than four thousand kilometers from its previous position," she said. Turning from the scanner, she moved to the table in the cabin's kitchen and pulled from a stack of papers a map of the United States. Drevina had acquired it several months ago, applying to the fresh copy all of the notes and other markings she had made on previous versions replaced over the years once they became outdated or worn. Opening the map, she laid it on the table before taking a pencil and circling one area.

"New York," said Glorick. "How is that possible? Your last check of the beacon showed it in its same position not a week ago. Could someone have found and repaired it so quickly?"

"No human could have done so," replied Canderon. "That ship was incapable of flight without substantial repairs that are beyond their current level of technology."

Glorick asked, "The Ptaen, then? Or someone from another advanced race?"

"It has been years since our last contact with any Ptaen," said Drevina.

"That does not mean they will abandon their search." Canderon shook his head. "If they are still here, then we are still a threat to them and of value to our own people."

Until their last encounter with a team of hunters more than a decade ago, Drevina had almost allowed herself to believe that the Consortium had given up its attempts to find her and her friends. It was foolish to entertain such notions, she knew, given the impetus for the unrelenting interest in their quarry. That motivation was reflected at her each day in a mirror, and on the faces of Glorick and Canderon. That the three of them were alive after so many years spent on Earth was cause enough to drive the Ptaen to find them. The salvation of the Iramahl people flowed through her veins, and if the Consortium was still pursuing them, that had to mean there was still a civilization on her homeworld to save.

To that end, Drevina and her companions had made every effort to hide themselves not just from potential Ptaen pursuit, but also curious human eyes. Her limited ability to shield the truth of their alien nature only worked in situations with small numbers of humans. Crowds and gatherings were all but impossible, amplifying her constant fear that she might run across a rare human who was immune to her influence. She and the others had decided that it would be prudent to avoid humans as much as possible. This decision required them to move at irregular though frequent intervals, between which they were able to find suitable if temporary shelter. The cabin they had come across in the wooded area surrounding the small town of Grover's Mill in rural New Jersey served their current needs well enough, but Drevina had already decided they would be moving again in short order.

They had come here after learning that the town had been popularized in some segments of American culture as the supposed landing site for an invasion by extraterrestrials decades earlier. The attack was fictional, but Drevina's research had led her to conclude that many groups who believed their government's elected and military leaders were conspiring to hide the truth from the citizenry had also concealed the truth of what had supposedly happened here. These conspiracy theorists were sure that evidence of the invasion was hidden somewhere in the vicinity, including remnants of advanced technology and perhaps even the remains of actual alien invaders. Even if no such evidence existed, Drevina had found the story fascinating, and she had persuaded her companions to help her investigate the possibility. She reasoned that if they did find something, it could lead to a way home.

Finding nothing would have no deleterious effects, as they had been moving and searching for a new temporary safe haven anyway, and Grover's Mill seemed a suitable location.

As it happened, Grover's Mill ended up being little more than a place to hide. Still, Drevina liked it here, far more than some of the other towns and cities they had visited in their quest to escape possible pursuit. The small population made it easier to avoid contact, and the cabin had been a nice find. Based on its condition, Glorick guessed that it had been abandoned many years earlier, and it had taken a moderate level of effort to make it secure against the elements. Its isolated location made it an ideal refuge, and in the months they had lived here, they had seen not a single human in the immediate area. Foraging for food and other supplies was easy enough, usually in the form of Drevina and one of the others accompanying her to the nearby town. Though necessity required them to acquire essential items, they endeavored to limit their theft to things of little or no value except in the interests of survival. Theirs was not the most laudable existence, she knew, but it was all they had.

The alternatives are even less pleasant.

An odd snapping noise erupted from the scanner, its display flickered, and Canderon grunted in irritation. "I think the data receiver is failing again," he said, moving to the unit and inspecting it with a critical eye. Even from where she stood, Drevina could see the warning indicator on the scanner's display screen. "I will probably have to disassemble it in order to locate the cause and make the necessary repairs."

It had become a regular occurrence to see such alerts. Much like her and her friends, Drevina knew that the unit had survived well enough across the many years of their exile, just as she understood that the scanner was nearing the end of its useful life. Despite Canderon's best efforts to preserve its functionality, the lack of viable replacement components to effect more than the most superficial repairs meant that there would soon come a day when the unit just stopped working. Though her friend had not stated with certainty that he would be unable to find suitable alternatives for the pieces needed to attempt yet another repair, Drevina could hear the resignation in his voice. Human technology, though it had evolved at an impressive pace since their arrival, was still generations behind Iramahl technological standards. She and the others had watched the first attempts at spaceflight with great interest, though they were both amused and saddened that the effort was driven not by a desire to explore and expand but instead to establish political, ideological, and military superiority among the planet's nations.

The two countries with the ability to further such goals, the United States and the Soviet Union, were frustrating with their veneer of civility that masked the deep-seated need to vanquish each other. Even as their people were locked in an ever-escalating conflict that was not even between themselves—at least, not directly—they had engaged in this odd competition to conquer first the space above their world and then its only natural satellite. Even as conflict drew to a close in Vietnam, a country Drevina had struggled to find on a map, American and Russian astronauts had worked together on a joint mission that was of nothing but symbolic value. The astronauts from both sides had shaken hands and made polite statements about forging lasting bonds and working together in peace before returning to their home nations, each of which was continuing to plot and plan its domination over the other. Whether the show of political niceties would lead to a lasting partnership between the two powers, in space or even just on Earth, remained to be seen.

Drevina had her doubts.

She and her friends had grown disillusioned as the humans' continued efforts in space, and their interest in pushing outward the boundaries of their knowledge and place in the universe, began to wane. Their reactions were admittedly selfish, as Glorick at one point thought that human space travel might progress to a point where it could provide an avenue of escape for them back to Yirteshna. That hope had dwindled with each passing year, until now it had returned to its place as one dream among many that taunted Drevina in her sleep. Whereas humans seemed on course to make bold leaps to distant planets in the decades to come, it had become apparent that such goals were mired in hopeless naiveté.

Political will had all but disappeared in the wake of

what leaders saw as the ultimate achievement of landing travelers on the nearby moon. The other planets of this system awaited, and yet the leaders of this world seemed content to allow all that vast potential to go untapped. Though automated craft had been dispatched to the system's other worlds and satellites, those efforts were limited as much by distance as technology. A machine could not do all the things of which a living being was capable, and neither could it experience the thrill of discovery. Much like the early civilizations on her own planet, this thirst for knowledge and even conquest had first driven the people of Earth to venture across their own world and eventually to their planet's lone natural satellite, but humans now seemed content to rest on those successes rather than trying to dwarf them.

Such a sad waste of potential, Drevina decided.

After spending several moments examining the scanner, Canderon looked up when the unit started beeping again, and Drevina saw the look of concern darken her friend's features.

"What is it?" she asked.

"The protection protocol," replied Canderon. "It has been enabled. I do not know why." After studying the readings for a moment, he added, "It may be a result of the move from the Arctic, or as a defensive measure when someone attempted to access one of the ship's onboard systems."

Glorick's expression was one of alarm. "Are you saying the destruct mechanism is armed?"

"Yes." Canderon continued to consult the readings. "It has raised its alert level from when you set it initially, Drevina, but not to final protective mode. However, if someone makes a further attempt at unauthorized access, that is not out of the question."

Drevina was already envisioning the scenario that would unfold if that sequence of events was allowed to transpire. "A detonation in a populated area? Hundreds of innocent people are at risk, and perhaps more."

The scanner punctuated her remarks by offering yet another indicator tone, one that Canderon seemed displeased to hear. Shaking his head, he placed the unit back on the table and dropped his diagnostic tool next to it. He released an audible groan that Drevina recognized as one of despondency.

"Can you not repair it?" she asked.

Canderon shook his head. "I do not know. The component that is failing is not one for which we have a replacement. If a repair is to be successful, I will have to fashion a new part from whatever materials I can find."

"I have every confidence that you will be able to do so," said Drevina.

"And what if that proves untenable?"

Glorick replied, "Then we will persevere. If you cannot repair the scanner, then we will find a way to replace the components you require. If we cannot do that, then we will construct replacements. If that is unsuccessful, then we will find another way. It is what we have always done. It is what our people have always done."

"I agree with Glorick." There was no other choice, Drevina decided. She was simply unable to think in other terms. Her entire existence had been predicated on survival, on making do with what one had in their possession rather than whining about a perceived lack of resources. After all, they had devised almost from nothing the medicine that might save her very civilization.

Assuming they are even still alive, and come looking for us.

"Very well," said Canderon, his demeanor seeming to improve. He placed a hand on Drevina's arm. "As Glorick says, we will persevere, but that cannot be our primary concern now." He gestured toward the map on the kitchen table. "What do you propose we do about the ship?"

There was only one answer, Drevina knew, and it served to pose still more questions. Did salvation await them, or final damnation at the hands of the Ptaen? There was a single way to find out, but they would first have to deal with the more immediate problem.

"We must go to New York."

Twenty-One

Wall, South Dakota
August 12, 1985

"Rijal."

His eyes closed and his senses focused inward, it took Rijal an extra moment to realize he was no longer alone. Drawing one more slow, deep breath and relishing in the sensation of the air filling his lungs, he opened his eyes to see Noceri standing before him.

"I apologize for the intrusion," said the younger Ptaen, and Rijal could hear the slight tremor in his apprentice's voice. "You asked to be notified if we became aware of something pertaining to our—"

"Yes, yes. I know what I asked you to do," said Rijal, cutting off what was sure to be an extended explanation. With his body stretched parallel to the ground and the palms of his hands pressed flat against the cave's stone floor, Rijal had achieved the perfect balance for meditation. On any other occasion, he would loathe having to sacrifice the harmony between mind, body, and earth, but it was apparent from his young learner's expression that something important had happened. "What have you found?"

Noceri replied, "A transmission from the Iramahl vessel. It has moved from its original location."

With practiced ease, Rijal pulled his legs toward his chest and shifted his body until he was suspending himself in a sitting position, holding that pose for one last breath before lowering himself to the cave floor. "You are certain?"

"Yes. We have verified the scans and confirmed that there is no equipment fault. The craft has moved, but we are unable to determine how this was accomplished."

Rising to his feet, Rijal followed his apprentice into the larger cave that had been their home for the past several cycles. A small fire was burning in the center of the chamber, over which Noceri likely had been preparing their evening meal before the interruption. Along the cavern's far wall was a portable worktable and before it stood his companion, Bnara, who appeared entranced by the scanning equipment arrayed on the table. Like him, she wore only the undergarment that helped regulate their body temperature, keeping them warm in the cave's cool environs. She likely had been involved with her own meditation before Noceri had called on her with this new development.

"So, it is true?" Rijal asked as he joined her at the worktable.

Bnara nodded. "Noceri verified the readings twice before informing me, and I corroborated his findings." She smiled. "You have trained him well."

"The ship remains on the planet?"

"Yes. As we confirmed when we examined it, the ship is no longer capable of flight or space travel, at least not without extensive repairs that likely are beyond its crew's abilities." Leaning over the table, she swept her hand across the scanner's biometric interface. "The ship has been moved to the eastern United States, a densely populated region the humans call New York."

Rijal was familiar with the location, having studied it and this planet's other major population centers from the scans conducted upon their arrival. Like those Ptaen who had come before them, he and his team had been forced to start their investigation with nothing, acquiring and scrutinizing all manner of information gleaned from multiple sources in order to formulate a strategy for hunting the fugitive Iramahl.

"It is a considerable distance," said Bnara. "I have no idea how it was accomplished."

Rijal considered the possibilities. "Perhaps they were able to utilize a ship or other technology from one of our other teams to assist them."

"Could they have found allies among the humans?" asked Noceri. When he received questioning stares in his direction, he added, "If it is true and the fugitives have been here all along, then they almost certainly would have interacted with the indigenous population. Is it not feasible that they may have befriended representatives of this civilization, who in turn aided them?"

"Of course it is feasible," Rijal snapped. "Surviving here for all this time would require at least some interaction." Realizing his reply carried with it more force than he had intended, he said, "It is good that you explore the possibilities. See the problem from multiple perspectives, apprentice. What is another alternative explanation that we have not yet discussed?"

Pausing a moment to consider his answer, the young Ptaen said, "Humans found the vessel on their own and moved it themselves."

"And what is the flaw in that theory?" asked Bnara.

It took him a moment, but then he nodded with obvious confidence. "The time required to excavate and transport the craft to its new destination would be far longer than what actually transpired. We have been monitoring the vessel's location since we found it, and the change in its location took place much too quickly for humans to accomplish with their present level of technology."

"Correct." Bnara offered an admiring nod. "Well considered, apprentice."

"Of course, this leaves us with an even more intriguing mystery," said Rijal. "Does it not?"

His mission here was twofold: locate the missing Iramahl dissidents and determine the status of the previous hunter teams dispatched to this world. Few messages from them had been received in the cycles since their departure from the homeworld. Though the presence of the fugitives had been established on this planet, there was no way to know whether they had found a means of escape. Some among the Consortium's higher leadership echelons had even postulated the idea that the Iramahl may have commandeered a craft from one of the hunter teams and now were well away from this planet and its primitive civilization. This theory had yet to be proven or refuted, and doing so was also one of Rijal's mission mandates.

For his own part, Rijal had concluded that the Iramahl renegades remained here, a notion he had despite any evidence to support his assertion. Other hunters had been sent into the void, including teams who had used this planet, Earth, as a starting point for continuing the search along likely vectors toward other star systems with habitable worlds, in hopes of discovering some clue, but they had found nothing. Given the enormity of the task, it was still ongoing, but Rijal believed that effort to be a waste of time and resources.

The fugitives were here. Of that, he was certain.

As for what may have happened to their fellow Ptaen, Rijal did not know. The hunters sent to Earth before he had been given his current assignment were soldiers he had not known, taken from other hunter units who had been more closely involved with overseeing Iramahl prisoners or factories and other work camps. Rijal's unit was a separate group, specially trained and reserved only for the most high-risk and high-value targets. Members of his unit had not been assigned to this effort because—in the beginning—it was felt that a mere handful of civilian dissidents could not hope to evade trained soldiers with access to weapons and equipment that far surpassed their own.

Only after the first teams were dispatched and cycles passed without word of success had the Consortium begun to realize they may have underestimated the resourcefulness and sheer audacity these "mere civilians" might be able to demonstrate. After all, the fugitives were running for their own lives, but in a very real sense they also were fleeing in the hopes of safeguarding the future of their entire civilization.

There also was the idea given voice by Noceri, that the dissidents had benefited from the assistance of human allies. That was possible, of course, but Rijal suspected there would be severe limits on the sort of assistance that could be obtained. Food, shelter, and transportation were obvious examples, and if that was the case, then his mission would be even more complicated. The Iramahl resistance had thrived in no small part due to the willingness of individual citizens as well as entire communities to risk their own lives in order to protect those who actively fought against the Consortium. They did so with full awareness of the consequences of their actions when they were found guilty of providing such support. If the fugitives here had enlisted the aid of humans, did that mean the people of this world might one day rise to stand against the Ptaen? It was an interesting if alarming thought, Rijal conceded. At their present level of technology, the humans posed no threat whatsoever, and he guessed it would be generations if not longer before they even ventured beyond the confines of their own solar system.

But what if they were to receive their own assistance, perhaps provided by the Iramahl or another spacefaring civilization?

It was yet another interesting yet troublesome notion, Rijal thought, and one best left for a more appropriate time. For now, there were more pressing matters.

"Bnara," he said, "are you able to ascertain the vessel's precise location?"

Studying the scanner for a moment, she nodded. "Yes. It appears to be housed within a structure. Though the city itself is home to a sizable population, the area where the ship is located is relatively free of habitation." She paused, and Rijal saw her features darken as she studied the readings. "This is interesting. I am detecting the presence of energy sources that are inconsistent with current human technology and which cannot be accounted for by the Iramahl craft."

"One of ours?" asked Noceri.

Bnara shook her head. "No, this is different." She turned from the scanner. "There may well be someone from another advanced race already here. That is the only logical conclusion, based on the available information."

His gaze shifting between her and the scanner, Rijal asked, "What sort of technology are you detecting?"

"I cannot answer that at this time. A form of scattering field seems to be in use, blocking attempts to scan the interior of the structure. Therefore, I am unable to provide information on what might be waiting for us when we arrive."

Rijal nodded. It was not the most encouraging report, but it was better than nothing. After all the time he and his team had spent here, hiding away from curious human eyes, they now had the opportunity to make some true progress with their mission. Were the Iramahl with their ship, or had the craft been salvaged by humans? If others from beyond this world were somehow involved, then to what extent and for what reason? What were their motives and true objectives?

"Begin your preparations," he said. "We depart with the setting of the sun."

Answers await.

Twenty-Two

"Admiral, with all due respect, would you kindly sit down before you wear a trench in my carpet?"

Lost in thought, it took Heihachiro Nogura an extra moment to realize that his longtime friend and the current Starfleet Commander, Harrison Morrow, was addressing him. Hands clasped behind his back, Nogura stopped his pacing and noted he had almost wandered into the large window that afforded Morrow a wondrous, unfettered view of San Francisco Bay.

"My apologies, Harry," said Nogura, turning to look at where Morrow sat in one of the two overstuffed recliners in the corner of his expansive office. The chairs were positioned before a stone fireplace, or what in truth was a fireplace constructed with modern materials that simulated the look and feel of stone. The fire itself was provided by a self-contained fuel source that also was installed with safety in mind, producing flames that were real but safely confined within the firebox.

The entire corner looked as though it belonged in

a cabin on a lake somewhere, which was the point, given Morrow's predilection for camping and being as far away as possible from technology and other trappings of modern society. The admiral was notorious for taking his infrequent bouts of shore leave in the mountains of northern California, and leaving behind his communicator or any other immediate means of contacting him. It often fell to one of his luckless assistants to transport from Starfleet Headquarters to apprise him of any legitimately urgent matters requiring his attention, though such instances were rare. His instructions while on shore leave were infamous: "If I can't see the flames from orbit, then it's something you can handle until I get back."

This was not born of a desire to shirk responsibility, Nogura knew. Instead, it was an outgrowth of Morrow's attitude that his senior staff should be able to function without the need to call him for advice and consent on every little thing. He preferred to delegate authority—while remaining conscious of the fact that as the Starfleet Commander, he could not defer responsibility—so that key decisions were made faster, rather than waiting on an ultimate arbiter: him. This required a level of trust in subordinate leaders that many of his predecessors had not engendered, and in Nogura's opinion, Starfleet and the Federation had suffered for it. Never again, Morrow had vowed, and it was a mind-set and direction for Starfleet's senior leadership that Nogura lauded.

"How come your office is nicer than mine?" Nogura

asked, making a show of admiring the sizable room and its lavish appointments.

Morrow chuckled. "If you want the office, you'll have to take the job that goes with it."

"Thank you, no. I've already done that once." Nogura held up a finger as though remembering something. "No, twice, now that I think of it. Can't say I liked it." He gestured to Morrow. "You're a better fit, but if I'd known they were going to upgrade the office, I'd have kept the job a bit longer."

He paused at the window, taking in the scene. At this time of late evening and with the sun long set, the city was illuminated and alive. Nogura recalled many nights from his youth as a fresh-faced, newly minted Starfleet ensign, on the town with friends and with an entire life and career ahead of him. Those days were further back in his past than he cared to admit, but the memories were as vivid as though his first shore leave was yesterday. Back then, he could stay up all night, drinking and carousing and perhaps even getting into a spirited bar brawl or two, all while doing his best to evade the shore patrol from nearby Starfleet Headquarters or the Academy.

Where had all the time gone?

The days had melted into years with startling speed, Nogura mused. That life and career that had seemed to stretch ahead of him to infinity had unfolded in dramatic fashion. Starfleet had put him to work early and often after he had demonstrated a consistent aptitude for unconventional and even brash thinking. By the time he was second-in-command of the *Thermopylae*, he had acquired a reputation for a total lack of fear when addressing or confronting superior officers—including telling them when he thought they were wrong, which was often. The captain of the *Thermopylae* had recommended him for accelerated promotion and command of a starship, forcing home to the upper levels of Starfleet leadership that more leaders like young Heihachiro Nogura were needed in the center seat, on the front lines and the edge of the frontier as the Federation welcomed new friends and confronted enemies familiar and untested.

Captaining starships had given way to commanding starbases and fleets, and eventually advancing to the admiralty, where he even had served in Morrow's role as the Starfleet Commander on two separate occasions. It had not taken him long to realize that while he might be capable of excelling in that assignment, it was not a role that called to him. Like some officers who felt most at home in command of a starship, Nogura had come to understand that his talents lay in big-picture thinking. To that end, he had immersed himself in the thick of Starfleet's operations and strategic planning as they dealt with escalating threats from the Klingon and Romulan empires as well as other adversaries ranging from the Gorn to the Tholians.

And those are just the ones I can talk about.

"I know that look," said Morrow, sitting with his feet up and nursing his preferred beverage, scotch. "You've been pacing like an expectant father for the past five minutes. Sit down and have a drink, Heihachiro. You're making me nervous."

Rather than take Morrow up on the offer, Nogura instead chose to renew his pacing. "I don't like waiting for other people to do things. It seems like all I do anymore is wait while other people do things for me. I was never very good at this part of the job."

"Understandable." Morrow sipped his scotch. "I've never been good at that either, but that's what admirals do. We give people orders, then sit around while they go and carry them out, hoping they'll do the job we gave them without screwing up, killing themselves or anybody else, or starting a war. We sit, we wait, and we worry." Then he offered a sly grin. "Or, we pace and we worry."

"It's not as though we don't have anything to worry about," said Nogura. "After all, I didn't wake up this morning thinking we'd be staring down the barrel of an interstellar incident."

Morrow nodded. "I read the reports. We've been contacted by the Ptaen Consortium."

"That's a mild way of putting it." Recent updates from the Federation Council and the Diplomatic Corps had been a bit more reserved as far as reporting this new development. Nogura had long ago learned the art of reading between the lines of any official correspondence generated by the council or any politician, to say nothing of some of the more verbose members of the admiralty, in order to get at the underlying issue.

"They're not very happy that the Iramahl have made

new friends," he said as he continued his pacing, reaching Morrow's desk and turning to head back the other way. "And they'd be most appreciative if we minded our own damn business and stayed out of their affairs. Of course, we were expecting that. What I'm worried about is whether the Ptaen decide this is worth pulling in some of the friends *they've* made over the years." He glanced at Morrow as he talked, watching his friend swirl the contents of his glass while contemplating the fireplace.

"There's no way the Ptaen come out on top in any sort of protracted conflict with us. You don't think they'd try to drag the Klingons into this, do you, Heihachiro? Even the Klingons know better than to let themselves be manipulated into doing someone else's fighting."

Nogura grunted. "Perhaps, but it's not like the Klingons have ever needed a reason to pick a fight. Their honor code might keep them from acting at the behest of the Ptaen, but that doesn't mean they won't find some other reason to kick some dirt in our faces while using this as the excuse. If there's one thing I love about the Klingons, it's how they're so consistent with their inconsistency."

A considerable portion of his career had been spent trying to figure out what adversaries such as the Klingons might be planning. Though the Empire had been relatively quiet in recent years, its disdain for the Federation continued unabated. Despite the best efforts of Starfleet Intelligence, much of the Klingons' goals and machinations remained a mystery, aside from the obvious. The desire for conquest had fueled their march across space for centuries, and though they tended to behave themselves with respect to the Neutral Zone established between imperial and Federation territory, there were notable exceptions to the agreement between the two governments.

Nogura was certain the Klingons had to be plotting something, if not a direct action against the Federation, then perhaps an effort at expansion that might place at risk nonaligned systems or those who had expressed interest in Federation membership. The truth was that the Empire was beginning to feel hemmed in by adversaries on multiple fronts, most of whom wanted no conflict. With their ability to expand their territory and harness the resources necessary to fuel their mammoth military becoming ever more limited, it was only a matter of time before the Klingons felt the need to take a more aggressive approach to protecting their interests.

And won't that be fun.

"Has the Klingon embassy had anything to say about this?" asked Nogura.

Morrow shook his head before finishing the last of his drink. "Not a word, which is surprising. I was sure their ambassador would take advantage of this to say something. It makes me wonder if he's on vacation, or dead."

The comment elicited a small smile from Nogura. He was more than familiar with Kamarag, the bombastic Klingon ambassador to the Federation, who could almost always be counted on to spice up Federation Council meetings. Though he tended to bloviate to the point that Nogura was certain sensors would detect a pronounced drop in the council chamber's oxygen levels, Kamarag was never boring.

"Either way," said Nogura, "you can be sure the council and the diplomatic people are already figuring out what they want to say to the Ptaen as well as the Klingons. We should probably start crafting our own message for the council, as well."

Rising from his recliner, Morrow crossed to the small wet bar tucked into one corner of his office. "Probably not a bad idea," he said as he reached for the scotch bottle and refreshed his glass. "And it wouldn't hurt to give them an updated report on the status of our border patrols and anything of note from our outposts along the Neutral Zone. Let's get Kirk in here."

"He'll love that." Nogura moved to the viewscreen set into the office's back wall and the communications station accompanying it. Activating the unit, he said, "Nogura to Starfleet Communications."

The viewscreen flared to life, and the image of a young human female in a Starfleet uniform appeared.

"*Starfleet Communications. This is Ensign Dagmar, Admiral. How may I assist you?*" Her smile and eyes were bright and wide, and she was just a bit too eager for this time of night, Nogura decided.

Trying to ignore how her voice sounded even younger than she looked, he replied, "Patch me through to Admiral Kirk. He should be at home."

"One moment, Admiral." Her image was replaced by a graphic of the Starfleet Headquarters logo. Then her moment passed, along with a second and then a third, by which time Nogura was wondering if the ensign had forgotten him. Just before he could ask about that, Dagmar returned to the screen. *"I'm sorry, sir. Admiral Kirk doesn't appear to be at home. At least, he's not answering the call."*

"Patch me through to the *Enterprise*, then." Nogura knew that Kirk looked for any excuse to revisit his old ship. Having it in Earth orbit with his best friends aboard while they helped with the current Iramahl situation was the perfect opportunity to escape his office, even if only for a few hours.

Once more, the viewscreen's image changed, this time to reveal a face Nogura recognized, though it was neither Jim Kirk nor the *Enterprise*'s captain, Spock, sitting in the command chair on the starship's bridge.

"This is the Enterprise. *Commander Hikaru Sulu in temporary command, Admiral. How may I help you?"*

"Where's Admiral Kirk, Commander?" asked Nogura. "Come to think of it, where's Captain Spock?"

On the screen, Sulu appeared nervous, as though he was about to say something Nogura did not want to hear. Then he replied, *"The admiral and Captain Spock are presently . . . away from the ship, sir. I've been placed in command until they get back."*

Nogura frowned. "Get back from where? I don't recall authorizing shore leave for either of them. Commander, you wouldn't be covering for them, by any chance, would you?" Before Sulu could answer, he stepped closer to the screen. "That could end up being a dangerous career move, son."

Morrow moved to stand beside Nogura. "Commander Sulu, why don't you save us all the awkwardness you're hoping to avoid and just tell us what Admiral Kirk and your captain are doing while leaving you there to mind the store?"

To Nogura's surprise, Sulu actually seemed relieved to receive such an order. *"I apologize for this, gentlemen. Admiral Kirk gave me explicit instructions to tell you everything you wanted to know once you attempted to contact him. He's authorized me to give you a full briefing of his activities while he's away from the ship."*

"Why didn't he contact us before taking off to . . . where exactly *is* he, anyway?"

Drawing what looked to be a very, very deep breath, Sulu replied, *"Sir, it's not so much where he is, but when."*

It took an extra moment for the response to sink in, but when it did, Nogura felt his jaw go slack.

"You're telling me he and Spock have . . . when?"

Time travel. Again.

"Yes, sir," replied Sulu. *"After their discussion with the Iramahl envoys, the admiral and Captain Spock theorized that while the missing scientists likely did not live beyond the twenty-first century, they might still be alive in the twentieth century. So, they enlisted the assistance of . . . some friends of ours from that time period to help find them. Perhaps you recall our previous encounters with a pair of humans, Gary Seven and Roberta Lincoln."*

For Nogura, Kirk's meetings with the walking riddle that was Gary Seven were among the most fascinating accounts recorded in the admiral's lengthy and rather remarkable Starfleet record. Nogura at first had found the reports in Kirk's file more than a bit fantastical, but *Enterprise* sensors and computer logs had recorded Seven's inadvertent visit to the starship during an actual, honest-to-goodness Starfleet-sanctioned mission to the twentieth century. What had begun as a strictly hands-off, observational mission of Earth and humanity during one of its most turbulent periods had ended up with Kirk and Spock assisting Seven to prevent a nuclear warhead from detonating in the planet's atmosphere. Since that first encounter, Seven and his assistant, Roberta Lincoln, had managed to find Kirk and the *Enterprise* more than once by traveling through time. They even had requested their assistance back in the twentieth century. It all tended to make Nogura's head spin, and it was more than enough to give anyone working for the Department of Temporal Investigations bellyaches for days.

"Tell me something, Commander," said Nogura, struggling to maintain his composure as he pictured Jim Kirk giving DTI a new round of fits. "Why didn't you report this to us sooner?"

Shifting in the command chair, Sulu looked around the bridge as though seeking support from one of the officers around him before replying, *"I was under orders, sir, not to say anything to anyone but you or Admiral Morrow, and only then if you contacted the* Enterprise."

Nogura made a mental note to have a long talk with Kirk, assuming the admiral returned from wherever he had gone, about his penchant for pushing the limits of operating "unless otherwise directed." The man's atypical definition of that term had gotten him into trouble with his superiors more than once. Of course, Kirk was often correct in the decisions he had made or the actions he had taken, but that did not excuse his maverick approach.

But isn't that why you promoted him and looked after him all those years? Isn't this just the sort of unconventional thinking Starfleet needs?

While Nogura did believe that, there were times when such attitudes threatened to cause more problems than they solved. There was no way to know if that was the case here. Only time—

Don't you dare say it.

Holding up a hand, Morrow said, "Now hang on. Are you saying that Admiral Kirk has some means of contacting these people? In the *twentieth* century?"

Sulu forced a smile. *"Well, Admiral, here's where the story gets really interesting."*

Twenty-Three

The Pentagon—Washington, DC
August 14, 1985

"Tell me, Major, how exactly an alien spacecraft just disappears out from under the noses of two dozen people."

Standing at attention before General John William Vessey Jr., Daniel Wheeler forced himself to keep his voice level and maintain his bearing. Yes, it was true that he was—for the moment, at least—the commanding officer of the United States government's preeminent covert operations unit and tasked with an assignment unlike anything else in the American military arsenal. Neither of those things granted him free rein to mouth off to superior officers, and while telling the chairman of the Joint Chiefs of Staff to kiss his ass might bring him momentary satisfaction, it was sure to drop a bomb on what otherwise had been a laudable military career to this point. At best, he might be able to get away with it once, perhaps twice, but it was a card best kept for just the right moment.

This was not that moment, Wheeler decided.

"We don't know what happened, General," he said. "One moment we were standing on the ice, studying the ship and preparing to excavate it, the next minute I'm looking up at the sky and an airman is standing over me asking if I'm all right. All of us—every single member of the team—were incapacitated, for a period of nearly ninety minutes. There were no injuries or fatalities, but the ship itself was gone. We have no explanation for what happened, sir." He paused, then added, "It's the damnedest thing I've ever encountered, General, and that's saying something."

Sitting behind his large oak desk, hands folded as they sat atop a blotter that was remarkably free of papers or anything else that might suggest he did anything within this room except interrogate subordinates, Vessey grunted in disapproval. Wheeler knew better than to say anything else at this point. Though the general was a slim yet still fit man in his early sixties and his thin light brown hair had gone gray, his eyes still burned with an intelligence and intensity that evoked fear in younger men. Vessey's reputation for being intolerant of waste or inefficiency in any aspect of military operations was common knowledge, as was his loathing of anyone who attempted to make excuses for failure. A combat veteran of World War II as well as the conflicts in Korea and Vietnam, Vessey had begun his military career as an infantry soldier in North Africa, receiving a battlefield commission to second lieutenant in 1944 after Operation Shingle, the amphibious landing and ensuing campaign against Nazi forces in Anzio, Italy. A long and distinguished career had unfolded after that, culminating in his appointment by President Ronald Reagan as chairman for the JCS. Vessey also held the distinction of being the lone remaining four-star flag officer who also had seen combat in World War II. The width and breadth of his military experience was staggering, and Wheeler genuinely respected the man, who like him had risen through the ranks as an enlisted man before earning a commission.

After nearly a full minute of silence, Wheeler heard Vessey exhale. "At ease, Major." Wheeler relaxed, and the general waved him to one of the leather chairs positioned before his desk. Once he was seated, the general leaned back in his leather chair, resting his hands in his lap.

"I've seen a lot of strange shit in my day, Major, but I'm still having a hard time wrapping my head around what you and that group of yours is doing." Vessey shook his head. "Aliens and spaceships? That's the sort of thing I dismissed as the junk my grandchildren watch on Saturday morning cartoons." He gestured around his office, which was tastefully appointed with a selection of photographs and other mementos that— like the several rows of ribbons on his uniform jacket— celebrated his lengthy service. "Then I get this job and people like you tell me we've had these things running around the planet for at least forty years, if not longer."

Wheeler released a knowing sigh. "There are days I feel the same way, sir."

"How the hell are we supposed to explain this to the president?" asked Vessey.

"With the truth, sir, as always. As far as I'm concerned, this just proves what we've been saying all along. Aliens are here, actively working at something. We don't know what it is, how many of them there are, or what it might be leading toward, but that ship didn't just disappear on its own; someone or something took it, somewhere." He blew out his breath. "I just don't have the first damned clue where."

Vessey said, "Well, whatever happened, it didn't fly out of there, at least as far as we can tell. I've already had SAC, Space Command, and NORAD verify that there were no satellite detections of anything resembling a launch anywhere around the world. The bird we retasked to cover the crash site shows that the ship was there on one pass, and gone the next. Whatever happened, it's like whoever moved the ship knew when the satellite would be overhead."

All of this information had been given to Wheeler even before he left the Distant Early Warning station at Tuktoyaktuk. Liaison officers from the Strategic Air Command headquarters at Offutt Air Force Base in Omaha, Nebraska, as well as the Air Force Space Command at Peterson Air Force Base in Colorado Springs and the North American Aerospace Defense Command at the adjacent Cheyenne Mountain facility had all contributed updated data. This telemetry, gathered from the network of American military satellites as well as other sensor equipment to determine the existence of any unidentified threat anywhere in the world, told Wheeler what he had suspected as he gazed at the hole in the ice where the alien ship had once rested: the craft had vanished.

Where had it gone? More importantly, who had taken it?

"This just helps to crystallize the problem, General," said Wheeler leaning forward in his chair. "There are those in this administration and within the military leadership who either have no idea what we're dealing with, or else they've somehow become convinced that there's no longer a threat. You and I both know better, sir."

Vessey gave him a sidelong glance. "You're telling me you know what I know, Major?"

Sensing he was being teased if not outright tested, Wheeler replied, "I know that you've spent a long career planning for the worst-case scenario, General, and that you've used your position as chairman to convince others to think along the same lines. That's why you've pressed the president to expand our reach around the world and to keep pushing back against the Soviets. It's why you recommended we not ignore the offensive and defensive advantages of satellites, space stations, and space-based weapons. You're the reason he's so hot about SDI, and why you lobbied for a unified command to oversee military space operations." He offered a small grin. "I've been paying attention, sir."

For the first time since the meeting began, Vessey smiled. "Glad to see someone is." Sitting up in his chair, the general rested his forearms on his desk. "And you're right. Despite my earlier comments, I've been aware of this alien business since the minute I was read into your group's activities. I'd heard rumors, of course, and twenty years ago things like Project Blue Book were a joke to most of us." He shook his head. "Of course, now I know that was the point, at least for the most part, right? Give cover for you and those who came before you. Damn fine job of keeping a lid on this, for whatever the hell my opinion's worth."

"Right now, it's worth a lot, sir." Wheeler tapped a finger on the general's desk. "We need you and your support, particularly now. This situation with the ship is just the sort of thing Majestic was created to deal with and to figure out how to fight. We can't go half-stepping now, otherwise it's forty years of work down the crapper."

Before Vessey could respond, the small box sitting next to the phone on one corner of his desk beeped, and a female voice said, *"General Vessey, sir, I know you said no interruptions, but I have a Marine lieutenant here who's requesting to speak with Major Wheeler. He says it's urgent, sir."*

Vessey eyed Wheeler. "One of yours?"

"Probably my aide, General." Lieutenant Joseph Moreno had accompanied him to the Pentagon and until at least a few moments ago had been working in a private office provided to him by one of Vessey's assistants.

Vessey frowned. "It's been my experience that when

262DAYTON WARD

a Marine says something's urgent, you pay attention." Pressing a button on the intercom, he said, "Send him in here, Sergeant."

"Yes, sir."

A moment later the door opened, and Wheeler shifted in his seat to see Moreno enter the office, dressed in a Marine officer's green uniform trousers and jacket over a khaki shirt and tie. The lieutenant was carrying a square canvas bag in his left hand. He closed the heavy wooden door before proceeding to within a pace of Vessey's desk and assuming a position of attention.

"Good afternoon, General. Lieutenant Moreno, reporting as ordered."

Vessey waved a hand toward the junior officer. "Well, I just invited you in, Lieutenant. You're the one who wanted to join the party. Stand easy, Marine."

"Thank you, sir. I apologize for the intrusion, but Major Wheeler instructed me to contact him immediately if we got any new information about a possible location on the missing alien craft."

"You're saying you've got something?" asked Wheeler.

Moreno nodded. "Yes, sir." To Vessey, he said, "You're going to want to see this too, General." He hefted the bag he still carried. "If I may?"

"Have at it, Lieutenant," said Vessey, gesturing for Moreno to move to the small round conference table in his office's far corner. The Marine laid the bag atop the table and unzipped it, withdrawing a blocky piece of off-white plastic that Wheeler recognized as a portable computer. Part of the unit operated on a hinge, and when Moreno flipped up this section, it revealed a monochrome monitor with orange text on a black background.

"Nice toy," remarked Vessey.

"It's a model developed for the DoD, sir," said Moreno. "Civilian versions that have some of this level of capability will be along in a year or so."

The general snorted. "Great. I've got a grandson who'll love that. I figure he's the one who's going to program all the robots to kill us in the future."

Moreno pressed a sequence of keys that Wheeler only half followed, and the result was the computer's compact monitor beginning to generate a map of the United States. Loath as he was to admit it, Wheeler had not yet jumped on the personal computer bandwagon with the same enthusiasm as the generation coming up behind him. On the other hand, Moreno was young enough that he likely had received some kind of computer training in high school before gaining greater exposure in college and later from the Marine Corps Computer Sciences School in Quantico, Virginia. Whereas Wheeler was competent enough to navigate a typical pocket calculator, Moreno was at home interacting with these far more sophisticated contraptions.

"What are we looking at, Lieutenant?" asked Wheeler.

Moreno said, "When we first examined the alien ship on site in Canada, we were able to detect a low-frequency transmission coming from it. We still have no idea what it was saying, General, or who was meant to hear it. When we were revived and saw that the ship was gone, we attempted to track the signal but it was long gone, and we thought that was that."

He tapped another handful of keystrokes, and a series of concentric circles appeared, overlaying the map with a small orange circle at its center positioned over what Wheeler realized was the Raven Rock Mountain Complex just over the border in Pennsylvania. Other smaller dots represented the Pentagon and the White House, but it was a third dot in the screen's upper right quadrant that drew Wheeler's attention.

"New York?" he asked, pointing to the display.

"Yes, sir," replied Moreno. "Our equipment picked up the transmission twice, on the same low frequency, and at both times the duration was less than two minutes."

Vessey, standing with his arms folded across his chest, asked, "How the hell were you even able to track it in the first place?"

"Well, that's a pretty interesting story, General," replied the lieutenant, who then paused to offer Wheeler an uncertain look.

Letting his subordinate off the hook, Wheeler said, "We've enjoyed the occasional technological breakthrough over the years, sir, thanks to various . . . items . . . we've acquired during our ongoing investigations."

His eyes narrowing in obvious skepticism, Vessey

pointed to the computer. "You're saying that thing is from an alien ship or other piece of equipment?"

"No, sir," replied Wheeler. "However, scientists with our organization have been successful in some limited reverse engineering of certain components, including the onboard computer systems of a vessel we retrieved back in the sixties." When Vessey opened his mouth to respond, Wheeler added, "The file for that and a select number of cases investigated over the years is not readily accessible beyond MJ-12 personnel, General. I didn't even know about it until Project Cygnus was initiated."

"I think I'm going to want to read those files," said Vessey.

"Already in process, sir." Indeed, Wheeler had requested authorization to have the general read into the entire scope of the missions of both Majestic and Cygnus, as well as unrestricted access to the extensive archives of both groups. Unlike some of his predecessors, Vessey had demonstrated during his tenure as chairman that he was serious not only about protecting the United States from foreign enemies, but also defending humanity from threats beyond the confines of its home planet. Though obviously unknown to the public, the real reasons for Vessey and the Joint Chiefs championing a greater emphasis on an American military presence in space was dictated less by concern over terrestrial threats as it was those from the stars, but selling the latter idea was of course a politically untenable option. Better to focus the fears of congressional leaders and concerned citizenry on an enemy they could see and understand, after all.

"The original technology utilized materials we can't reproduce," explained Moreno. "Some really crazy additions to the periodic table, sir. However, in most cases we were able to find workable alternatives, but our substitutes resulted in our being able to only partially recreate the functionality of the original components." He gestured to the computer. "While we've made significant progress in our computer miniaturization and processing efforts, we're still years or even decades away from the kind of power and portability the alien tech promises." He sighed. "But when that gets here? Watch out."

"What about this signal?" asked Vessey. "How were you able to track it?"

Moreno cleared his throat. "Once we had a recording of it, along with notes about its frequency, signal strength, duration, and rate of cycling, we input all of that information to our mainframe at Raven Rock, then hit the switch and let the machine start chewing on it. The process took the better part of the day, mostly due to our equipment still having issues with detecting anything broadcast on such a low frequency and power level. To be honest, we would've missed it the first time if not for the signal technician who was on duty. She caught it just by sheer luck, then was able to figure it out when even the computer wasn't sure."

"Can you pinpoint its location?" asked Wheeler.

The lieutenant's expression fell, and he shook his head. "Not to an exact spot, sir, but we can get within spitting distance." Reaching for the portable computer's keyboard, he tapped another sequence of keys and the map shifted to focus on New York, then refreshed with a larger image of the state. The orange dot turned into a circle, inside of which was the recognizable landscape of Manhattan and the northwest area of Brooklyn.

"That's it?" Doubt laced Vessey's question.

Wheeler replied, "With all due respect, General, it's a lot more than we had this morning." He studied the map, noting that the center of the circle fell over the waters of the East River running between Brooklyn to the south and Manhattan to the north.

"You're from New York, Moreno," he said after a moment. "What's our best bet?"

Without hesitation, the Marine said, "The Navy Yard, sir. That area's been going downhill for years. There are dozens, maybe even hundreds of buildings in or near that area that'd be perfect for hiding. You could probably stay there for years without anybody noticing. Once we're on the ground, we should be able to hone in on the signal and get a fix on its location."

"That's our play, then," said Wheeler, nodding with renewed confidence. "We'll start at one end and make a complete sweep until we find it."

Whoever had taken the ship from him would not do so a second time.

Twenty-Four

Seldom did a day go by that Leonard McCoy did not want to take a phaser to a piece of equipment that had wronged him in some real or perceived manner. There also were rare occasions when he thought of taking some offending piece of technology to the nearest airlock and jettisoning it into space.

Today was shaping up to be one of those days.

"I've seen a lot of strange things in my time," he said, pushing himself away from the computer terminal and slumping even deeper into his chair, "but this is a whole other ballgame, right here."

Sitting across from him at the table they had been sharing in his lab, Doctor Christine Chapel looked up from her own work and regarded McCoy with what he recognized as an expression of sympathy. "Maybe you need to take a break. How long have you been at that, anyway?"

McCoy glanced at the computer display's chronometer. "A while." He sighed. "What else am I going to do?

I can't just sit here, waiting for Jim and Spock to come back from wherever the hell they've gone off to. Who knows what kind of trouble they're stirring up, and without me to clean up their mess."

"Are you saying you wanted to go with them?" asked Chapel.

McCoy cast a sidelong glance in her direction. "Christine, how long have we known each other?"

"About twenty years, give or take."

"Then you should know by now that I hate the idea of time travel even more than I hate transporters." He shook his head. "Traveling through time is like playing with fire. It's dangerous, even when it's done for the most noble of reasons."

Upon hearing Kirk's proposal to utilize time travel in order to make contact with Gary Seven, McCoy thought his friends had taken leave of their sanity. Though he had participated in time travel on more than one occasion, it was not something McCoy viewed with a casual air. The very real risk of altering the course of history, even as a result of the most innocent of acts, was something he, Kirk, and Spock had debated before and after each of their previous journeys through time. They had repeated that discussion before Spock's launching of the probe and revisited the topic prior to his and Kirk's departure with Roberta Lincoln to the twentieth century.

"I can only imagine what Admiral Nogura must be thinking right now," said Chapel. "There's no way he would've authorized a mission like this. I wouldn't want to be anywhere near his office right now. Or Admiral Morrow's, for that matter."

"Why do you think I came back out here?" The facilities at Jupiter Station were the real reason for his return, but being five hundred million miles away from Starfleet Headquarters also had a definite appeal. As a favor to Kirk, he had joined the admiral along with Spock and the rest of their friends on the *Enterprise* once the situation with the Iramahl and their reasons for coming to the Sol system became clearer. However, after taking some initial blood samples from Jepolin and Opirsa and conducting a series of preliminary screenings and other tests on the Iramahl representatives, McCoy had decided even the starship's wide-ranging lab spaces and services would be insufficient for further research. Once the *Enterprise* had been transferred to Starfleet Academy as a training vessel, it no longer was a priority for receiving the latest system upgrades and enhancements to its onboard facilities. With that in mind, he opted for his much more comprehensive laboratory and other resources here on the station to assist him in his research. Still, it saddened him to see the once state-of-the-art starship reduced or diminished in this way, even though he knew he was being overly emotional.

Spock would raise both of his eyebrows if he heard you talking like this.

"Thing is," McCoy said after another moment, "Jim's right. Or Spock's right and he was able to convince Jim to go along. Sure, them taking off without asking permission is probably going to raise a lot of hackles, but getting approval for something like this could take weeks or months. For that matter, it's even money on whether the brass would sign off on the idea in the first place. You could argue that Jim was right to go before anyone could tell him not to."

A small smile on her lips, Chapel replied, "You think there's a chance Nogura will see it that way?"

"Not a snowball's chance in hell." He shrugged. "Besides, he was smart to keep it to just him and Spock. There's no need for me or any of the rest of us to go stomping around three hundred years in the past. Of course, he'd have been smarter not to go at all, but I guess he didn't count on Miss Lincoln coming to get him."

Chapel shifted in her seat so that she could rest her elbows on the table. "So, why did she come to get them? I don't understand that."

"She and Seven are shorthanded. It's just the two of them back there against the whole world, and I guess she needed some extra help. It makes sense for Spock to go. He knows everything so far as the Iramahl and their technology, and he's smart enough to avoid doing anything stupid that might change history." McCoy sighed. "Jim went because he's Jim, and he's not about to let Spock or anybody else go on a dangerous mission if he's not out in front or right there beside them."

It was a trait that had defined Jim Kirk as a leader throughout his career and made him the bane of policymakers and other bureaucrats within Starfleet's upper echelons. When Kirk had commanded the *Enterprise*, more than one admiral had taken him to task for his habit of taking the lead during landing parties and other dangerous situations, and he had fought them all on this point. He had always placed the safety and well-being of his ship and crew above all other considerations no matter the personal cost. His refusal to sidestep personal risk when forced to subject those under his command to danger had produced the sort of loyalty that was a rarity for any kind of leader. Such devotion was an invaluable asset in an age where starships and their crews could be out of touch with command and out of reach of support or assistance for months or even years at a time. In short, Starfleet needed more leaders like James Kirk, not fewer, even if those in charge had to endure his occasional unorthodox or just plain insane stunts.

Like now, for instance.

Blowing out his breath, McCoy leaned back in his chair and lifted his feet to rest them atop the table. "If there's a way to find those people, then you and I both know Jim and Spock working together is the best shot we've got." He gestured to the computer display. "Besides, we've got enough to keep us busy."

Chapel indicated the terminal she had been using to assist him with the research. "I've never seen anything like this, not even as a theory in a journal."

"We've seen different examples of genetic engineering," McCoy replied. "Some that went right, and some that went horribly wrong. You can argue that the people on Sycorax had a handle on what to do and what to avoid, but remember that other planet we found way back when, where they were messing around with trying to prolong human life spans and ended up killing the entire adult population?"

Nodding, Chapel replied, "I remember you almost died from whatever it was they turned loose on that planet."

"Yeah, well, that happened a few times. And how about what the Klingons did to themselves a hundred years ago?" McCoy sighed. "And don't even get me started on the craziness we stirred up ourselves."

"You mean the Eugenics Wars." Chapel's expression turned somber. "There's still a course about eugenics at the Academy. It's provoked some pretty interesting debates over the years."

McCoy snorted. "It made a few of my guest lectures pretty interesting." Lifting his feet from the table, he straightened in his chair and leaned across the table. "Do you know what all of those examples have in common? Those, and pretty much every other one I can come up with off the top of my head? Every single one of them was born from a desire to improve the status quo. Life prolongation. Cure birth defects or other abnormalities. Make people stronger and healthier. However misguided many of those attempts might have been, they started out with the best of intentions. That was always a big part of those debates."

"It sure was."

McCoy pointed an accusatory finger at his computer

terminal. "But this is nothing like any of those other examples. This was a deliberate effort to impede the Iramahl, to make them something less than they once were. That's appalling. There's no other word for it. I can't even begin to fathom the mindset of someone who could imagine something like this, let alone find a way to make it a reality and to justify it in the name of . . . well . . . whatever the hell reason the Ptaen came up with back then." The lengths to which the Ptaen had gone in order to maintain their grip on the Iramahl people had to rank the oppressor race among the worst conquerors the galaxy had ever known, as far as McCoy was concerned.

Chapel said, "But can we cure it? That's the big question." Once more, she looked to her terminal. "Or, barring that, at least find a way to mitigate it."

"If Jepolin and Opirsa are right," McCoy said, "it's certainly possible. On the other hand, the people who supposedly did it took years to do it, and they went missing four hundred years ago. Meanwhile, you and I have been working for about a day, starting from scratch, and I'm just not that smart. You have to think other Iramahl scientists—or anybody else, for that matter—had to be working on it too. How is it nobody else has found the answer?" Could the injustice perpetrated against the Iramahl over uncounted generations truly be reversed? Were he and Chapel the ones to do it? At the moment, it just did not seem likely.

"Number one, you're plenty smart," said Chapel, and he noted the admonishment in her tone. "Self-deprecation doesn't suit you. We'll figure this out. I've been running tests and comparisons for hours against the medical banks, and so far, I've got nothing, but I'm nowhere near giving up. It's just going to take some time. That's all."

"Fine. How's your schedule for the next couple of centuries?"

Shrugging, Chapel said, "I'm not going anywhere."

The door to the lab opened, and Commander Tonia Barrows entered the room. Like McCoy and Chapel, she was still dressed in her Starfleet uniform despite McCoy knowing she had been off duty for at least two hours. She caught sight of them and offered a warm smile of greeting.

"I figured I'd find you two here." Looking to Chapel, she said, "Good to see you, Christine."

"Same here, Tonia. How's life upstairs?"

Barrows made a show of rolling her eyes. "Are you kidding? The Iramahl are the most exciting thing to happen around here in ages." She snapped her fingers. "And just like that? Back to business as usual, which means I'm bored. How are things down here?"

Gesturing to his computer, McCoy said, "We're just trying to do the impossible. You know, the usual. What brings you down to the basement?"

"Dinner. I'm hungry. Let's eat."

"I think that's my cue," said Chapel, starting to rise from her chair.

"Don't be silly." Barrows nodded toward the door. "Join us. You both look like you could use the break. Come on. I'm buying."

Chapel smiled. "You sold me. Let's go."

Her computer terminal chose that moment to beep for attention, making McCoy scowl at it. "What does that thing want now?"

Leaning over the table and swiveling the terminal to face her, Chapel studied whatever information was on it, and McCoy saw her eyes widen. "I'll be damned." She turned the screen in his direction. "Look at this."

On the screen was a computer-generated representation of an Iramahl DNA strand, labeled with various notations Chapel had applied as a part of her own research. McCoy recognized most of the notes, but there were a few new ones, including a new message flashing at the bottom of the screen.

"You've found something." He smiled. "I think you found something, Doctor."

"It's a lot of guesswork," said Chapel. "I compared their DNA against samples from other genetically engineered species in the medical data banks. Nothing's a one-to-one match, of course, but there are a few similarities at the building-block level we might be able to do something with."

McCoy had seen those comparisons for himself, but he had not reached that conclusion. What had he missed?

"I know what you're thinking," said Chapel. "I know that look. You didn't miss anything. Neither one of us just thought to look at it from this particular angle. Take a look again."

Staring at the computer model, McCoy almost overlooked it one more time, but when he caught the obscure connection, he could not help the grin that threatened to break his face. "You're kidding."

"Nope." Now Chapel was smiling.

"Somebody want to clue in the rest of the audience?" asked Barrows, crossing her arms.

"Klingon DNA," said Chapel. "Specifically, one of the nucleotides in their DNA that was affected by the Augment virus a century ago and caused—among other things—the cranial ridges in so many Klingons to dissolve."

Barrows frowned. "And you think this might be able to help the Iramahl somehow?"

Chapel sighed. "It's still a theory, but it's more than what we had an hour ago."

Unable to suppress a chuckle, McCoy said, "Wow. Jim's going to love this. Nogura's going to love this, and the Klingons are *really* going to love this." He had heard the new rumblings about the Ptaen Consortium perhaps allying themselves with the Empire, if for no other reason than to get the Federation to reconsider its pledge to assist the Iramahl. "I want to be in the room when they get the news."

Shifting her gaze between the two doctors, Barrows said, "I think I know what this means."

McCoy nodded, feeling the first hint of excitement since beginning this task. "Yep. We're eating in."

Twenty-Five

Brooklyn Navy Yard—Brooklyn, New York
August 15, 1985

Standing next to the worktable they had positioned alongside the Iramahl vessel, Spock watched as Mestral, dressed in a pair of dark blue coveralls, emerged from the vessel's open hatch.

"The new components appear to be serviceable, following our modifications," Mestral said as he descended the short ladder standing beside the hatch. "Though I suspect their usefulness will be limited."

Spock replied, "I believe you are correct, but what you have provided should be sufficient." He had been maintaining a constant scan of the ship's active systems with his tricorder, after Mestral had substituted the damaged or deteriorated pieces of computer hardware with replacements they had configured with the help of the Beta 5.

"It is unfortunate you did not accompany us to obtain the new components," said Mestral. Moving away from the ladder, he brushed dust from the sleeves and knees of his coveralls, which Roberta Lincoln had provided for both Vulcans while they worked on the alien ship. "You would be intrigued by the wealth of information and artifacts the people of this era have collected that pertains to extraterrestrial beings and their technology."

Nodding, Spock replied, "So Miss Lincoln said, though her suggestion that Admiral Kirk and I remain behind was a prudent one."

Given the uncertainty of being able to find the Iramahl refugees—assuming they were even still alive—and concerned that the Ptaen might somehow determine the wrecked ship's location, Lincoln had advised Kirk and Spock to stay at the warehouse. At least here they would be able to protect the alien vessel as well as reduce the likelihood of them doing something that might alter or otherwise interfere with the historical events. Meanwhile, Lincoln and Mestral had set off via Gary Seven's transporter to what Lincoln had described as one of the United States government's numerous sites around the country that contained information about various encounters with extraterrestrials as well as examples of their technology.

"It was a logical decision," said Mestral. "Still, it was a fascinating repository. The instances of other civilizations visiting Earth, particularly during his era, is quite interesting."

"Perhaps. Then again, Vulcans and humans, along with a good number of other spacefaring civilizations, have long used covert observation and even limited interaction to study primitive cultures while assessing their potential as friends or adversaries. Indeed, it is common practice for Federation science teams."

Mestral nodded. "It was the same for our people in this time period, as well." He paused, and Spock noted the softening of his features. "Odd, that I should so casually discuss time periods in the plural, as though I have always accepted time travel as a valid premise. It was not until my encounter with Miss Lincoln and the Certoss agents, and my subsequent visit to your starship, that I realized the total fallacy of the Vulcan Science Directorate's stance on time travel."

"There was a time when I believed as the directorate did," replied Spock, setting his tricorder on the table and moving to the desktop computer provided by Roberta Lincoln. "Even after they began to modify their stance in the twenty-second century, there still were professors and instructors who held to the outdated views. I encountered more than one such individual during my primary education period."

"And now," said Mestral as he moved to stand next to Spock, "at least if what Miss Lincoln has told me is true, you have encountered this phenomenon more than any other Vulcan."

Spock had never before considered that possibility, but he could recall no information that might refute such a claim. Instead, he said, "It was not something I set out to do. If there is anything that has been a constant during my time in Starfleet, it is that the unknown has a tendency to reveal itself in numerous, often unanticipated ways. This was true with respect to our encounters with various temporal phenomena." He paused in the midst of reaching for the computer. "Of course, it's been my observation that the likelihood of such odd encounters tends to increase when one is in the company of Admiral Kirk."

"Interesting," replied Mestral. "I shall note that for future reference."

Using the interface cable Miss Lincoln had produced from wherever she or Gary Seven procured such things, Spock connected his tricorder to an input port on the side of the computer. While the desktop model looked contemporary on the outside, he had learned the shell contained a sophisticated mechanism that was a stand-alone unit in its own right, but which also could interface with the Beta 5 back in Seven's Manhattan office. This allowed Spock to access and analyze the scan data stored within the tricorder at a rate that was on par with the *Enterprise*'s main computer.

Satisfied with the connection as data began to scroll on the computer's orange-hued display screen, Spock said, "It will take a few moments."

Mestral nodded. "Very well." When he said nothing else, Spock sensed a tension emanating from the younger Vulcan.

"Is there something else?"

Turning away from Spock, Mestral looked about the room as though verifying that they were alone. "There is a . . . personal matter . . . I wish to discuss, if you would agree to such a conversation."

"By all means," Spock replied.

His facial features taking on an almost human expression of embarrassment—understandable given his prolonged stay here on Earth—Mestral said, "As you know, I have been here for . . . some time. Twenty-seven years, ten months, and eleven days, as time is measured on Earth. During most of that time, I have been without . . . Vulcan companionship."

Spock understood where this was going. Out of respect for Mestral, he also took a moment to confirm they were alone in the work bay before replying, "You speak of the *pon farr*." The time of mating, which affected Vulcans throughout their adult life span, had caused problems for Spock more than once.

His embarrassment evident, Mestral nodded. "That is correct. I have endured the blood fever four times, and on each of those occasions, I was able to employ meditation to mitigate the symptoms. However, the difficulty of doing so has increased with each occurrence. Though I do not expect to be faced with the problem for some time, I would ask if there are . . . other techniques I might employ in order to properly handle the condition when it returns."

"Perhaps your relationship with Mister Seven and Miss Lincoln might allow them to transport you to Vulcan," Spock suggested. "Even if such a visit is only . . . temporary."

Mestral shook his head. "I wish to remain on Earth. I have considered the possibility of a human female to assist in such matters, but that presents an unwarranted risk of my being exposed as an extraterrestrial."

"There may be some additional meditative techniques I can teach you," Spock offered. "They have proven successful for me on more than one opportunity." It was an interesting dilemma, he decided, viewing Mestral's situation strictly from the viewpoint of considering the biological and psychological factors that contributed to the *pon farr* condition. Though meditation had been of assistance to him, it was not a foolproof method. In truth, there was but one course of action that guaranteed a successful navigation of this chaotic, even violent time. It intrigued Spock that Mestral had chosen this life of solitary exile without apparent regard for the personal difficulties he had to know he would encounter.

Before Spock could say anything further, a door opened behind them, and he saw Admiral Kirk emerging from the office at the room's far end. Kirk was dressed in contemporary civilian attire, consisting of blue denim trousers with brown boots and a dark red button-down shirt with open collar that he wore loosely rather than tucked into his trousers.

"It'll be dark soon," Kirk said by way of greeting. "You two have been at this all day." He nodded to the Iramahl ship. "How's it going?"

Spock replied, "We have made some progress, Admiral, thanks to the efforts of Miss Lincoln and Mestral."

"I heard," replied Kirk. Looking to Mestral, he asked, "Where did you two find the parts you needed?"

"The computer interface module was salvaged from an automated drone retrieved by the air force in 1965, Admiral," said Mestral. "The craft crash-landed in a rural region of the southern United States." He indicated a file folder resting on the table. "We copied the relevant information from the archive facility when we appropriated the component."

Opening the folder, Kirk reviewed its contents. "February 1965." After a moment, he looked up. "James Wainwright? That name rings a bell."

"Indeed," replied Spock, having also recognized the name of the air force officer who had written the report, as well as the stamp covering part of the report's first page: TOP SECRET/MAJIC—EYES ONLY. Wainwright's report was a detailed accounting of the craft's discovery and eventual removal from its crash site by members of Project Blue Book.

"However, I must admit that I was unfamiliar with the area in which the craft was found." To Mestral, Spock said, "Booger Hollow, Arkansas, no longer exists in the twenty-third century." What he did not say aloud was that in decades to come, that region of the United States would not fare well during the nuclear exchange that ushered in World War III. For Mestral, such events had not yet occurred. Would he still be on Earth seventy years from now, when the war would take place? Spock did not know, and he made a mental note to review any pertinent historical information stored in the *Enterprise*'s computer data banks upon his and Kirk's return to the starship and their own time.

Mestral said, "The probe was transferred to a classified subterranean military facility in San Francisco. During my time assisting Agents Wainwright and Marshall with Project Blue Book, I learned that the American government had established several of these repositories around the country. Most of them operate—or operated—independently of one another, with the complete list of locations and items stored at each facility known only to key members of the project and Majestic 12."

"We learned some of this during our last mission with Miss Lincoln," said Kirk, "when she brought us to help her with the Certoss agents. It was a rather eye-opening experience."

During their previous encounters with Seven and Lincoln, Spock and Kirk had learned that world government and military leaders, the Americans in particular, had acquired such materials over the course of decades and perhaps longer. One of the fascinating yet puzzling aspects of humanity's desire to learn more about the beings who chose to visit Earth was that those who acquired such knowledge then made every effort to hide that information from the public while doing their best to exploit it.

"Except for the items of greatest interest," Mestral continued, "which are stored at bases in Ohio and Nevada, most of the collected artifacts and data are moved to one of these other sites. These materials are usually classified under nondescript names such as *Project 9* or *Operation Deep Ice*. Miss Lincoln also learned that after the dissolution of Blue Book, other initiatives were put in place to continue oversight of these facilities, presumably while Majestic's primary mission of identifying and developing defenses against extraterrestrial threats pushed forward."

"If I remember correctly," replied Kirk, "there also were a number of disinformation campaigns, designed to keep amateur enthusiasts occupied and away from any important facilities and material."

"That is correct, Admiral. I read some of the documentation produced to support the campaigns. It is an impressive level of effort, and it has largely succeeded with respect to keeping the public away from the military's true efforts."

The computer emitted a high-pitched beep, and Spock noted that its screen now displayed a high-resolution image of a complex, multicolored technical schematic that under normal circumstances would be well beyond the capabilities of computer technology available to the general populace. The enhancements made to the unit by Mister Seven and Miss Lincoln, however, saw to it that the monitor's depiction of Spock's scan data was rendered with comprehensive detail. It was not as advanced as what he might expect to see using equipment aboard the *Enterprise*, but it would be more than sufficient for their current purposes.

"Interesting," he said as he regarded the diagram. "Our enhanced access to the ship's onboard computer has only served to confirm our suspicions."

Stepping closer so that he could better see the information being displayed, Mestral studied the schematic and its accompanying sensor telemetry for a moment before saying, "It appears the self-destruct protocol is protected by its own separate layers of encryption and security access that are distinctly different from the procedures used to lock out the main computer."

"It would seem so," replied Spock. He and Mestral, combining their individual computer expertise with assistance provided by the Beta 5, had managed to bypass the intrusion countermeasures that had been protecting the Iramahl ship's onboard computer and data storage systems. This in turn had given them access to the operating system as well as several programs and processes that the Vulcans had determined were used to operate autonomously, such as life-support, navigational and long-range sensors, defensive systems, and other functions better served by the computer's ability to respond faster than a living being.

"The self-destruct procedure operates in a self-sufficient manner like these other automated processes," said Mestral, "just as it has since its activation more than a century ago. If I understand these readings correctly, the system has been operating in a low-power mode, its monitoring processes remaining active while everything else was transitioned to a hibernating state, waiting for a command from the master control protocol to awaken from that mode."

Kirk said, "That sounds like something you'd find aboard a sleeper ship."

"Precisely," replied Spock. The systems aboard the Iramahl vessel contained many similarities to mechanisms used aboard such vessels, which were a common development by many civilizations once their technology advanced to the point of attempting interplanetary or interstellar flight. "However, even those systems contain override protocols in the event of an emergency or other unexpected situation."

He pointed to the screen, indicating one particular section of the software diagram. "In this case, the self-destruct protocol has such an override, but it is keyed to a specific code entered by a particular individual, which I assume in this case to be the ship's commander."

"Just like the self-destruct procedures used on Starfleet ships," said Kirk.

"Based on a preliminary study of this design," said Mestral, "I do not see an alternative to entering the exact deactivation code. It appears that any attempt to circumvent the process will only result in its being executed."

Spock replied, "It would be best to avoid such a scenario."

"I second that." Kirk crossed his arms. "What about some kind of containment or force field? Just something localized, around the ship itself. Do we have what we'd need to do something like that? At least then, if the thing does go off, we can keep it from blowing a hole in the city."

"That may be a possibility," said Mestral, "but it likely would require obtaining additional components from the classified repositories, assuming we can find the appropriate items or viable substitutes. I shall consult with Miss Lincoln, Admiral."

On the table, Spock's tricorder began emitting a steady beeping. Spock reached for the unit and noted the messages on its compact screen. "Ptaen life signs, Admiral, within one hundred meters of this location."

Twenty-Six

There was something interfering with Noceri's scanner readings, but Rijal had seen enough.

"The ship is inside that structure," he said. Crouched behind the rooftop parapet of a neighboring building, he peered through a pair of binoculars, which like several other items he and his companions carried had been stolen from humans. They were not as efficient as an optical targeting scanner, but they were adequate for his purposes.

Beside him, Noceri continued to study the scanner. "The power readings are definitely not normal for indigenous technology, but I am unable to identify the energy signature."

Rijal had considered the implications of this enigma during their transit here. Had a group of humans found a way to study and replicate technology from an advanced race? Were members of such a civilization hiding among the human population, as he and his team had done?

"Though we are able to detect the Iramahl ship's transmission and the energy field that is active inside the structure," said Noceri, "I am unable to determine whether there are any security measures in operation."

Kneeling to the other side of the apprentice, Bnara said, "I wonder if the Iramahl also have found this place."

"We have to operate under that assumption," said Rijal. "There is only one way to be certain." Direct action was required in order to make a proper determination. He preferred this approach, as he had grown weary of hiding and waiting.

Removing his sidearm from the equipment satchel he wore slung over his left shoulder, Rijal verified its power level. He had been unable to fully charge the weapon, owing to the dwindling battery packs in their cache of supplies. The extended stay on this planet, coupled with the numerous, fruitless attempts to locate and detain their quarry, had done much to consume their limited resources. If this hunt continued for a protracted period, he and his companions would be forced to rely even more on weapons, tools, and other items procured from their unwitting human hosts.

Bnara was now using the binoculars to study the target building. "There are several entrances, though we must assume they are secured or monitored in some fashion that belies their appearance." She patted the satchel she wore slung over one shoulder. "We have ways of combating that."

Another tone from the scanner made Rijal turn to his apprentice, who was studying the device with renewed confusion.

"What is it?"

Shaking his head, Noceri replied, "This is detecting

the presence of another scanning field." He looked up from his equipment. "It is aimed at us."

"They can detect us?" asked Bnara. "How is that possible? Humans do not possess such technology."

Rijal frowned. It was an interesting development, but not insurmountable. "It seems these humans have numerous remarkable qualities." Reaching under the collar of his uniform, he activated the garment's masking field. Noceri and Bnara mimicked his movements. He did not even know if the fields would defeat whatever was being used to track them, but it did not matter, not now.

"Select the entrance that places us in closest proximity to the vessel," Rijal said, reaching into the satchel to retrieve other items he would need. "It is time."

Using himself for bait was not something with which Kirk had ever felt comfortable.

He had done it, of course, more than once, but that did not make it any more desirable a prospect now as he and the others waited. Waited for what, exactly?

"Let's try to keep this from spinning out of control," he said, taking a moment to exchange glances with Spock, Roberta Lincoln, and Mestral. "There's no way to know how they'll react when confronted. Based on everything we know, the Ptaen aren't actually looking to kill or even harm the Iramahl. They just want to take them back, presumably to learn how the Iramahl were able to reverse their condition."

"That doesn't mean they won't kill anybody who gets in their way," replied Lincoln.

Kirk nodded. "Exactly, but at least here we have something of an advantage." Spock's tricorder had tracked the three Ptaen life signs as they maintained their position some one hundred meters or more from this building. Were they surveying their surroundings, waiting for an opportune moment to launch an attack? Perhaps they were waiting for their Iramahl quarry to arrive. Jepolin and Opirsa had told him back on the *Enterprise* that neither the Iramahl nor Ptaen of this period had scanning technology on par with tricorders or sensors. They could track communications and energy readings, but not life signs. This alone gave Kirk and the group an edge, but they also had this building, which, while not impregnable, was at least a place that provided cover and concealment.

Crossing the room to where Kirk and Spock stood with Mestral at the worktable before the Iramahl ship, Roberta Lincoln reached out to touch the green cube sitting atop the contemporary desktop computer's monitor. "I've done what I can. There's a force field around the building's perimeter that should keep anyone from entering. We don't use it very often, as that's the sort of thing that might attract unwanted attention from casual passersby, but we can run it for a while without raising too much suspicion." She gestured to the alien vessel. "Admiral, we could move this, but if you're right about these Ptaen, they don't want the ship. They're just hoping it attracts the Iramahl."

"That's our best guess," replied Kirk. "Based on what Spock and Mestral have told us, there's really not

anything aboard the ship the Ptaen would want." He
frowned. "Well, except maybe for the bodies of the
dead crew members." After the ship had been relocated
here from the Arctic, Lincoln had taken the step of
transporting the remains of the two Iramahl from the
wrecked section of the vessel and placed them in stasis
tubes in another part of the warehouse. They would be
handled in accordance with Iramahl customs, once the
immediate issue was resolved.

Like not blowing up Brooklyn, Kirk mused.

"Admiral," said Spock, his attention focused on his
tricorder. "Something is wrong. My scans are being
disrupted."

"What do you mean?" asked Kirk, feeling his hand
move toward the phaser tucked into the pocket of the
blue nylon jacket provided to him by Lincoln.

The Vulcan's eyebrow rose. "I'm uncertain. The readings were nominal a moment ago."

Sitting in silence on the computer monitor until
now, the green cube flared to life, pulsing from within
while emitting a shrill whine.

"Computer," said Lincoln. "Report."

"*Fluctuation in force field energy readings,*" replied
the Beta 5. "*Interference from outside power source.*"

Standing next to Spock, Mestral said, "Perhaps the
Ptaen are employing a form of electronic countermeasures to mask their movements."

"Spock?" Kirk prompted.

"That would seem to be a logical development."

Spock adjusted the controls on his tricorder. "I'm attempting to compensate."

It was at that moment that something exploded, punching a hole through the cavernous room's high ceiling.

Kirk and the others scattered as debris rained down near the room's far end, with chunks of cement and roofing materials crashing to the floor and bouncing along its concrete surface. The explosion itself was not that loud, but Kirk's ears still rang from the effects of the muffled blast. Turning in that direction, he fumbled the phaser from his jacket pocket as he saw first one, then two more dark figures descending through the hole. Rappelling on ropes into the room, the new arrivals dropped toward the floor too fast for Kirk to target them.

"Admiral!"

In the midst of bringing up his phaser to aim at one of the intruders, Kirk caught sight of the third assailant tossing something in his direction. Then Mestral was lunging at him, the Vulcan crashing into him and driving both of them to the workshop floor. The thrown object, whatever it was, clattered across the floor on the other side of the Iramahl ship and exploded.

This time Kirk heard and felt the effects of the device, realizing an instant after it detonated that it was not designed to injure, only disorient. His vision disintegrated into white nothingness and his hearing felt as though he was underwater. He blinked in rapid fashion, trying to shake off the momentary blindness even as he heard the sounds of muted running.

"Spock!" he shouted, almost not hearing the sound of his own voice. His vision was clearing, and he saw someone kneeling over him. It was Mestral, extending his hand. Kirk allowed the Vulcan to help him to his feet, but his gaze was already shifting to look around the room in search of the intruders. A shadowy figure darted past the wreckage of the Iramahl ship, but was gone before Kirk could get a good look at it.

"Miss Lincoln!"

Kirk looked to where he had last seen her, but she was gone, though the green cube on the computer was flashing with even greater urgency than before the explosion. Any thoughts about whether the advanced mechanism might be trying to broadcast an alert or warning were lost as he saw Mestral turn and aim the servo in his right hand at . . . nothing.

"Stop where you are," the Vulcan called out. "We do not wish to harm you, but we will defend ourselves if necessary."

Reaching with his free hand to rub his eyes and clear away the last of the ghost images plaguing his vision, Kirk raised his phaser in that direction, but still saw nothing. "Mestral, what . . . ?"

Wait.

"They are Iramahl, Admiral," said another voice— Spock's. His friend appeared from around the front of the alien ship, phaser and tricorder still in hand, though his usually neat hair was somewhat disheveled.

"They were using the ability Jepolin demonstrated for us back on the *Enterprise*."

"I guess it's working," said Lincoln as she stepped around the craft's aft section, servo in her right hand. "I don't see a damned thing." She moved toward the worktable and touched the green cube, silencing its audible alert even though the device continued to flash.

Mestral and Spock converged on each other, Spock releasing his tricorder to hang from his shoulder before extending his hand toward something or someone that remained invisible. Then he was forced to blink again as three figures seemed to coalesce out of thin air, and one of them handed Spock what appeared to be some sort of weapon. Each of the aliens was dressed in a formfitting dark garment that by itself was not remarkable, but their skin pigmentation as well as facial and cranial features denoted them without question as Iramahl.

"And Vulcans aren't affected by whatever it is that they do," Kirk said, nodding. "Of course."

"I do not know who you are," said one of the Iramahl, a female, "or how you are able to do what you have done here, but you are in grave danger. It is imperative that you grant us access to our ship."

Holding up his hands and aiming his phaser away from the Iramahl, Kirk said, "It's not our intention to harm you in any way, and of course the ship is yours. I'd be happy to explain all of this to you, but right now we've got bigger problems. Spock?"

"Whatever is disrupting my tricorder is still in

operation," replied the Vulcan. "I am still unable to scan for the Ptaen life-forms."

The female Iramahl's expression darkened. "Ptaen? They are here?"

"We were able to monitor their movements," replied Mestral, "until you activated your disruption device prior to entering the building."

One of the female's companions said, "We did no such thing."

Why did I know you were going to say that?

The thought came an instant before Kirk heard the sound of what had to be an energy weapon's discharge from somewhere behind the ship, followed by something heavy falling to the concrete floor. Spock and Mestral backpedaled away from the ship, and the three Iramahl followed them as Kirk and Lincoln turned toward the source of the disruption. A cloud of smoke and dust was shining through, and Kirk could see a beam of light coming from what now had to be an open doorway. Lying on the floor inside the room was one of the metal security doors at the room's far end, warped and twisted as it was ripped from its frame by extreme force.

The device had renewed its shrill alarm, demanding attention, and Kirk tried to ignore the alert that was an assault on his still tender eardrums. Then he heard the sound of new footsteps running across the workshop floor and realized they seemed to be moving toward the computer. Spock and Mestral were continuing to hustle the three Iramahl out of the way as the footfalls grew louder and more insistent.

"Watch out," he said in a low voice, using his free hand to maneuver Lincoln out of possible lines of fire and lifting his phaser as he saw a shadow on the floor near the Iramahl ship's bow. He was taking aim when he felt Lincoln grab his arm.

"Down!" she snapped, and Kirk had a heartbeat to realize she was pulling him to one side and firing her servo at a target he had not seen. A sharp, piercing whine erupted from the slim silver pen, and though there was no beam, Kirk still saw the tool's effects as the dark figure staggered in the face of the weapon's assault, but did not fall.

"Uh-oh," said Lincoln, just as the figure seemed to shake off the servo's effects before ducking back around the side of the craft.

"Spock, get them out of here!" Kirk barked, pushing himself to a kneeling position and firing his phaser in the direction of the ship's nose. The weapon's blue-white beam struck the front of the craft, and he was certain he heard a cry of surprise from somewhere beyond the ship. He did not expect to hit anyone or anything, but his shot did seem to have the effect of making the new intruders think twice about revealing themselves. That would provide only a moment's respite, Kirk knew.

"Come on," he said, pushing himself to his feet. "We've got to move." Aside from the Iramahl craft, the middle area of the workshop provided nothing to use for cover. Only storage lockers and the doors leading to the other parts of the building were of any use, but getting to any of them or even the transporter vault in the office without exposing themselves to enemy fire would be all but impossible, and the alternative was to stand and fight.

A dark-clothed figure vaulted over the Iramahl ship, landing with exquisite grace less than ten meters in front of Kirk and Lincoln, and the admiral got his first good look at a living, breathing Ptaen. Its formfitting black garments covered it from the neck down, leaving exposed the indigo hue of its head and hands. Long black hair seemed to be fastened at the neck, and the Ptaen's pronounced brow and forehead seemed even larger thanks to its elongated skull. A vertical crease ran from the bridge of the alien's narrow nose up and over the top of its head.

The Ptaen hunter recovered from its jump as Kirk was raising his phaser, but Lincoln was faster, her servo aimed and firing. The intruder dodged to its left with startling speed. Kirk tried to adjust his aim but the Ptaen was raising something and aiming it at him.

Then, for the second time in as many minutes, Kirk's vision exploded in a flash of blinding white.

Twenty-Seven

"Mister Spock, we must go back."

Drevina and her companions stood in a passageway beyond a portal leading to the building's larger workspace. Through the still open doorway, she could see part of their spacecraft. Between her and the door were the two beings with the odd pointed ears who had been able to defeat her masking gift.

How had they managed that?

Every higher order life-form they had encountered since arriving on this planet had been susceptible to her manipulations, aside from one other individual. Like that extraordinary being, were these two males from another world? If so, what species did they represent?

It was the younger being who had implored his older comrade about returning to the warehouse, likely in a bid to render aid to the two other people—human, as far as Drevina could determine—who remained inside.

Standing at the door, the older alien held it open with one hand. "Mestral, take our guests to the secure holding area beyond the utility room. It has an emergency anti-intrusion system. You and they will be safe until we can take control of this situation."

Another round of energy discharges, what Drevina recognized as coming from a Ptaen weapon, echoed from the larger room beyond the door, seizing the attention of both aliens. When they moved away from the door and toward the commotion, she used the distraction to her advantage. Lunging forward, she struck at what appeared to be the older alien, knocking him off his feet and sending him tumbling to the floor. Drevina darted past him, forcing closed the heavy metal door leading to the building's larger workspace. She felt it latch into place and then heard the sounds of locks engaging. A control pad set into the wall next to the door changed colors, and Drevina guessed this was an indication that the hatch was now locked.

Turning back to her companions, she saw that Glorick and Canderon had combined to attack the alien's younger companion, who was employing some form of defensive unarmed combat tactics. Her friends expressed no concern over this, with Canderon leading the way. He stepped closer, lashing out with a speed the alien did not seem to anticipate. This was coupled with Canderon's strength that also seemed to be unexpected, though the alien was able to parry the attack. What he could not do was deal with Canderon as well as Glorick, who chose that precise moment to launch a vicious strike to the side of the alien's head. That was enough to drive the alien off his feet and send him toppling to the floor, where he lay unmoving.

"Did you kill him?" asked Drevina as she retrieved from the unconscious older alien his weapon as well as her own. The other sidearm was of a sort she had never before seen, but its functions seemed simple.

Glorick replied, "He is incapacitated, but not severely injured." He gestured toward the locked door. "There is no time. We must leave."

"But the ship," Drevina said. The scans she had taken of their former vessel prior to entering the building had shown her that the destruct protocol remained in a passive state, but interference by the Ptaen hunters or these strangers would be enough to push the protocol to its active—and quite final—mode.

"If we stay here, the Ptaen will take us," said Canderon. "We can regroup and try again once we regain control of the situation, but for now we must go."

"What of the humans in there?" she asked, then indicated the fallen aliens with her weapon. "And did you not hear these two talking? They did not speak like enemies, but as hopeful allies."

"We can discuss this later," snapped Glorick, grabbing her by her arm. "And elsewhere."

Exiting the building was easy, thanks to Drevina employing her weapon at its maximum strength against the reinforced door that appeared to have been the building's main entrance. Despite whatever materials were used in its construction as well as its magnetic locking mechanism, Drevina's sidearm tore it from its mounting, and it fell back and onto the sidewalk. Without concern for being seen by any humans who might be walking past the building—a negligible risk now that darkness had fallen—she led the way into the open air, and the trio sprinted toward the nearby water. She could hear activity in the distance, but she saw no signs of ground vehicles in the immediate vicinity. The lights of Manhattan were visible across the East River, and there was the faint, rhythmic drone of an aircraft somewhere in the skies above them. Drevina glanced over her shoulder to see Glorick and Canderon both checking behind them for signs of pursuit, but saw nothing.

You knew this would happen.

Predicting the Ptaen's attempted ambush had been a simple affair. The hunters had doubtless been monitoring their quarry's ship since their arrival, the same way Glorick had been doing for decades. Once the wreck was moved from the Arctic crash site, the Ptaen surmised she and her friends would attempt to investigate, and of course they had. What choice did they have? With the destruct procedure activated, the craft was a danger to innocent people here in New York.

We have to go back.

What they had to do was evade the Ptaen, draw them away from here in some manner, and keep them occupied long enough to backtrack and disable the ship's destruct mechanism, hopefully before the humans or their odd companions did something to push the protocol to its final mode.

Running around the building's corner, Drevina darted across a section of cracked concrete that was riddled with grass and weeds. A similarly dilapidated walking path ran parallel to the waterway and crossing it brought them to the revetment composed of thousands of massive wooden piles and other shapes. Then she saw the boat. It was a sleek affair, long and thin in a way that reminded her of the beauty to be found in Iramahl space vessels. Only a canvas top over the boat's console area disrupted its graceful lines. With the paltry illumination provided by a few streetlamps and lights from the building behind them, the boat's black paint helped it blend into the near darkness. They had taken it from a private marina some distance from here with the intention of returning it before its owner knew it was missing. To say that plan was now in jeopardy was something of an understatement.

"Glorick," she called over her shoulder. "Activate the watercraft." As he made his way across the seawall, she turned back to Canderon. "You will remain here."

Her friend eyed her with confusion. "I do not understand."

"Glorick and I will lead them away. You hide, and wait for them to give chase, then go back and deactivate the protocol."

Shaking his head, Canderon replied, "But you may need my help."

"There are far too many other people who need your help now."

Though he displayed understandable discomfort at the thought of separating from his friends, Canderon's expression showed that he appreciated the situation. "You are correct, of course. Good luck."

Drevina made her way to the boat, where Glorick was activating its engine. She looked back toward the building to see that Canderon had already blended into the darkness and disappeared from sight around the structure's far side. As for the building itself, who were its unusual occupants? Were they not of this world? Had they somehow learned to avail themselves of technology from other extraterrestrials? Perhaps they were benefiting from the assistance of such beings, but to what end? Drevina hoped those and so many other questions received answers.

Without waiting for her order, Glorick guided the boat away from the seawall and accelerated across the basin, heading north toward the river. The watercraft had been his idea, as it provided the best option for getting to and from the target once they had pinpointed their ship's location. After more than a century on Earth, during which they had observed so many advances in human technology, Drevina and her friends had become proficient in operating most forms of ground- and water-based transportation, as well as smaller rotary and fixed-wing aircraft.

"Drevina," said Glorick, raising his voice to be heard over the sound of the boat's engine, "Do you hear that?"

It took her a moment to realize what he meant. The drone of aircraft she had heard a few moments earlier was now louder and getting closer. Glorick was pushing the boat faster, but they both knew that excessive speed in this area might attract the attention of police or other curious parties. Moving around him, Drevina peered out from beneath the boat's shade cover and saw a dark shape moving above them.

It was a helicopter, and then she was all but blinded as an intense beam of light flared to life from the craft and aimed at her.

Standing at the water's edge, Rijal watched the boat powering away from shore and into the river. They would have countless places to lose themselves among the people of this massive metropolis. Indeed, they did not even need to remain in the city, but could instead head along the coastline, out into the ocean until they had eluded all remaining pursuit.

"What do we do now?" asked Noceri from where he stood near the edge of the wooden wall forming a barrier for the water. "Should I recall our ship?"

We were so close!

How long had they been here, vainly searching for some sign of the Iramahl fugitives? How many hunter teams had been sent to this world for the same purpose? Finding the Iramahl ship's signal and learning that the craft had been moved from its tomb in the frozen wastes had been a stroke of good fortune, the first he and his fellow hunters had enjoyed since their arrival. This might well be their best, if only, chance of apprehending the fugitives, and it was slipping away with every passing moment.

One had to wonder about the futility of this action, but Rijal was not the one to do so. He had been given a task; he would see that task completed, no matter the cost or the time required.

Despite the immediacy of the situation, Rijal was reluctant to use their own scout craft to give chase. It appeared from its course that the watercraft carrying the fugitives was heading toward the city. Even with the darkness, the risk of discovery was a concern. After all, he and his fellow hunters lacked the bizarre gift possessed by certain Iramahl, including the fugitive Drevina, and he wondered if she had used that ability to any effect on this planet's indigenous inhabitants.

Of course, for all Rijal knew, she could be using her gift right now, to stand within easy reach of him and his companions while they laughed.

They lack the courage for such a brazen act.

Behind him, Bnara said, "From the ship, we can still track their movements and follow covertly."

She was correct. Why had he not considered this himself? Was his judgment being affected by the failure to capture the fugitives when they had possessed such great advantage? Perhaps, along with the humans who had somehow become involved with the Iramahl. Who were they? How had they managed to take custody of the ship, and what of the other technology they had employed? It had taken several of Bnara's tools to defeat the structure's intruder control measures as well as whatever had been used to track the hunters' movements. Much of this was very confusing and there were many questions, but Rijal found he did not care about the answers, at least not now.

"Recall the ship."

Whoever was beating on his skull, Kirk wanted that person dead.

"Admiral? Are you all right?"

Opening his eyes, Kirk saw Spock looking down at him, and then he realized he was looking up at the warehouse's ceiling. Then he remembered his head hurt.

"I'm starting to think I might be getting too old for this sort of thing." With Spock's help, he regained his feet, then held on to the Vulcan's arm long enough to steady himself. "What happened?"

"You and Miss Lincoln were stunned by a Ptaen energy weapon. Fortunately, the weapon's effects are temporary, and my tricorder has detected no lasting effects."

Kirk grimaced. "Tell that to my head."

To his left, Mestral was helping Roberta Lincoln up from where she had fallen. Despite her tousled appearance, Kirk thought she seemed none the worse for wear.

"Are you all right?" he asked.

Lincoln nodded. "I'll be okay, in about a month."

His thoughts beginning to reorder themselves, Kirk looked to Spock. "The Iramahl—where are they?"

"I am afraid they have fled, Admiral," replied Mestral. "Mister Spock and I were incapacitated in the confusion."

"Which means the Ptaen are chasing after them," said Lincoln.

Holding up his tricorder, Spock said, "We can track their movements. However, there is another problem." He paused, looking toward the Iramahl ship. On the nearby worktable, the green cube's flashing had increased to the point that it resembled a strobe light.

Kirk eyed the device with dread. "That doesn't look good."

"Computer," called Lincoln. "Status."

From the desktop computer, the voice for the Beta 5 announced, *"Destruct system triggered by proximity of unauthorized personnel. Contingency protocol enabled. Countdown under way. Translation of temporal measurement units indicates destruct sequence activation in twelve minutes, forty-nine seconds."*

"Can we stop it?" Kirk asked.

Spock replied, "We are unable to circumvent the security encryption, Admiral. We need assistance from the Iramahl."

Looking to Lincoln, Kirk asked, "Can you bring them back here with your transporter?"

"No," she replied with an irritated expression. "I can activate the beam close to their location, but it can't grab them while they're on the move."

That made it simple, Kirk decided. "Then we'll have to go and get them. Spock, I need you to stay here and keep trying to deactivate that thing. We can't let it go off."

"I believe I may be of assistance."

Everyone turned to see one of the Iramahl standing before them. He appeared unarmed, his hands held away from his body.

"My name is Canderon." He pointed to the Iramahl ship. "I was the technical specialist aboard that vessel. I should be able to assist in deactivating the destruct protocol."

Lincoln said, "That'd be awesome, right about now."

Canderon did not appear to understand her tone. "Drevina, the leader of our group, seems to think you are allies, rather than enemies."

"That's right," Kirk said, taking his phaser and, in very deliberate fashion, placing it in his jacket pocket. "We've come a . . . long way to find you. We want to help you and your people, if you'll let us." He gestured to the ship. "It'll be easier if you can stop that."

Canderon nodded. "I understand. I have only one request: please help my friends."

"We can do that," said Lincoln, and when Kirk looked at her, she nodded toward the door. "Come on. I'll drive."

"Drive?" Kirk asked.

Lincoln smiled. "You'll see."

Twenty-Eight

Major Daniel Wheeler felt his heart leap into his throat as the helicopter's spotlight focused on the speedboat below them. After several minutes of the boat's driver attempting to evade pursuit, Wheeler finally found himself staring into the face of an actual, honest to goodness alien.

"Son of a bitch. Right there." Reaching over, he tapped the chopper's pilot on his shoulder. "Get after them," he said into his helmet microphone, his voice filtered through the helicopter cabin's communications system.

Captain Peter Edwards, one of a handful of air force pilots detached to Project Cygnus at Raven Rock, guided the MH-53J helicopter closer to the water.

"They're making a run for it," said Wheeler.

Edwards shook his head. "From this distance, taking them out is easy."

"No. We want them alive." It was the first time since his taking command of Project Cygnus that such an opportunity had presented itself. Encounters with extraterrestrials had happened more than once to other case officers during his tenure with Project Blue Book, and he had been on hand when remains were recovered and studied. Though he had been an outspoken skeptic about such things at the beginning of his tenure with these assignments, Edwards had seen far too much by this point to doubt the existence of aliens, let alone the threat they represented.

And now here he was, looking into the face of an actual specimen.

Tracking the alien transmission had been a stroke of incredible luck, even if it had still left them with a sizable area to search. The Brooklyn Navy Yard, all but abandoned, provided a huge number of potential hiding places. They had been attempting to hone in on the signal when Edwards had spotted an explosion from one of the buildings along the waterfront. With nothing to lose after several fruitless hours of searching, it was their best lead of the day, and it had panned out in spectacular fashion.

Would you just look at this damned thing?

Though seemingly humanoid at first glance—as seemed to be the case with so many others they encountered—the differences in this alien's physiology were stark. Its pale yellow skin and hairless head gave it an odd, sickly appearance, at least to Wheeler. It wore a dark bodysuit that both served to highlight its human-like build while at the same time helping it to blend into the darkness that was broken now only by the helicopter's spotlight. As far as Wheeler could tell, this specimen was a female, accompanied by a male companion who currently was driving the boat.

"I don't think we've ever seen one like these," he said, looking over his shoulder to where Lieutenant Moreno stood hunched between Wheeler and Edwards. Behind the young Marine was Master Sergeant Dwayne Wallace, an older enlisted man who also was the helicopter's gunner, sitting behind the M60 machine gun mounted just inside the open hatch just aft of Edwards's seat on the craft's flight deck.

Moreno, wearing a helmet like the rest of the crew, shook his head. "Me neither, sir. I don't think anyone has."

Another triumph for Project Cygnus, Wheeler thought. While he had the support of General Vessey and therefore the rest of the Joint Chiefs of Staff, capturing live specimens of a newly encountered extraterrestrial race and being able to study and exploit whatever advanced technology they possessed was at the heart of the mission he had been given. It would serve as a harsh wake-up call for those who had expressed doubt about the worth of efforts like Cygnus, or who continued to live in ignorance of the very real danger hiding and living among them all.

If the aliens could be taken alive.

"Can we disable the boat without hurting them?" he asked.

Edwards replied, "If we can get them to slow down, then maybe, but there's no guarantees, Major."

"Let's give it a shot." Wheeler shifted in his seat, angling for a better look at the boat as the pilot guided the helicopter even closer to the water. For a few brief

seconds, he was reminded of his own time behind the
stick, flying low and fast over treetops and rivers before
deciding that there were challenges to be found elsewhere. He still felt the rush, though, and it was hard to
keep from smiling.

Such thoughts vanished right along with the boat
as it disappeared without warning from the spotlight's
beam.

"What the hell?" Wheeler twisted in his seat, trying
to track the boat even as Edwards was slowing the helicopter and beginning to turn it back the way they had
come. It was obvious that the boat had just decelerated,
using the cover of darkness to provide a few precious
seconds as the aliens aboard it made some desperate
bid at evasion.

Edwards completed the turn so that the helicopter
now faced up the East River leading back to the Navy
Yard, but the boat was not there. Using the controls
for the spotlight, Wheeler swept the beam from left
to right until he saw the wake trailing the boat as it
headed back the way it had come. Wheeler realized
what the aliens were planning.

"We've got to cut them off before they go ashore,"
he said, pointing through the windshield. "Otherwise,
we'll lose them."

Turning in his seat, Wheeler pointed to Master Sergeant Wallace. "Fire across their bow."

"Yes, sir," replied the gunner, adjusting his position
in his seat as Edwards banked the helicopter to give

Wallace a shot. The master sergeant let loose a string
of fire from the M60, every fifth round a tracer that
produced a bright orange streak that let Wheeler see
the shots plowing into the water ahead of the boat.
With Edwards continuing his approach, Wallace adjusted his aim to keep his fire ahead of the craft. With
the spotlight now once more capturing the boat in its
harsh glare, Wheeler could see the two figures moving
beneath the protective canopy, and then the female
turned to face him.

There was something in her hand.

Wheeler pointed toward the boat. "Pull up!"

The aircraft was moving low enough to the water and
at a sufficiently slow speed to make targeting it a simple
matter.

Drevina waited until Glorick decelerated the boat as
they approached the wooden-and-metal seawall before
firing her weapon. The single burst cast off a sphere
of intense light as the energy pulse spat forth, striking
the nose of the helicopter. The craft's response was immediate, its pilot attempting to maneuver it away from
danger as she fired again. This time the pulse slammed
into the helicopter's flank, and she could see its ar-
mored metal siding buckle from the impact. There was
a noticeable change in the pitch of the craft's engine,
and it seemed to wobble in midair as its pilot regained
control and guided it away.

The seawall was within reach as Glorick slowed the

boat and deactivated its engine. "Come," he said, reaching for his own weapon and moving to climb onto the wall. "We must keep moving."

With Glorick leading the way, they set off running away from the water. This area of the Navy Yard was all but deserted. No buildings here featured any internal light sources, with only a few dim lamps scattered the length of the nearby street making any attempt to ward off total darkness.

"Which way?" asked Glorick. "And what do we do about Canderon?"

Drevina had already been considering that part of the problem. They could not leave their friend behind, not now. With Ptaen hunters and now human agents pursuing them, the chances of being captured or killed was increasing by the moment. They already knew what would happen if the Ptaen found them, but what of these humans and their odd, obviously alien companions? Had she heard them correctly? Were they potential allies? As for those now giving chase in the helicopter, it was not difficult to surmise their intentions: capture, at any costs.

There also remained another, more pressing issue: the ship and the destruct protocol. Drevina could not allow that to happen, regardless of what happened to her, or Glorick and Canderon.

Then you have but a single course of action.

Taking a moment to survey her surroundings and orient herself according to the map she had memorized,

Drevina pointed toward a cluster of buildings to the west.

"That way."

It was time to end this.

"Wait, something's wrong."

Kirk scowled as he adjusted the tricorder's settings. Was the unit malfunctioning, or was he just reading the display wrong? His gut told him it had to be the latter.

"What is it?" asked Roberta Lincoln from where she sat behind the steering wheel of her car, guiding the vehicle down the Navy Yard's darkened streets.

"The Iramahl," he said. The readings were correct. "They've changed direction. They're no longer on the water. I think they're moving on foot." After first escaping the area in a boat they must have brought with them, the other two Iramahl now were back on land. Had they changed their minds? Were they worried about their companion, who was helping Spock and Mestral? That made sense, particularly with the Ptaen still in the area.

At least Kirk was sure they were still in the area. Unlike the Iramahl, he had been unable to track the Ptaen's location with the tricorder since leaving the Aegis building. Were they able to evade the scans somehow?

One thing at a time, Admiral.

Adjusting the tricorder's settings again, he said, "Three hundred yards west of our present position."

"Hang on." Lincoln stomped on one of the car's pedals, and Kirk braced himself against the dashboard as she spun the steering wheel to her left. The vehicle's speed dropped in dramatic fashion and its tires screeched in protest as Lincoln guided the car onto a side street. She hit the accelerator again, and the car jumped forward, its engine howling with power and purpose and its rumble echoing off the metal and brick facades of the abandoned buildings they passed. Kirk noted how she handled the vehicle with the confidence of an experienced driver well versed in the capabilities of the vehicle under her control. What had she called it back at the Aegis building? Her *baby*? Painted a bright red with a retractable black top, she called the car a Mustang. Manufactured nearly twenty years earlier and given to her by her father, the vehicle was subjected to meticulous care, which now was bearing fruit as the vehicle raced down the dark, empty streets.

"You're enjoying this, aren't you?" he asked, unable to resist despite the gravity of their current situation.

Her eyes on the road, Lincoln smiled. "I live in New York City. I never get to drive like this. Hell, I hardly ever get to drive at all."

"But you know how, right?"

Instead of replying, Lincoln made the car go faster.

Trying not to cower in the front seat as he braced himself against the dashboard, Kirk divided his attention between the tricorder and the road ahead of them, which to his critical eye looked to be suffering from neglect. Lincoln seemed unfazed by any of that, however, navigating the car around those potential hazards with deft precision.

"Haven't you ever driven a car, Admiral?"

Kirk frowned. "There's been some debate." Before he could clarify, the tricorder beeped in response to one of the prompts he had programmed it to provide. Looking at the road ahead, he saw a junction where the road intersected with another thoroughfare to the right. "Turn here."

"Got it."

Gripping the door handle as Lincoln executed the turn at speed, Kirk felt inertia pulling his body toward her at the same time the car's tires squealed on the pavement. She eased off the speed until the Mustang was at the turn's midpoint, then hit the accelerator again. The car's engine roared with new power.

"They're up here," Kirk said, his eyes on the tricorder. He pointed toward two large, abandoned buildings standing along the waterfront. Aside from the headlights on Lincoln's car, a lone streetlamp provided the only illumination. "They've stopped. Probably holding position and waiting to see what we're about."

Lincoln slowed the car, pulling it to one side of the road and extinguishing its headlights before turning off its engine. With his side window rolled down, Kirk was struck by the near silence of their surroundings. Aside from the sound of water lapping against the nearby sea-wall, the odd bell from a buoy somewhere in the East River, and insects, there was almost no other ambient sound.

No, Kirk realized. There was something else.

"What is that?" he asked, unable to identify the odd,

rhythmic thump that seemed distant and yet close at the same time.

Lincoln said, "Helicopter."

"Is that what we saw before?" Kirk had noted an odd, wingless aircraft flying fast and low over the water as they had made their way down the street running parallel to the waterfront. Then he reviewed the scan data collected by the tricorder during the past few minutes. "That's it. They must have been chasing the Iramahl."

"Sure, because why not?" asked Lincoln, though he could tell from her tone along with whatever else she muttered under her breath that she was not seeking an actual answer. Instead, she pushed open the door on her side and exited the car.

By the time Kirk got out, the sound from the helicopter seemed to be fading. No, he decided, that was not it. Instead, the aircraft's engine sounded as though it was powering down. Had the helicopter landed somewhere nearby?

Wonderful.

When his tricorder beeped again, Kirk glanced at its display, and for an instant the image on the unit's compact screen seemed to break up before refocusing itself.

"Something wrong?" asked Lincoln.

Eyeing the tricorder, Kirk frowned. "I'm not sure. For a second, it was acting like it was getting some kind of ghost or double reading, almost as if—"

He flinched at the sound of Lincoln's servo whining and a burst of energy erupting along the side of the warehouse building ten meters from the road. Only with the flash did Kirk see the figure hugging the wall, all but invisible with its dark clothing. Its black hair and violet skin identified the alien as a Ptaen. Lincoln's shot missed but not by much, the servo's energy bolt chewing into the side of the building now that she had upped the device's power level. The resulting blast sent brick and mortar shrapnel exploding in all directions. The Ptaen was cowering to protect itself, and it stood still long enough for Kirk to take aim with his phaser. His weapon's blue beam lanced across the open space, but the Ptaen somehow avoided the salvo. Then it was running again, using the darkness to its advantage as it plunged between two abandoned warehouses.

Searching the area for other threats, Kirk saw nothing. Then the dark retreated somewhat as Lincoln activated a silver flashlight she had taken from her car. She shined its beam along the nearby building, but Kirk saw nothing.

"Come on," he said, checking his tricorder again. "The Iramahl are close."

Kirk started jogging, Lincoln fell into step beside him, and they set off into the night.

Twenty-Nine

The cockpit was cramped, with just enough room to accommodate Spock, Mestral, and Canderon, but it pulsed with a power it had not known for more than a century.

"Access enabled," said Canderon from where he sat at one of the workstations facing away from the center of the confined chamber. The Iramahl had been working at a brisk pace since the three of them had boarded the vessel, and though his species did not appear to perspire, Spock was able to see the strain on the alien's face as he focused on the tasks before him. Canderon's long, thin fingers moved across the workstation's smooth surfaces with an assuredness that communicated his skill with the equipment, which Spock found remarkable given the amount of time that had passed. His efforts were being rewarded, as several of the consoles and displays around the cockpit had come to life and were beginning to communicate an array of information Spock only partially understood.

"Detonation in five minutes, twelve seconds," reported Mestral. "I am detecting no change in the destruct protocol."

"There will be no change," said Canderon, not turning from his console as he worked. "We will either deactivate it, or it will execute. The ship's intruder control efforts have removed all but the most extreme options that would normally be available to us."

Mestral said, "I find it interesting that we did not somehow accidentally trigger the protocol ourselves."

"Several of the oversight systems are compromised or inoperative," replied Canderon, "including most of the safety protocols. However, there are contingency processes in place, designed to prevent premature execution of the protocol when the system detects the presence of what it has determined are innocent parties. What I do not understand is how it did not interpret your attempts to infiltrate the computer system and disengage the protocol to be an attack. In theory, that is the sort of penetration it is designed to prevent."

"Then it is fortunate that part of the system is compromised," said Spock.

Canderon's hands paused above his workstation, and he turned to regard the Vulcan. "Yes, it is most fortunate."

"The happenstance will have more meaning if we are able to completely disable the protocol," said Mestral. "Detonation in four minutes, forty seconds."

"Are you always so precise in your measurements of time?" asked Canderon.

Mestral replied, "I endeavor to be accurate in all such measurements."

Returning to his work, Canderon said, "Neither of you is a human, and I am unfamiliar with your species."

"We are Vulcans," replied Spock, "though in point of fact, I am half human. My mother is from this world."

"How long have you been here?"

Mestral said, "I arrived here twenty-eight years ago. Like you, my ship crashed while my crew and I were surveying this world. I have been living in secret since then."

"The rest of your crew died in the crash?" asked Canderon.

"Our captain perished, but three of us survived. Two were rescued after a short time, but I elected to remain behind."

This made Canderon turn from his station. "You chose to stay here?"

"Yes. I wished to observe humans as they continue to advance both technologically and sociologically. So far, it has been a most interesting experience."

Canderon seemed to appreciate this. "I have similar thoughts about the time we have spent here. We have observed many great strides in technological advancement, but also far too much that is not to be celebrated. War, poverty, social injustice—these are many of the same issues that have plagued the Iramahl, even without Ptaen influence or subjugation. I have often wondered how my people have carried on in the time since we made our escape."

Spock exchanged glances with Mestral, who now was regarding him with a quizzical expression as though expecting him to contribute to the conversation. Before he could formulate a reply, an alert indicator sounded in the cockpit, and he pointed to his workstation. "I do not recognize this reading."

His statement was punctuated by a series of flashes and sparks erupting from a wall-mounted workstation module. Smoke seeped from around its edges, and Canderon pushed himself from his seat to press a control at an adjacent station. In response to his action, Spock heard a powerful vacuuming sound from behind the bulkhead, and the smoke and small licks of flame emanating from the damaged console receded. He next heard a fan activating within the wall itself.

"At least the fire-suppression systems are still functional," said the Iramahl. Turning, he moved to stand next to Spock and peered at the workstation monitor. "That overload was within a hub of our ship's network of optical data pathways. In this case, it was the hub transferring information from the central core to the ship's subordinate processes. The diagnostic routines have detected a fault in the optical data pathways leading to and from the hub, which is interfering with our ability to properly access the computer core and the data storage cells. I am unable to route the proper commands to the subprocessor overseeing the destruct protocol."

"Can we access the subprocessor directly?" asked Mestral.

"No. Any attempt to do so in its current condition would be interpreted as a hostile penetration of the system and immediately trigger the protocol.

Spock said, "Then we must repair the pathways."

"That would be an option if we had more time," replied Canderon. "With the interval remaining to us, it will not be possible."

His right eyebrow rising, Mestral asked, "You are saying the protocol cannot be avoided?"

His expression turning somber, the Iramahl shook his head. "I do not see how."

"There is a way," said Spock. "Abandon ship."

After ensuring that Canderon and Mestral evacuated ahead of him, Spock emerged from the Iramahl craft and moved to the worktable. On the desktop computer's monitor was a schematic of the ship, along with a clock he recognized as counting down the time until detonation, blinking with each passing second. Sitting on the monitor was Roberta Lincoln's green cube, the interface for the Beta 5.

"Computer," he said, "are you able to transport the craft from this location?"

"Affirmative, but doing so will trigger detonation upon arrival at its destination."

Canderon asked, "Why did you not just do this before, when the protocol was activated?"

"We feared doing so would trigger detonation," replied Spock. "From the beginning, we have been trying to preserve the craft."

Mestral said, "That appears to be academic, at this juncture."

"Agreed," replied Spock. "Computer, scan the surface coordinates of the Atlantic Ocean corresponding to the Laurentian Abyss. Verify that there is no shipping traffic in the immediate vicinity."

The Beta 5 said, *"Scanning. No indications of shipping vessels at that location."*

"Lock onto the craft and transport it there immediately. Place the ship at a depth of one hundred meters below sea level."

In response to his command, a high-pitched whine emitted as though from the air around them, and Spock looked up to see the first tendrils of a blue fog coalescing into existence around the Iramahl ship. Within seconds, the field had enveloped the craft, and Spock could feel its energy playing across his exposed skin. The whine of the transport beam escalated as the effect grew larger and more powerful, before the fog and the vessel it contained faded from the room.

"Computer," Spock said, "report from the site of transport."

On the desktop unit's monitor, a monochrome map was drawn in rapid fashion, and Spock recognized a portion of the east coast of the United States dominating the image's left side. The remainder of the screen was dominated by the ocean east of Nova Scotia. An icon near the boundary between land and ocean was blinking, with another, larger indicator flashing at a position in the water. The scale depicted in the map's lower right corner indicated a distance of five hundred miles between the two points.

"Transport complete," reported the Beta 5. *"Detonation occurred at coordinates forty-four degrees, zero*

minutes north, fifty-six degrees, zero minutes west, and at a depth of one hundred meters."

Despite custom and a life spent mastering his emotions, Spock permitted himself a small sigh of relief.

Looking at the empty space where his ship had sat mere moments earlier, Canderon said, "The technology needed to accomplish such a feat is astounding." He turned toward Spock and Mestral. "We have been here so long, it seems our people have forgotten us, or perhaps they no longer have need for us." The Iramahl offered a small smile as his gaze seemed to drift toward something in the distance that only he could see. "That actually would be satisfactory." Holding out his arms, he regarded the Vulcans. "Perhaps this world was meant to be our home, after all."

Spock replied, "On the contrary, your people still have great need of you. Where I come from, they have fought back against Ptaen oppression and are now a free people. However, they have never been able to replicate a response for the genetic condition the Iramahl continue to endure. You and your companions are their salvation, Canderon."

The alien's expression clouded with confusion. "Where you come from? I do not understand."

Nodding, Spock replied, "Yes, I know. As it happens, it is a rather lengthy yet fascinating story."

They were running out of options.

Crouching low and staying close to the side of the building, Drevina and Glorick used the darkness to mask their movements, watching and listening for signs of their pursuers, who seemed to multiply with each passing moment.

"Wait." Glorick's warning was almost inaudible, but Drevina did feel his hand on her arm and she stopped, holding her breath and listening. The military helicopter that had been pursuing them had left the immediate area, but she could still hear its engine somewhere in the vicinity, likely closer to the water, where there were fewer obstacles to landing. Her weapon had inflicted some damage to the craft, but Drevina suspected it was not serious. It was more likely the helicopter had landed so that its occupants could continue their pursuit on the ground.

"We need to keep moving," she said, casting a glance over her shoulder at Glorick. He was standing with his back pressed against the building's wall so that he could keep watch back the way they had come. The alley between this building and its neighbor at least prevented anyone from approaching from their flanks, but that did not rule out the possibility of them becoming trapped as pursuers blocked both ends of the passage. They could not remain here.

How many people were chasing them now, representing how many factions and interests? At least the Ptaen had a clear agenda, but Drevina could not be certain about any of the others. Even the humans, who had expressed an apparent desire to help her and the others, brought with them more questions than answers. How they had come into possession of the ship remained unexplained, as was their command of technology far beyond the capabilities she had observed from this society. The two males with the very much nonhuman ears were another mystery. Who were they? From where had they come to be here? Were they a potential ally to the Iramahl, or an enemy? They had not mistreated her and her companions, despite being on the defensive end of an assault on them.

What had the human male said, about having traveled a great distance to find them, and that he wanted to help her help her people? Did he somehow understand their plight, and the salvation she and her companions carried within them? How could he know? Despite the tense nature of the confrontation, a part of Drevina had felt compelled to believe and trust the human, but after all this time, was it still possible to find a true ally here?

Approaching the mouth of the alley, Drevina stopped, pressing herself against the wall and listening for signs of movement. Ahead of her was a thoroughfare, a road linking the numerous deserted buildings surrounding her. Other streets linked to this one, offering several avenues of possible escape, but only one mattered to her. From her vantage point, she could see the building housing their ship. From the outside, it looked as vacant as its neighbors, which Drevina now realized was by design. Its owners—whoever they were—had chosen ideal camouflage for their activities in this isolated, neglected area of an otherwise immense, thriving city. On foot, it would take her and Glorick several minutes to return to the building. Where was Canderon? Had he made his way back inside, and was he assisting the humans to disable the destruct protocol? How long until detonation? In the chaos of the pursuit, Drevina had lost track, but she knew that time had to be running short.

A flash between two buildings across the street caught her attention, and instinct made her squat closer to the ground and extend her weapon arm in that direction. Immediately recognizable was the report of the Ptaen weapon, but so too was the blue energy beam she saw piercing the darkness in response. The humans at the warehouse had wielded such weapons and now appeared to be engaging the hunters.

"Come," she said, rising from her crouch and sprinting across the road. With Glorick following behind her, she remained in the shadows and avoided the pools of weak illumination offered by the security lamps. Ahead of her, she heard more weapons fire as well as indistinguishable shouts of warning. The building they approached was a square, three-story construct, situated at a point where two streets intersected. Like many of the other buildings, its interior was dark and its exterior had fallen to neglect, with wood covering many of its windows while others remained open to the elements.

From behind that building emerged a figure, lithe and muscled and wearing a formfitting dark garment.

Its hair flowed freely around its head as it backpedaled, firing its weapon at a target Drevina could not see.

It was a Ptaen hunter.

The large green container on wheels carried a putrid smell, but Kirk ignored the offensive odors as it absorbed the brunt of the Ptaen's weapon. Another energy pulse slammed into the container, rocking it on its wheels and nearly toppling Kirk to the cracked asphalt, and he saw the gash sliced along its metal flank as the energy pulse tore through it.

Hunkering next to him, Roberta Lincoln flinched as sparks and bits of hot metal peppered her. "Okay, I'm getting really tired of this. I do not want to get killed hiding behind a dumpster."

They had almost walked into the Ptaen attack. Kirk, following the Iramahl life readings with his tricorder, had led Lincoln down a narrow passage between two dilapidated warehouses, straining to listen for the sounds of footsteps or other movement between the constant lapping of water against the nearby seawall. For a second time, the tricorder readings had become scrambled for a fleeting moment, which Kirk realized was some byproduct of whatever cloak or stealth field was employed by the Ptaen. The trouble with this revelation was that it was only helpful when they came within proximity to the seemingly invisible hunters.

As they just did.

Kirk looked for his tricorder, which he had dropped during the scramble for the dumpster. He could not see it within easy reach, and another round from the Ptaen energy weapon made him give up the search. Instead, he leaned around the dumpster—as Lincoln had called it—aiming his phaser at where he thought the shot had originated. He fired the weapon in a sweeping motion, hoping to catch one or more Ptaen with the beam, but he saw nothing.

These guys are good.

Another shot, from a different position, shattered the darkness and slammed into the dumpster, and this time Kirk did fall backward to the ground. Hearing footsteps to his left, he aimed his phaser while still lying on his side and fired, and this time he saw a figure skirting the circle of light provided by a lone lamp. Then another report crackled in the air, and the lamp's bulb shattered, casting the area into greater darkness. There was some visibility thanks to the ambient light cast off by the surrounding city, but there were far too many shadows in which to hide.

"Stay down," Lincoln snapped, using her free hand to hold him on the ground as she leveled her servo and fired once, then a second time. She then grumbled a rather vile Klingon oath under her breath before pushing herself to her feet. "Come on. We can't stay here."

"Where'd you learn to talk like that?" Kirk asked, rolling to a kneeling position before standing up.

"Ask me later." She was studying their current position. To the west was another alley separating a pair of delapidated brick buildings. Any thoughts that there might not be any innocent civilians to catch in a crossfire vanished when he saw a trio of men, dressed in worn, soiled clothing, jump through an open first-floor window of the closer building before stumbling and running away.

"Homeless people," said Lincoln. "Drifters, people down on their luck. I can't believe we haven't run into more of them."

"Maybe they're being smart and keeping their heads down." Kirk gestured toward the alley. "That way?"

Lincoln nodded. "Beats staying here."

As though agreeing with her, another salvo from a Ptaen weapon struck the wall behind her, prompting Kirk to grab her hand and dash for the alley, firing his phaser in a sweeping arc behind them as he moved. The tactic must have had at least some effect, because there were no more shots aimed at them before they reached the passage. The alley's entrance was consumed by shadow, and Lincoln aimed her servo ahead of them as though searching for potential targets. They reached the darkness and Kirk pressed himself against the wall, debating the merits of running inside one of the buildings for cover. He decided against it, considering he did not know where the other two Ptaen were and not wanting to be trapped if the hunters tried to approach from multiple directions.

"There," Lincoln said, her voice low as she aimed her servo out of the alley and across the street to where Kirk now saw a figure darting toward the dumpster.

Then another bolt of energy from his right made him flinch as it drilled into the green metal container with enough force to push it several meters to one side. The Ptaen using it for cover scrambled out of sight, just before Kirk felt a hand on his shoulder. Whirling around phaser up, he found himself staring into the face of the Iramahl female. She held her hands away from her body, her weapon aimed in the air.

"Come with me."

As they started to move deeper into the alley, Kirk heard something new. It was a whine, faint but growing louder. At first, he thought it was another aircraft, but his gut told him that could not be correct.

"That is a Ptaen ship," said the Iramahl. "It is coming for us."

Thirty

Rijal felt his irritation growing with each passing moment. The situation was evolving beyond his grasp. It was useless now to question how or why it had had happened. His only concern was to halt this descent toward chaos and reassert control. The humans who had involved themselves were not a concern. Bystanders were not an issue. Only the Iramahl mattered.

"The ship is on approach," said Noceri, who carried the scanning unit. "It will be here momentarily."

Even as he nodded in acknowledgment, Rijal could hear the soft whine of the scout craft's engine growing ever louder as his apprentice used remote guidance to bring it there.

"Good," he said, gesturing for Noceri to follow him. The humans and at least one of the Iramahl had chosen this darkened passage in their latest attempt to flee, but Rijal was beginning to understand the area's topography. The water ahead limited the options for escape, as did a nearby collection of buildings. Upon exiting the passage at its far end, his quarry would have fewer options from which to choose. He had anticipated this maneuver.

Keying the communications node affixed near the auditory canal on the side of his head, he said, "Bnara, are you ready?"

"*Yes, Rijal,*" replied his fellow hunter, her voice clear and distinct as it filtered through the node's receiver. "*They are coming.*"

Rijal increased his pace, feeling his blood surging within him as he ran. Behind him, he heard the sounds of Noceri's breathing as the apprentice maintained stride. They already had traversed the alley to its midpoint and were gaining on their quarry.

This had always been the part of the hunt he had most enjoyed: the moment of anticipation as he closed in for the final confrontation, feeding off the energy of his prey as they began to realize there was no escape, and no alternative but to turn and fight. It was in such moments that a hunter's true skill and spirit were tested to their fullest. Though the Iramahl had not made the most formidable opponents, they had taxed him far longer than many he had been sent to hunt. What they lacked in strength they had more than compensated for with ingenuity and guile, and that earned them some measure of respect from him. While he was duty-bound to return them home in accordance with his directives, Rijal hoped they might decide to pose one final challenge once it became obvious there remained nothing to be lost.

Dim illumination was visible ahead, at the alley's end, and Rijal saw three figures silhouetted against that light for just a moment before they dodged to one side as though remembering to use the darkness as a shield. He almost attempted another shot, but opted not to give away his position just yet.

Patience, he reminded himself. *Always patience. Let the prey commit the error.*

A beam of blue energy lanced outward from the darkness. Rijal recognized it as coming from whatever weapon one of the humans was carrying. A shout of alarm accompanied it, and then all three figures, one of which could only be the female Iramahl fugitive, sprinted across the lit area at the alley's mouth and out of sight. Then he heard a more familiar report from another weapon, Bnara's. Rijal knew she was waiting for the Iramahl, but was perhaps unprepared for their actions upon emerging from the alley.

More weapons fire erupted beyond the alley as Rijal emerged from the darkness in time to see the two humans using their mysterious weapons against an elevated target along one of the buildings. Rijal saw that Bnara had perched herself on a metal balcony suspended before an open window and now was firing toward the ground. The humans and the female Iramahl had taken up position behind a large, multiwheeled ground vehicle that appeared long abandoned. Bnara's tactic had worked, and now their quarry was trapped between them, as evidenced when first the female Iramahl and then the human male fell to her weapon.

Beams of light swept across the ground, and Rijal looked up to see their scout craft moving into view, slowing to a hover over the area above the skirmish. It was small enough that it could land here between the buildings, offering Rijal and the other hunters all they needed to take the fugitives into custody.

"Noceri!" he shouted, turning to see that his apprentice was still guiding the ship. "Proceed with the landing!"

An energy burst flashed to his right and Rijal turned in that direction in time to see another of the Iramahl firing his weapon. The salvo sailed past Rijal, but he heard a grunt of shock as the bolt struck Noceri. His apprentice stumbled and fell against the side of the building, stunned from the attack, but Rijal's attention was focused on the new threat. He fired back, striking the Iramahl in the leg and spinning him around. The fugitive fell to the ground, his weapon dropping from his hand and bouncing out of reach. Though injured, the Iramahl was trying to regain his feet, and Rijal closed the distance. With his free hand, he grabbed his quarry's arm.

"This is over," he said, forcing the words between gritted teeth.

Instead of replying, the Iramahl lashed out, striking Rijal's other arm and knocking away the weapon. Rijal reacted without hesitation, slashing across the Iramahl's face with the edge of his hand. The fugitive weathered the attack and tried to fight back, only one of his punches connecting as Rijal's superior skill kept him at bay. Rijal felt the Iramahl grab a handful of his hair and pull his head closer, and then searing pain shot through his face as his opponent's teeth sank into his skin.

Roaring with pain and fury, Rijal responded with a lifetime of training and instinct. His hands gripped both sides of the Iramahl's head and twisted with such force that the snapping of bone echoed off the nearby buildings.

"Glorick!"

Ignoring the cry of distraught grief behind him, Rijal released the Iramahl's head and allowed the limp body to fall to the ground, where it collapsed in an unmoving, lifeless heap.

Only then did Rijal see the human standing before him, carrying a large weapon in both hands and aiming it at his chest.

Not quite sure he could believe his eyes, Daniel Wheeler stood in mute horror as one alien broke the other alien's neck.

Following the sounds of the fighting had been easy. With the helicopter damaged and both its gunner and Lieutenant Moreno injured during its emergency landing, Wheeler had left the pilot, Captain Edwards, to tend to the wounded while he set off in pursuit of the aliens. Not for the first time, he had cursed himself for not thinking to bring a larger team with him. What had begun as an uneventful survey of the Navy Yard in an attempt to track the alien ship's transmission had unraveled within the space of moments, first with the boat chase and then the aliens damaging the helicopter with their strange weapon. Now those aliens were here, fighting other aliens as well as what at least appeared to be a pair of humans, and Wheeler had just witnessed one murdering the other, and all of it illuminated by the spotlights shining down from a hovering alien spaceship.

No one's ever going to believe this.

A flash of energy ripped into the concrete near his feet and Wheeler flinched, ducking to his right. The shot had come from somewhere above the ground, and then he saw the figure standing on the fire escape of a building forty yards away. From this distance and beyond the light cast off by the alien ship, the shooter was more shadow than substance, but Wheeler could see it crouching against the balcony's railing, angling for another shot.

Dropping to one knee, Wheeler pulled the Heckler & Koch MP5 to his shoulder, sighting and pulling the trigger in one fluid, practiced motion. The submachine gun unleashed a torrent of nine-millimeter rounds that raked the balcony, at least five of those first ten shots finding their target. The body slumped forward and over the railing, falling to the ground.

"No!"

The alien Wheeler had seen killing the other with its bare hands roared in unchecked rage before charging him. At the same time, a third one who had been leaning against the wall staggered away from the building, holding in its hand what could only be a weapon. Wheeler pushed himself to his feet, backpedaling at the same time he heard the whines of other energy weapons piercing and illuminating the darkness.

Reacting to the immediate threat, Wheeler adjusted his aim and fired the H&K at the rushing alien from a distance of less than ten feet. The weapon barked and the alien's body absorbed the salvo, its momentum continuing to carry it forward. Wheeler was able to side-step his attacker, just avoiding being bulldozed to the concrete. Seeing movement in his peripheral vision, he twisted in that direction in time to see the third alien aiming its weapon at him. Though he tried to swing the H&K in that direction, Wheeler knew he would never make it.

Damn.

Then energy howled one more time, and the alien's body went rigid as something struck it in the back. Its body twitched in response to the attack before it seemed to lose all control and dropped face-first to the ground.

"I didn't want to do that," said Roberta Lincoln, her voice taut.

His left arm was on fire, but Kirk did his best to ignore the pain as he divided his attention between the Ptaen ship that had settled to a landing less than thirty meters away, the dead Ptaen lying on the ground between him and the ship, and Lincoln. Pushing himself to one knee, he reached for her arm. Tears were welling up in her eyes as she tried to cope with what she had been forced to do.

"I know," he said, gently squeezing her arm. "But you did what was necessary."

Lincoln shook her head. "No, you don't understand. We *don't* kill. We're not *supposed* to kill. Seven, he's been adamant about that from the beginning. That's not our job. We're supposed to be *helping* people here."

"You were left with no choice," said the female Iramahl. Like Kirk, she was injured and he noted the pain in her face. A burn darkened her left side, though Kirk saw no blood. "You saved our lives. There is no shame in that act."

Pushing himself to his feet, Kirk was about to add something in the hopes of comforting Lincoln when a new sound began to echo around them. He turned toward the Ptaen ship and watched as a blue mist formed around it, growing larger and more solid for several seconds before the odd cloud and the ship disappeared.

A moment later, there was a beeping from inside his jacket, and despite the pain in his arm, he smiled and retrieved his communicator.

"Kirk here."

"*Spock here, Admiral. You'll be pleased to know that the Iramahl ship is no longer a concern, and that we've taken possession of the Ptaen scout craft and moved it to our location. Mestral is assisting our Iramahl friend with deactivating it.*"

"Iramahl friend? When did that happen?"

"Canderon," said the female Iramahl. "I sent him to help deactivate our ship's destruct protocol. I am pleased to hear he was successful."

Kirk grunted. "That makes two of us." To the communicator he said, "Well done, Spock."

"*We are becoming most adept at utilizing the technology at Mister Seven and Miss Lincoln's disposal, Admiral. It's unfortunate that we cannot remain here longer, so that I might better understand it.*"

Hearing this, Lincoln's expression softened. She did not smile, but there was a definite easing of the turmoil she was experiencing. "You're a natural, Mister Spock."

With luck, Kirk hoped, they would only need to avail themselves of that technology one more time. Then he winced as new pain shot through his arm.

Okay. Two more times.

"We've got injuries here, Spock. Myself and . . . ?" He looked to the female Iramahl.

"Drevina," she said.

"*Acknowledged,*" replied the Vulcan. "*Assuming your injuries are not life threatening, we should be able to treat them here.*"

"Maybe then somebody can tell me what the hell is going on."

Looking up, Kirk saw the human military officer, dressed in a camouflage uniform and staring at them with intense interest. He carried a rifle, though Kirk noted that its muzzle was pointed at the ground as it hung from a sling on his shoulder. A tag above the man's shirt pocket read WHEELER.

"We can explain everything, Major," said Lincoln, and Kirk heard a quiet tone as she raised her hand and aimed her servo at Wheeler. Before the man could respond, she triggered the device and his body stiffened before all emotion drained from his face.

Lincoln shook her head, releasing an exasperated sigh as she regarded the stunned major. "Because the day just wasn't complicated enough already."

Kirk could not help a small chuckle. "I suppose it's not the nicest way to thank him for saving our lives."

"I'll apologize to him later." Rising to her feet, she extended her hand to Kirk. "Come on. Let's get that arm looked at."

His attention now on Drevina, Kirk said, "Right. We're not quite finished with all of this, are we?"

The female Iramahl regarded him with curiosity. "I am afraid I do not understand."

Kirk smiled. "Don't worry. Everything will make sense soon." Then he shrugged, an action that made his arm ache. "At least, it'll make a sort of sense."

Thirty-One

San Francisco, Earth
Earth Year 2283

Even though Heihachiro Nogura appeared calm and collected, Kirk could see the annoyance lurking beneath the admiral's veneer of civility.

Yeah, there's definitely a yardarm in my future.

"Admiral," said Jepolin as she stood before Nogura, "on behalf of all Iramahl, I cannot thank you enough for your assistance. The brave, selfless actions of your officers have given my people new hope. We are in your eternal debt."

Nogura gestured past the envoy to where Kirk stood alongside Spock and McCoy, as well as Drevina and Canderon. "The credit belongs to Admiral Kirk, Captain Spock, and Doctor McCoy. They are three of our finest officers."

Oh, he's going to keelhaul me for sure.

The thought made him aware of the low throb that was the lingering effect of the injury he had sustained from the Ptaen weapon. Spock had tended to their wounds once everyone had regrouped at the Aegis building, after which preparations were made to return to the twenty-third century.

Maybe we should've stayed back there.

Straightening his posture as Jepolin turned to him, Kirk offered a formal nod. "The honor to serve was ours, madam, but we didn't act alone. If not for our friends, none of this would have been possible." He held out a hand and indicated the other two guests in Nogura's office, Gary Seven and Roberta Lincoln, who had used the technology at their disposal to return Kirk and Spock along with the Iramahl refugees to the twenty-third century. Standing near the windows overlooking San Francisco Bay, Seven was dressed in a black business suit of the sort he had worn the first time Kirk met him, whereas Miss Lincoln sported a fashionable blue skirt and jacket over a white silk blouse.

For his part, Seven looked just a few years older than when Kirk had first encountered him nearly two decades earlier. This, despite the fact that Seven as an older man had visited him years ago, after that initial meeting. The complexities and contradictions of time travel along with the frenzied collision of past, present, and future would be something Kirk never fully understood.

You should probably stop trying to think about it so hard. You're going to blow a warp coil.

Seven, holding his black cat, Isis, said, "My associate, Miss Lincoln, deserves the congratulations, Envoy Jepolin. Due to a number of unusual circumstances taking place in our own time, she's been forced to take on a great deal of additional responsibility in my absence when I'm called away for various . . . assignments."

Recalling what he knew about Seven and Lincoln's activities during the 1980s and 1990s, Kirk suspected Seven was being deliberately modest, even coy with respect to their work on Earth. They would never get the credit they deserved for the trials they faced as they helped to guide humanity toward a more prosperous future.

"Only through her initiative, resourcefulness, and perseverance was any of this possible," continued Seven. "She also enlisted the assistance of Mister Mestral, who's been something of a guest on our planet for some time." Though he had been tempted to accompany the group through time to the twenty-third century, Mestral instead had elected to remain in 1985, deciding it best that he not receive too much knowledge about the future of humans on Earth.

Seven turned to regard Lincoln. "Though some of her methods were a bit unorthodox, and I know she was forced to do something she would rather have avoided, I've come to understand that in our line of work, even distasteful actions are sometimes necessary." To Lincoln, he said, "I'm proud of you, Roberta."

Lincoln's face flushed. "Thank you. I don't know what to say."

Though she offered nothing else, Kirk could see she had not yet come to grips with having to kill the Ptaen hunter. It would, he knew, haunt her for a time, if not for the rest of her life.

"We also would like to reiterate our thanks to Miss Lincoln," said Drevina, "and Admiral Kirk, Captain Spock, and Doctor McCoy. I must admit that I am still struggling to understand all that has happened and how we have come to be here." She paused, and Kirk watched her gaze fall to the carpet for a moment before she added, "When we left Yirteshna so long ago, we knew we were leaving behind loved ones we likely would never see again. Still, to know that so much time has passed is a bit unnerving." She lifted her head and looked to Kirk. "But to know we still have purpose is gratifying. My only sadness is that Glorick, Lvonek, and Mranzal are not here to share this with us."

Jepolin said, "You will be welcomed as the heroes you are, Drevina. Both of you, as well as your comrades who died on Earth, will receive every honor we can provide. It is the least we can do for the saviors of our civilization."

Looking to McCoy, Drevina said, "Doctor, I am told you have found something that can make our cure even more effective than we originally imagined."

Not one for official gatherings of any sort, McCoy cleared his throat and shifted his feet, offering sidelong glances to Kirk and Spock before replying, "Yes, that's right. Doctor Chapel and I discovered an interesting commonality between your DNA and a portion of Klingon genetic code that was affected by a virus they battled more than a century ago. It was really Doctor

Chapel who made the connection. We think that once we're able to re-create the solution from all those years ago, applying this enhancement will accelerate the restorative process."

Nogura said, "In fact, Doctor Chapel has volunteered to head up a Starfleet Medical team that will travel to Yirteshna to aid in the development of this new version of the regimen. I've already approved the orders for her temporary duty assignment, and she's organizing her team and equipment as we speak." His expression softened into a broad grin. "I don't mind saying that I rather enjoyed informing the Klingon ambassador about this. Apparently, the Empire and the Ptaen have been getting quite chummy, so you can imagine this little development is rather awkward for both sides. As though the Klingons needed another reason to dislike us."

"You're welcome," said McCoy.

"What of the Ptaen?" asked Canderon. "I do not believe they have so readily accepted what has happened."

Stepping forward and continuing to stroke his cat, Seven said, "Part of that is likely our fault, Admiral Nogura. Once the situation with the Ptaen was resolved in our time, we reprogrammed their ship to return to their home planet. We also included a message in its computer saying that the Iramahl were no longer on Earth." He shrugged. "Technically, it wasn't a lie, but I imagine the Ptaen government won't be amused if they ever learn the details of this little caper."

Canderon asked, "But how will you explain this?

Our being here, centuries after we were thought to have left the planet or died?"

"I can't speak for anyone else," replied Nogura, "but I don't plan on bringing it up. I'd just as soon not get into a discussion about time travel. There may not be enough liquor on this planet to make me want to start a conversation about that." Moving away from his desk, he regarded the two former fugitives. "Not that it really matters. There's nothing they can do about it anymore."

Jepolin said, "The admiral is correct, Drevina. Much has happened since you left our home. The rebellion you helped spread was compelled to carry on in your absence, particularly when it was learned you had found a cure for the genetic affliction the Ptaen had imposed upon us. Driven by the example you set for all our people, the Iramahl continued to stand and fight, to harass and push back, to resist and ultimately break the will of our oppressors. They did it because you gave them something to fight for beyond simple freedom, which by itself is absolutely worth defending. You also gave them hope that we would reclaim everything the Ptaen took from us, denied us, and indeed used against us: our very existence." She held out her hands to them. "You have given us our future."

Farewells were exchanged, at which time Nogura summoned the escort detail from the Federation Diplomatic Corps that had been waiting outside his office. There would be at least a few more meetings, Kirk knew, before the Iramahl departed for their homeworld.

"Admiral Kirk," Drevina said as she stopped before him on her way out of the office. "Captain Spock. Thank you again. I hope this is not our last meeting."

"I hope so too," replied Kirk, taking her extended hands in his own. "Good luck to you and your people."

Drevina glanced at McCoy. "With the talents of people like you, I do not see how we could fail."

Once the Iramahl were gone and his door once more sealed, Nogura turned to his remaining guests. "This is normally the part where I initiate court-martial proceedings." He eyed Seven and Lincoln. "Not that there's anything I can do about you two, of course."

"I take full responsibility for everything that happened, sir," said Kirk.

"Damned right you do." Nogura began to pace his office. "Time travel. You know, once we found out we could do something like that, I swore I'd never get involved with it, for any reason." He shook his head. "As you can see, that's working out well for me." He stopped pacing as he came abreast of Kirk. "I'd ask you if you had any idea the risks you were taking when you decided to attempt this ridiculous stunt, but I already have the answer to that question."

Here we go, Kirk thought.

Nogura sighed. "Did you know the Department of Temporal Investigations has a file on you bigger than your Starfleet personnel record? They're thinking about starting up a special section just to deal with all of the trouble you cause them. I'm not sure, but I think you may even have your own code name. 'Clock Wrecker,' or some such damned thing. I don't know if that's true, but it's a rumor I can get behind."

His previous encounters over the years with their representatives were enough to tell Kirk that the Federation agency had taken a keen interest in the *Enterprise* and him specifically. That much was understandable, he conceded, given the number of times he had been involved in temporal incidents. He suspected that at least a few people within that organization had lost significant amounts of sleep wondering and worrying about what he might do—or undo—during such events.

Can you really blame them? You give them ulcers.

"Admiral, if I may," said Spock. "From the beginning, Admiral Kirk and I took steps to minimize our involvement in historical events. Even when Miss Lincoln decided she needed our assistance in the twentieth century, we did everything possible to mitigate our presence in the past."

"Look," said McCoy, and Kirk could tell from the single word that his friend had already reached his limit for tolerating Starfleet bureaucracy. "If Jim thought this was the only way to help the Iramahl, then it was the only way, and it was the best way. And you know he didn't do it without weighing the consequences, either for the mission or himself. That he knew he'd get into hot water and went anyway should tell you something." He punctuated the statement with a snort. "You'd think Starfleet would know this by now."

"Bones," said Kirk, his tone one of warning.

His eyes narrowing, Nogura shifted his gaze to regard McCoy. "Doctor, I'm quite familiar with your reputation for eschewing authority."

"I've worked very hard to nurture that reputation."

"Perhaps you've never been aware of my feelings on such things."

McCoy scowled. "With all due respect, Admiral, if you're familiar with my reputation, then you already know my response to that."

"Fair point." As quickly as Nogura's annoyance appeared, it faded.

"Admiral," said Lincoln, "their involvement is my fault. I made the decision to bring them back with me." Her expression was one of apology. "In our line of work, there aren't a lot of people we can call on for help. It's not the sort of job where you can just run an ad in the classifieds." When her comment evoked stares of incomprehension from the Starfleet officers, she waved a hand as though to dismiss what she had said. "Anyway, you'll be happy to know that we've decided to take some steps to address that, at least on a very limited basis."

Kirk nodded in understanding. "You mean Major Wheeler."

"Right. Though we're not going to tell him everything, we'll give him enough to know we're on the level."

Nogura asked, "What did you tell him about the Iramahl ship?"

"That it was lost while attempting to leave Earth,"

replied Seven. "As for its actual fate, Mister Spock chose well when selecting the Laurentian Abyss. Even though the explosion all but disintegrated the ship, whatever survived will never be found. It's one of the least accessible places on the planet. The Russians apparently lost a nuclear submarine there last year, and even we couldn't find it." He paused, adopting a wistful expression. "A year ago from mine and Miss Lincoln's point of view, of course."

Holding up a hand, Nogura said, "Don't even get me started on that."

"As for Major Wheeler," continued Lincoln, "considering his unique position within the government and the military, he and his Project Cygnus team are in the perfect position to help us if we ever have to deal with extraterrestrials again."

"Does that mean you're not going to make a habit of absconding with my officers to go gallivanting through time?" asked Nogura.

With a fleeting look toward Lincoln, Seven replied, "We can at least try to minimize the need for such extreme measures."

"I guess that'll have to do."

Still stroking Isis, Seven said, "And I think that's our cue." He nodded to Lincoln, who reached into her jacket to retrieve her servo. "Gentlemen, it's been a pleasure."

Lincoln activated her servo, and the door to Nogura's office opened to reveal the familiar blue fog of Seven's transport beam. Along with Isis, Seven and Lincoln moved toward it.

"Live long and prosper, Mister Seven and Miss Lincoln," said Spock, holding up his right hand and offering the traditional Vulcan salute. "And you as well, Isis."

"Until we meet again," replied Seven with the faintest hint of a smile on his lips, before he and Lincoln disappeared into the shimmering blue mist, which vanished a moment later.

After they were gone, Nogura turned his attention back to Kirk. After a moment, he released an exasperated breath. "You three could drive a man to drink. Do you know that?"

"Is that an offer?" asked McCoy.

Ignoring the comment, the admiral moved toward his desk. "Don't misunderstand me, gentlemen; I'm grateful for what you did. Your actions may very well save an entire civilization and gain us a new ally. That's probably worth a commendation or two." He eyed Spock. "Don't you have a starship and a class of cadets to deal with, Captain?"

The Vulcan nodded. "Indeed I do, Admiral." He glanced to Kirk. "Though I must admit that this was an interesting diversion."

"And you," said Nogura, pointing at Kirk. "You missed one of your scheduled lectures. I've already informed Commandant Rouviere to expect you no less than four times this month. Plan accordingly."

Knowing better than to protest, Kirk forced himself not to smile. "Understood, sir. I look forward to speaking with our cadets."

"I'll bet you do." Nogura stood in silence for another

moment, then shook his head. "And in the future, if you three could keep your antics to your own century, I'd appreciate it."

"Works for me," replied McCoy.

"A reasonable request," said Spock.

Kirk nodded in agreement. "We'll certainly do our best, Admiral."

That seemed to satisfy the admiral, at least for the moment. "Good," he said. "Then let's have that drink."

ONE LAST THING

Thirty-Two

New York City
June 25, 1986

There were times Roberta Lincoln loathed the Beta 5.

Such feelings often, but not always, manifested themselves early in the morning, when the computer deigned to summon her before she had enjoyed her first cup of coffee. On those occasions, she imagined herself taking a sledgehammer to the advanced construct's polished obsidian control console and reveling in the resulting devastation.

Then there were times like these, when the call came just as she was contemplating a glass of wine and a hot bath.

"We've got to stop meeting like this," Roberta said, emerging from the concealed doorway that connected Gary Seven's well-appointed office with her own apartment. "People are going to start talking. Besides, just because I'm twenty feet away doesn't mean you can call me whenever you get a glitch in one of your files." One of the first things Seven had done upon recruiting her to work with him was provide her with a new place to live, liberating her from the shoebox she had called her old apartment in the Village. While her accommodations were quite practical as far as being available in the event something urgent came up and required her attention, it also meant she was all but at the beck and call of Seven as well as the Beta 5. Whereas Seven himself preferred to exercise restraint when it came to imposing upon her after whatever passed for "normal business hours" in their rather odd line of work, the Beta 5 had no such compunctions.

The computer, which had already revealed itself from its hidden wall alcove as Roberta crossed the office toward it, appeared content to ignore her remarks and instead reported, *"Scanners have detected the presence of an unidentified space vessel entering high orbit."*

"Unidentified?" Roberta frowned. "You're sure it's not the Russians? They've been pretty busy lately." Even as the United States manned spaceflight program had come to a halt following the tragic loss of the Space Shuttle *Challenger*, its Soviet counterpart was proceeding ahead at full speed. There already had been several launches earlier in the year to their *Salyut-7* space station as well as sending up the first component of what would become that orbital facility's replacement, *Mir*. Further missions were planned in the coming years in order to complete the new station's construction. Designed for continuous habitation and long-term research, *Mir* would be the largest manmade object outside the Earth's atmosphere.

Not quite a moon base, but we're getting there.

The Beta 5 said, *"Spacecraft is not of human origin. Scans indicate it is a Klingon vessel."*

"What?" While Roberta knew what a Klingon was, and had even seen one or two of their ships over the years, those incidents had taken place well away from Earth, in more ways than one. There also was the fact that first contact between humans and the Klingon Empire was not due to occur for another two hundred years. "A Klingon ship, here? Why would Klingons be here now?"

"Purpose unknown." The computer paused, as was its habit when it was collating and analyzing data newly received through its array of scanners and receivers. The only outward indication of this work in progress was the flashing of indicators on the flat black panel housing its display screens. *"Vessel configuration is consistent with design utilized during mid-twenty-second and twenty-third centuries."*

Roberta studied a wire-frame schematic of the Klingon ship as depicted by the Beta 5, noting that the vessel was of a smaller scout-class design, intended for operation by a limited crew. "Are you saying it traveled through time to get here? Since when do the Klingons know anything about time travel?" Realizing the double meaning of her question, she rolled her eyes. "Never mind. How'd it get here?"

"Unknown. Review of its trajectory indicates a course from the vicinity of the sun in order to arrive at Earth."

Now that, at least, sounded familiar, Roberta decided. As Gary Seven had explained it to her, accelerating at faster-than-light velocities toward a star and then breaking away from the star's gravitational pull at the precise moment was one known method for traveling through time. It was, however, a crude method and one fraught with any number of risks. The calculations required to achieve the proper course and speed while factoring the mass of the ship attempting the maneuver required pinpoint precision. While she held no doubts that Seven himself could accomplish such a feat, even he would need the assistance of the Beta 5 to ensure total accuracy. As far as Roberta knew, only one other person had ever arrived at the correct formula, and he most certainly was not Klingon.

"Scan the ship for life signs."

The Beta 5 chewed on that for a moment before replying, "*Seven life-forms: six human, one Vulcan.*"

"You have *got* to be kidding me." Realizing she had given voice to the errant thought, Roberta asked, "What's the ship doing now?"

"Ship has entered standard orbit. Though it has activated a cloaking device, I am able to track the field's energy distortion."

Kirk. It has to be.

A *twenty-third*-century Klingon vessel with a Vulcan among its handful of passengers, traveling through time to Earth? Only James T. Kirk would be so brash as to undertake such a bold action, but why? What had brought him back to the twentieth century yet again? Roberta reminded herself that there was, of course, another potential wrinkle, in that she did not yet know from what precise point in time Kirk—if indeed it was Kirk—had traveled. Was it a younger Kirk, who had not yet met her and Gary Seven? Perhaps he was far older than the last time Roberta had seen him. If time travel possessed any single point of consistency, it was an ability to induce headaches in anyone who dared think too much about the concept. Like her, for example.

It had only been a year or so since she had last seen Kirk, and how many times had they crossed paths since their first meeting? It seemed ridiculous that she would have so many encounters with a man who hailed from three hundred years in her future, but in point of fact it was but one of the more normal aspects of her job.

Even discounting the occasions when Roberta or Gary Seven had called upon the intrepid captain's assistance, the man still managed to find a rather troubling number of methods and reasons to return to the twentieth century. Still, she knew that Kirk, perhaps more so than most people from his century and certainly anyone from hers, understood all too well the risks associated with time travel. If he was here after traveling nearly three hundred years into his own past, then he had done so for good cause. As for whether anyone else agreed that such a motive was valid, either here in 1986 or from whichever year Kirk had traveled? That remained in question. If it *was* Kirk who now orbited Earth, then the fact that he had come not with his own vessel but instead a Klingon ship seemed to imply a very peculiar set of circumstances.

Realizing she was tapping her fingernails on the Beta 5's console, Roberta asked, "When's Gary due back?"

"*Supervisor 194 is on assignment in Bhopal. He has*

not communicated any change in his itinerary. He is due to return by zero nine hundred hours tomorrow."

"Yeah, I think we need to call him back early."

"Recalling Supervisor 194 at this point may jeopardize his current mission. He is pursuing a high-value target."

"I know, but he's going to want to hear about this. If he decides to send me on my own to check it out, so be it. I promised him no more time-travel shenanigans without warning him first."

Seven had traveled to India in order to obtain fresh information on the whereabouts of one of the numerous people whose movements he and Roberta were monitoring. The subject in question had a rather annoying habit of evading most attempts at tracking him. This left Seven with no choice but to conduct his own onsite reconnoitering of the individual's last known location. Though he preferred to let the Beta 5 gather and collate relevant data on targets deserving of such continuous scrutiny, there were times when direct action was required. Such was the case with a number of persons who had earned special notice in the files kept by Gary Seven and his amazing though not all-knowing supercomputer.

I could write a book about the trouble some of these people have given us. Maybe two.

The Beta 5's displays and other indicators were continuing to stream a litany of information, and after another moment it said, *"Miss Lincoln, my scanners detect a change in orbiting vessel's status. It appears to be aligning for a descent through planetary atmosphere."*

"It's landing? Where?"

"Current trajectory suggests a landing point some-where along the west coast of the United States."

"Is there any sign the ship's been detected? Military or civilian satellites? Anything?"

"Scanning. Indications negative at this time."

Roberta blew out her breath. "I guess that's some-thing. The last thing we need tonight is us or the Rus-sians deciding they're under attack and to start launching missiles."

"Update on ship's current status. Predicted landing point is somewhere in or near San Francisco."

That was enough, she decided. Even without Seven, she could at least transport out to California and ob-serve the activities of the ship and its crew. At this point, Roberta was hoping it *was* just Kirk and his crew. Of course, from what she recalled of her previous visits to San Francisco, it was possible that Klingons wandering the streets might not even attract much in the way of attention.

"Track it to its landing point," she directed, "and relay those coordinates to Seven, and tell him I'm going ahead to check it out."

"What are your intentions, Miss Lincoln?"

Roberta shrugged. "For the moment, I just want to see what's going on. We'll take it from there." If it was James Kirk, then she wanted to be there in case he got himself into trouble while doing whatever it was that had brought him to twentieth-century San Francisco.

Of course, trouble has a way of finding Kirk, doesn't it?

ONE MORE THING
AFTER THAT

Thirty-Three

"Good morning, General."

The air force sergeant's crisp salute greeted Brigadier General Daniel Wheeler as the elevator doors parted, and he stepped from the car into the foyer. Standing alone and at attention behind a dull-gray metal desk, the sentry rendered the proper military greeting. Atop the desk were a pair of notebooks as well as what Wheeler took to be a textbook of some kind, along with a coffee cup. He also recognized the cover of a popular techno-thriller paperback novel resting beside the other clutter, of the sort sold in the bookstore several floors above where he now stood.

The anteroom was an uninviting affair, with the desk and its matching chair the sole furnishings save for the arrangement of flags posted on stands along the far wall and flanking a large bronze plaque bearing the official Pentagon seal. Aside from the plaque, there was no other indication as to Wheeler's present location. There was not even a clock, which was a good thing, as it spared him from being reminded of the ungodly hour at which he had been summoned to this most furtive of locations. Indeed, neither this room nor any attached appeared on any list or diagram available to anyone outside a very small, tight circle of personnel. Even the floor these rooms occupied, B14, did not officially exist. Fourteen stories below the Pentagon's ground level, it was accessible via four elevators—two each for passengers and freight—which also were closely guarded secrets.

Switching his briefcase to his left hand so that he could return the salute, Wheeler eyed the sentry and realized he did not recognize the young man who was doing his best to maintain his bearing. The sergeant likely was a recent addition to Wheeler's military-police detachment and therefore saddled with this most undesirable of duty shifts, and his nervousness was obvious as he stood still and silent, awaiting orders or—more likely—for the general to be on his way so he could begin breathing again.

Wheeler smiled. "At ease, Sergeant. I've already had an airman for breakfast this morning. You're safe." The comment had the desired effect and the younger man relaxed, though he did not go so far as to return the smile. "You're new here, aren't you?"

"Yes, General," the man replied, offering a curt nod. The nametag over his uniform shirt's right breast pocket identified him as HESS, and Wheeler realized he recalled seeing that name in the list of new personnel he had reviewed over the weekend.

"Hess," Wheeler read aloud. "You came from Mac-Dill. Is that right?"

Again, the sergeant nodded. "Yes, sir. I was an MP at CENTCOM."

"From Florida to DC just in time for winter?" Wheeler chuckled. "Lucky you." Wheeler himself had been stationed more than once at MacDill Air Force Base in Tampa, Florida, including two assignments at the United States Central Command. He much preferred the warm beaches and blue waters of Tampa Bay to winters spent in Virginia and Maryland.

"I go where they send me, General," offered Sergeant Hess, opting to smile for the first time.

"Don't we all." Proceeding to the large metal door set into the concrete wall at the room's far end, Wheeler removed a magnetic key card from his pocket and inserted it into the reader installed next to the door. A keypad mounted above the reader allowed him to enter an eight-digit code, after which the door's lock disengaged and it began to slide aside. Before stepping through the now open portal, he cast a look over his shoulder. "Good to have you with us, Sergeant."

Hess saluted once more. "Thank you, sir." Like the rest of the military-police detachment assigned to his command, the sergeant knew nothing about what waited beyond the doorway through which Wheeler now stepped. The man's duties were simple: prevent unauthorized personnel from attempting to access the door. In the unlikely event anyone meeting that description made it this far underground, Hess and

anyone else charged with manning that desk was em-
powered to utilize deadly force in order to comply with
his standing orders, even if he never was to know what
he was defending.

Ours is not to reason why, Wheeler mused as he
waited in the vestibule protected by the door behind
him. Only when that barrier was once more in place
did he insert his key card into the reader for the door
on the opposite side of "the airlock," which was the
nickname bestowed upon this closet-sized room. The
metal door before which he now stood was a twin of
the hatch he had just accessed and would not open unless or until the inner hatch was locked. Wheeler was
able to override this procedure, of course, but regulations called for him to do so only in the face of dire
emergency. As he had often ruminated, should such
a situation ever come to pass, respect for established
protocol would without fail be one of the first things
cast aside, for there would be matters of more immediate import requiring attention. Most issues fitting that
description would, Wheeler figured, pertain to the very
survival of humanity.

In the meantime, the general followed procedure,
just as he required of the people serving under his
command.

A separate eight-digit code was required for the
inner door, which opened after Wheeler punched the
proper keys on the pad mounted above the card reader.
The hatch slid aside, and the vestibule filled with the
sounds of activity as he stepped onto a raised walkway

overlooking the main floor of the situation center that was the heart of this facility. Called "the Trench" by many who worked there, the chamber reminded him of Mission Control at the Johnson Space Center in Houston, or one of the NORAD operations centers buried deep within the Cheyenne Mountain Complex in Colorado, where he had been assigned twice during his career.

Below him, twenty workstations arranged into one of three curved rows—seven consoles along the forward and rear aisles and six in the middle—faced a trio of massive flat-screen video monitors, each of which was further divided into quarters with their own separate feeds. Despite the early hour, 0238 hours according to the digital clock high on the room's forward wall, personnel representing each of the United States Armed Forces as well a few on loan from allied military organizations, along with some civilian employees, sat at each of the workstations. Wheeler knew this was not typical for this time of night and that the majority of those now working had been called in just as he had. The bullpen was at full capacity, and he recognized several faces from the prime duty shift, with everyone having responded to a message sent to the pager each of his people were required to carry at all times: the emergency code *19470704*.

July 4, 1947. Wheeler allowed himself a small smile at the subtle humor and nod to history. After all, it was that date and its significance that—over time and thanks to a winding trail of fate and circumstances—had brought him to stand in this place, commanding these people while charged with a most unique task. The room he now overlooked, along with everything else tucked away within this undisclosed sublevel of the Pentagon, was but the latest iteration of the effort that had spanned five decades. Majestic 12 had grown from its modest genesis as a response to the crash landing of an extraterrestrial craft in Roswell to a point that it now accounted for nearly five percent of the operating budget for the entire Department of Defense. That was just the up-front money, as every president since Truman had authorized without question additional funding and other resources in order to address new or unexpected needs. Derivative operations such as the Groom Lake facility and the efforts of Projects Sign, Grudge, Blue Book, and Cygnus had been born out of necessity to support or—in some cases—deflect away from MJ-12's sole, unwavering objective to be prepared for any threat that might originate from beyond the confines of Earth.

Gone now were the fancy names or other designations, or the need to present a public face for a clandestine mission. There was only Daniel Wheeler and the people he commanded, here in this "secret lair" far beneath the nerve center of America's military might as well as at other satellite locations around the world, none of which existed in any official capacity. That would be the case, now and for all time.

Among the shadows of history shall we forever lurk.

"General?"

Wheeler turned to see his chief of staff, Colonel

Kirsten Heffron, walking toward him. Dressed in an officer's green uniform that appeared tailored to the same mathematical precision that was typical of any Marine, Heffron appeared unfazed by the early hour.

"Good morning, sir," she offered, moving to stand next to him as they both overlooked the Trench. "Did you say something?"

Wheeler realized he must have spoken the words aloud. A flush of embarrassment warmed his cheeks, and he waved away Heffron's concerns. "I'm sorry, Colonel. I guess I was lost in thought about something I'd read."

"Shadows of history," Heffron said. "Forever lurk. That's from the book we just scuttled, isn't it?"

As always, Wheeler was impressed at her ability to recall such details. "That's the one. A damned shame too. It actually was one of the more entertaining ones." The book, a tell-all written by a former member of his command, had been discovered less than a week before its author was set to deliver it to an editor at a major New York publishing house. A disgruntled DoD civilian employee terminated for cause a year earlier, the man had secured a modest advance fee in exchange for his purported airing of dirty laundry from deep inside the Pentagon. Managing to entice the publisher by and convincing her that many of his claims were real, he had saved what he was calling "the best parts," namely Wheeler and his group, for last. This was fortunate, as it had given Wheeler enough warning to see to it that the manuscript was never delivered. As for the employee, he currently was serving a lengthy prison sentence after being convicted for the unauthorized release of classified information. The publisher who had been expecting the manuscript was more than happy to forget about the whole thing in exchange for not being the focus of any further government scrutiny, such as an exhaustive audit by the Internal Revenue Service. Meanwhile, the manuscript itself now occupied a place in Wheeler's office library alongside the handful of other attempted and aborted exposés. He had decided he would wait until he retired before revisiting those accounts, just to see how well they withstood the test of time.

Waving a hand toward the Trench, Wheeler said, "Looks like you managed to corral everybody."

"Sorry for the all-call, sir," Heffron replied, "but I figured it was better to err on the side of . . . well, whatever."

"Agreed. Do we have anything new?"

"Not since the initial sighting. That video's been blasted to every major outlet around the country by now. It'll be global by this time tomorrow." Heffron shrugged. "People will talk about it for a couple of days, then move on to something else. By the end of the week, the only place you'll hear about it is from MUFON and the fringe groups."

"Maybe, but this wasn't some blurry picture or jumpy tape. I have a feeling this one might have some legs." In truth, Wheeler was not worried by groups like the Mutual UFO Network, which were benign if persistent with their ongoing calls for greater government transparency when it came to the subject of unidentified and unexplained phenomena that may or may not have connections to extraterrestrial activity. Even the conspiracy pushers who filled hours of late-night talk radio speculating about secret agendas and cover-ups for alien encounters posed no real threat. After all, one of the jobs with which his organization was tasked was leaking disinformation to such parties as a means of keeping their focus and attention away from the truth, which at times could be more frightening than any theory or fantasy. How many a night's peaceful sleep had reality cost him—at least, reality as it had been defined for him for so many years since his being ushered behind the veil that was Majestic 12 and its mission?

Add one more.

Stifling a yawn, Wheeler said, "I want to see it again." He gestured toward the Trench's video wall. "Cue it up." He waited as Heffron relayed his order to the army warrant officer sitting at the floor director's workstation, and a moment later one of the quadrants on the center video screen shifted from a map of the United States to a fleeting image of a city skyline at night. High above the ground, what could only be a craft streaking across the sky, moving with the speed of a jet fighter. Across the bottom of the image was a red banner highlighting a caption: AMATEUR VIDEO.

Wheeler lost any thoughts of returning to sleep.

Over the room's loudspeakers, a male voice said,

"Incredible footage was caught just an hour ago by a man using his camcorder to tape a backyard barbecue."

"Freeze that," Wheeler snapped, and the warrant officer halted the image, providing him and everyone else in the room with a still frame of the craft. Crossing his arms, he reached up to stroke his chin. "What do you think, Colonel? Look familiar?"

Heffron nodded. "Absolutely. It looks a lot like something photographed by recon satellites thirty years ago." She pointed to the screen. "Same basic configuration, with a hull flanked by more or less cylindrical components: two above and one below. This one looks more streamlined. More advanced, but there's no denying their silhouettes are similar."

"I was thinking the same thing." Wheeler had made the same connection upon his first viewing of the footage, which had been broadcast by a television station in Los Angeles the previous evening. It had taken a couple of hours for the video to make it across three time zones to the east coast, but he knew that local television outlets around the country would be making this a part of their morning news programming in just about two hours. He waved to the warrant officer down in the Trench. "Go." In response to his casual order, the video resumed its playback with the mysterious craft once more zooming across the California night sky.

"The massive unidentifiable object does not appear to be a meteorite, weather balloon, or satellite, and one aviation expert we've spoken to has stated that it's definitely

not any kind of U.S. aircraft currently in use. We're awaiting investigation by local authorities, and we'll keep you updated as news develops on this incredible story."

Heffron said, "All our attempts to track it are coming up empty. I hate to say it, but the damned thing looks to have vanished without a trace."

How many files from Majestic's voluminous library contained reports of similar sightings? Wheeler had long since bothered trying to maintain a count of such things, secure in the knowledge that the actual number was well above what had been acknowledged by the United States government in the form of public-facing groups like Project Blue Book and its predecessors, and far beyond those examined by even the most enthusiastic UFO watch groups.

Stepping away from the walkway's railing, Wheeler moved toward the set of stairs that would take him up to his office. With Heffron following, he said, "It had to come from somewhere. The ship we photographed thirty years ago was in a higher orbit than the satellites we had up there at the time. It really was just blind luck that we caught anything at all. Thing is, we've got better satellites now."

"Maybe it has some kind of advanced tech that lets it hide from our satellites," Heffron suggested. "Or they're able to track our birds' orbits and just avoid them."

"There's a comforting thought." Wheeler reached the landing at the top of the steps and walked past the desk where his aide sat. Though no one occupied the chair behind the desk, Wheeler noted the coffee cup and the active, locked computer station. "You really did wake up everybody, didn't you?"

"All hands on deck, sir. I've already got people scrubbing that tape for anything we can cross-reference against our files. Unfortunately, what was shown on the news is pretty much all there is. Unless someone else comes forward with their own video, there might not be a whole lot we can do with it."

For a brief moment, Wheeler considered the silver pen in his jacket pocket, the special properties it possessed, and the woman who had given it to him. What were the odds that the mystifying Roberta Lincoln already knew about the strange ship? Perhaps she was aware of its origins and intentions. Would she share that information with him?

I can't, he reminded himself. Lincoln had cautioned against his attempting to contact her except in cases of extreme emergency. The images on one videotape did not warrant sounding such an alarm. Not yet, anyway.

Wheeler led the way into his office, dropping his briefcase on the small round conference table that occupied one of the room's front corners. "Maybe not by itself, but it can still serve a purpose." Unbuttoning his uniform jacket, he draped it across the back of one of the table's chairs. "It's time to beat back the naysayers again, and this is just the thing to do it with."

Scowling, Heffron shook her head. "Budget cuts?"

"Yep." Gesturing for the colonel to take a seat in one of the chairs positioned before his large oak desk, Wheeler made his way to its opposite side and dropped into the leather high-backed chair. "The trouble with being a black project is that you're not always able to bring your masters down for a guided tour so they can see where all their money's going." This dilemma had plagued Majestic 12 almost from its very beginning. Despite support for the organization from the executive branch, the nature of the project required it to operate in total secrecy, folded into and mixed in with other, more conventional military expenditures. As a consequence, there were occasions when Wheeler and his group were obliged to justify their existence, all while maintaining the shroud of mystery concealing their activities.

Heffron said, "If we could show them the thinnest slice of the truth, we'd never have another budget meeting ever again."

"Not just that," Wheeler replied, "but think of how many men and women have dedicated their careers and their very lives to this cause. Wouldn't it be nice if even a handful of them received just a piece of the recognition they deserve?" Over the course of five decades, hundreds of people had worked toward a common goal while passing up awards and promotions, destroying marriages and other relationships, and forgoing anything resembling a normal life as they toiled in obscurity.

And what of those who had been sacrificed in the name of maintaining that secrecy? Principled men and women like James Wainwright and Allison Marshall, who, as with the others attached to efforts like Blue Book, were thrown to the lions in order to cast attention away from MJ-12's true mission. Wainwright and the others had known the truth from the beginning and had pledged themselves to the cause of being ready for the aliens' eventual return.

"Hopefully," Heffron said, "we'll be able to properly honor those people."

"Maybe one day, after you and I are long gone. Until then, I think the best we can hope for is that the public never has any reason to know what we're doing down here or even any of our names. If that's the price for working in the shadows for the rest of my life? I'll take it." Wheeler rose from his chair, moving to the large window at the front of his office so that he could stare out at the men and women manning the Trench. Like their predecessors, they carried out their work in isolation, and if they succeeded in their mission, they likely would never even receive the thanks of a grateful nation.

Will we be that lucky?

There was no way to know, of course. Indeed, there was only one immutable truth: the threat against Earth was real, regardless of the opinions offered by skeptics and deniers. Wheeler knew that such doubters would remain blissful in their ignorance until the inevitable happened, and they faced subjugation or annihilation. Only he and the group of patriots he now commanded, along with counterpart organizations around the world—to say nothing of the "special friends" he had acquired as a consequence of this rather odd job—were humanity's sole means of protection.

Did they have any real chance against such a threat? Perhaps not, but any prospective invaders would have to prove that. No, Wheeler vowed; they would have to earn it. To that end, his people's vigilance would be unwavering, their preparation continuous, and their resolve absolute.

Because if the people of Earth possessed a single line of defense, then that line began where Daniel Wheeler now stood: Pentagon Sublevel B14, Section 31.

Acknowledgments

Thanks once again to my editors, for allowing me to write this follow-up to what probably was one of the most fun *Star Trek* writing projects I've ever done, *From History's Shadow*. Reader response to the first book was overwhelmingly positive, and though I didn't write it with the idea of revisiting characters or threads I set up in that book, it certainly was fun to go back and play in this little corner of the *Star Trek* sandbox. Will there be another such adventure? Only time and sales will tell.

Thanks again to Greg Cox, not for anything in particular he did this time around, but for writing *The Eugenics Wars: The Rise and Fall of Khan Noonien Singh*, the books to which I try to remain faithful while writing these little stories. Any missteps in that regard are mine alone.

And, of course, thanks to you, my readers. Your comments about the first book are a big reason I decided to write a sequel. I hope you found it worth the wait.

Until next time!

About the Author

Dayton Ward has been modified to fit this medium, to write in the space allotted, and has been edited for content. Reader discretion is advised.

Visit Dayton on the web at
www.daytonward.com